DARE
TO BE, M.E.!

Other Avon Camelot Books by
Anne C. LeMieux

FRUIT FLIES, FISH & FORTUNE COOKIES

Writing as **A.C. LeMieux**

DO ANGELS SING THE BLUES?
THE TV GUIDANCE COUNSELOR

Anne C. LeMieux is the author of seven books for
young people, including another book featuring Mary
Ellen and Justine, *Fruit Flies, Fish & Fortune Cookies*.
Using the name A.C. LeMieux, she has written two
books for older readers, *The TV Guidance Counselor*
and *Do Angels Sing the Blues?*

Anne LeMieux lives in Southport, Connecticut, with her
family.

Avon Books are available at special quantity discounts for bulk
purchases for sales promotions, premiums, fund raising or edu-
cational use. Special books, or book excerpts, can also be created
to fit specific needs.

For details write or telephone the office of the Director of Special
Markets, Avon Books, Inc., Dept. FP, 1350 Avenue of the
Americas, New York, New York 10019, 1-800-238-0658.

DARe TO BE, M.E.!

ANNE C. LEMIEUX

Illustrations by Marcy Ramsey

AN AVON CAMELOT BOOK

This is a work of fiction. Names, characters, places, and incidents either are the product of the author's imagination or are used fictitiously. Any resemblance to actual events, locales, organizations, or persons, living or dead, is entirely coincidental and beyond the intent of either the author or the publisher.

AVON BOOKS, INC.
1350 Avenue of the Americas
New York, New York 10019

Copyright © 1997 by ACL Limited, A Connecticut Limited Partnership
Interior illustrations copyright © 1997 by Avon Books
Interior illustrations by Marcy Ramsey
Published by arrangement with the author
Visit our website at **http://www.AvonBooks.com**
Library of Congress Catalog Card Number: 96-36034
ISBN: 0-380-72889-3
RL: 4.9

All rights reserved, which includes the right to reproduce this book or portions thereof in any form whatsoever except as provided by the U.S. Copyright Law. For information address Avon Books, Inc.

First Avon Camelot Printing: June 1998

CAMELOT TRADEMARK REG. U.S. PAT. OFF. AND IN OTHER COUNTRIES, MARCA REGISTRADA, HECHO EN U.S.A.

Printed in the U.S.A.

OPM 10 9 8 7 6 5 4 3 2 1

If you purchased this book without a cover, you should be aware that this book is stolen property. It was reported as "unsold and destroyed" to the publisher, and neither the author nor the publisher has received any payment for this "stripped book."

Dedicated with love
to RiRi Willinger,
whose best-friendship was and is the bedrock
for this book,
and to her two beautiful daughters,
Emily and Sarah

ACKNOWLEDGMENTS

The author would like to thank Nancy Kolodny, M.A., M.S.W., author of the book *When Food Is Foe*, for sharing her expertise, her insights, and her compassion, and Patty Roche of Black Rock, Connecticut, for giving a candid glimpse into the world of creative catering.

DAre
TO BE, M.E.!

Chapter 1

"My last day of torture!" Mary Ellen announced as she came through the back door. Stopping next to her mother's small study off the kitchen, she waved a pink, fifty-dollar check. "I swear, those two terrors make Nicky look better behaved than a—a police dog puppy!"

Dr. Bobowick looked up from the stack of final exams she was grading.

"Put it with your bankbook, honey, so it won't get swallowed by your room before you have a chance to deposit it, like the last two. It's a pain in the neck for Mrs. Alexander to have to cancel payment, not to mention paying the extra bank fee."

Mary Ellen saluted, stepped over to the kitchen desk,

opened the top drawer, and pulled out her bankbook. She smiled in satisfaction at the balance. Twelve weeks of baby-sitting for the four-year-old twins next door, nine to noon, five days a week, and as far as she was concerned, she'd earned every last cent! Taking care of Timmy and Tommy Alexander all summer had been like taking care of two sets of monkey triplets. But she'd had the chance to earn six hundred dollars toward the two-hundred-gallon, marine fish tank she wanted; her parents had promised to match her savings if she earned half. She folded the check and tucked it in the savings passbook, then slipped it back into its plastic envelope.

"Is Nicky still next door with the twins?" Dr. Bobowick called out.

"Yep. They're in the backyard, working on their tunnel to China," Mary Ellen reported. "Two feet down, seven thousand, nine hundred miles to go. Mr. Kelly's gonna go bananas when he sees the condition his lawn's in after a year of renting to the Alexanders." Closing the drawer with her bankbook safely inside, Mary Ellen glanced at the mail-pile on the desk. The return address on the top envelope read Dexter Junior High School. She groaned.

Finish one kind of torture and another one starts! Her course schedule for her new school. Sticking her index finger under the envelope flap, she tore it open, snatched the sheet of thin computer paper, and leaned against the study doorway, reading it.

"Mary Ellen Bobowick. Grade 7 / Homeroom 103 / Teacher: Mr. Gumble," the top line on the computer print-out said. On the left side her courses were listed, each assigned a number. On the right, columns for six days, labeled A-day through F-day, each day divided into eighteen twenty-minute time modules with three minutes in between each one. Most of the classes spanned either two or three time modules each. *But six days a week??*

"That's it, I quit!"

2

"What's wrong?" Her mother looked up, her red pen poised in mid-correction.

"You need an advanced degree in calculus even to figure this out. Plus they want us to go six days a week! I give up! I'm not ready for junior high. I'll go back to sixth grade."

"Six days a week? That's the first I've heard of that. Let me see." Dr. Bobowick took the paper from Mary Ellen's hand and studied it for a moment, then smiled. "You didn't read the fine print. You don't have school six days a week. Dexter's on a rotating schedule—probably to make sure that Monday classes won't wind up getting canceled on all the long holiday weekends. Week one, which starts on Wednesday, will be A-day. Then B and C, and the following Monday will be D-day."

"Oh." Mary Ellen leaned over her mother's arm and examined the schedule more closely.

"It looks like you'll have English, Social Studies, French I, Math, and Earth Science four times most weeks," Dr. Bobowick said, running her finger down the paper.

"Okay, I get it. And Study Hall three times, Phys. Ed. and computer twice and—hmmm—I don't know what this is." She pointed at the A-day column, then scanned over to match the numerical code to the course key on the side of the column. 'Number 3217. DTBDDTBY.' Huh?"

"Must be an error. Maybe it's for Library," Dr. Bobowick said.

Mary Ellen checked again, and shook her head. "That's in the Media Center. This course meets in the All-Purpose Room—APR. With Ms. Coville."

"Do you want me to call and see if it's a mistake?" her mother asked.

Mary Ellen shook her head. "That's okay. I'll find out soon enough, anyway."

Dr. Bobowick handed the schedule back to Mary Ellen. "You better go put this with your new school things. You don't want to—"

"I know, lose it before the first day of school. I'll have a hard enough time figuring out where and when I'm supposed to be, even *with* a schedule." She folded it and tucked it in the pocket of her cutoffs. "Can I use the computer first, though? I want to check my e-mail."

"Yes, I won't need it for at least another half an hour." Dr. Bobowick turned back to the exams.

Lifting a stack of biology textbooks off the wooden chair near the window, Mary Ellen set them carefully on the floor, then pulled the chair over to the computer desk, which stood against the wall opposite her mother's regular desk. The best present she'd gotten for her birthday last December had been an account with the Parlinet Information and Communications service. Her budget was twenty-five dollars a month, to explore the cyberworld or do research. But the best thing about it was being able to send and receive electronic mail from her best friend, who'd been living in Paris since last September. Justine's father had gotten a job working as a corporate efficiency consultant for a year. E-mail made Justine seem so much closer when Mary Ellen sent her a letter and got a response back, sometimes within hours, instead of days or weeks. It was sort of like the difference between eating fresh-out-of-the-oven cookies and stale graham crackers.

After switching on the computer and the monitor, Mary Ellen opened the computer file—actually, the latest of sixteen files where she kept all the letters she sent to Justine, along with all of the replies which Justine sent back from her father's office computer. Reading them was almost like reading an ongoing, two-person diary, Mary Ellen thought; although for the past month, the correspondence had been pretty one-sided. She started tapping out a new letter on the keyboard.

Dear Justine,

I can't believe summer's almost over. You being away, and

my being held prisoner by two preschool dungeon-masters every morning made it seem like the longest one ever. But hanging out with Ben at the beach and knowing he was going to be moving away made it seem like the shortest. I can't figure that out. One of those paradox thingymabobs, I guess. Anyway, the big news is (drumroll . . . . . .) I'm now officially a 32 triple-A. Well, okay, it's not *SO* big, but like Einstein says, it's all relative—and it sure beats 28 negative-Z!! I hope you'll be back in time to go to Ben's moving-away barbecue party. It's the Sunday afternoon of Labor Day weekend.

LMKWUWY (Let Me Know What's Up With You) Love, your best friend and e-pen pal, M.E.

After Mary Ellen clicked on the Parlinet icon, the modem dialed its short telephone melody, connected to the network, and the service asked for her password. Parlinet suggested members choose passwords that no one else would be likely to guess or use, but that the user would be sure not to forget. *Drosophila.* Mary Ellen smiled as she typed it in. The scientific name for fruit flies, which, after the Great Fruit Fly Disaster last fall in school, was a word she would *never* forget.

The Parlinet welcome screen flashed on.

"Welcome to Parlinet," the mechanical-sounding cybervoice greeted her. Then it was silent. Mary Ellen sighed. No mail. Frowning, she copy-and-pasted her letter into the e-mail field, addressed it to Justine's Internet address, then zapped it on its electronic way. After signing off, she switched windows and scrolled up to the last decent letter Justine had sent to her, back at the beginning of August.

Dear Mary Ellen,

My mother finished the gourmet Cuisine de la Belle France course she's been taking. Boy, don't ever let anyone in your house take a French cooking class if you want to stay skinny. I mean major butter, heavy duty sauces, nonstop baked goodies and TERMINAL chocolate! We're talking serious *femurs de tonnerre* (thighs of thunder). I swear, I've eaten so much of her homework, I'm going to look like a walking puff pastry by the time we get back.

Anyhow, to celebrate her graduation, Mom made this whole huge nine-course dinner last Friday. It took her two days to get it all ready. Then my father called and said he couldn't make it home from the office. Mom went hysterical and took the baguette bread she'd baked herself and pounded the spinach souffle into a pancake with it. Olivia tried to calm her down by saying *"Plus ça change, plus c'est la même chose,"* which means "The more things change, the more they stay the same." I think she meant it was no big deal about my father not showing up for dinner, because even back in the States, he was hardly ever home for dinner. But her saying that made my mother go even crazier, and she started raving about how she hated France, and wished we'd never come to live here. Finally she went into her bedroom and didn't come out till noon the next day. My father was sleeping on the couch when I woke up.

You won't recognize my father, by the way. He has a goatee beard now, and he dyed all the gray out of his hair! It looks kind of strange with the way his hairline recedes. Olivia says he's freaking out about going into male menopause. Anyhow, life over here is tres bizarre.

SYBFAEPP (Still your best friend and e-pen pal) Love, Justine

P.S. Olivia got her left nostril pierced with a little gold ring. Totally gross. I asked her what she was planning on doing the first time she got a cold and had to blow her nose. Can you imagine the booger backup? Eeewww. I expected Daddy to have a cow when he saw, but this is the weirdest thing of all—he didn't even NOTICE for two days!

Mary Ellen scrolled down, skimming over her own reply to the next letter from Justine:

Dear Mary Ellen,

This city is totally dead right now. Everyone who lives here goes on vacation in August. It is a GHOST CITY, just about. I am dying of ennui. (That's Boredom with a capital E!) I wish you were here. No, make that—I wish I were there!

Love, Justine

P.S. I'm trying this new diet from JeunnElle magazine—so far I've lost 6 pounds.

She scrolled through three more of her own long gabby letters to an even shorter one from Justine:

Dear Mary Ellen,

Thanks for all the mail. I'll write longer soon.

Love, Justine.

"I'll write longer soon." *Humph*. Well, she could hardly write shorter, that was for sure. Something prickled Mary Ellen's brain, a sensation like annoyance mixed with hurt feelings, that after all the news-packed mail she'd sent her, Justine couldn't be bothered to write a decent reply.

Mary Ellen turned off the computer, pushed the chair back where it belonged, and bent down to replace the stack of books. Her mother's study was too tiny not to keep neat, and part of the deal with Mary Ellen being allowed to use her mother's computer was that she had to leave everything exactly the way she found it, or she'd be banned. The bargain was too important to mess up, no matter how naturally messy she was.

"News from abroad?" her mother asked.

"Nope," Mary Ellen said grumpily.

Dr. Bobowick swiveled around in her chair and looked at her thoughtfully. "Is something wrong, honey?"

Mary Ellen shrugged. "I don't know, " she said slowly. "Justine's letters have been different this past month."

"Different how?"

"I don't know," she said again, frowning. "Different short. Really short. And not saying much."

"I'd think Justine would be fairly busy now, getting ready to move back home," Dr. Bobowick said.

"Maybe," Mary Ellen admitted. "But what if . . ." She paused, her frown deepening.

"What if what?" her mother prompted.

"What if Justine is different—I mean *really* different—now? What if when she gets back, she's so different we don't like each other anymore? What if she's so—so—Frenchified—she's too cool to hang around with me?"

Dr. Bobowick leaned back in her chair. "Mary Ellen, I can't promise you that things will be the same. They probably won't. I'm sure Justine's grown up a lot this year. But so have you. Relationships grow up, too. That's part of what keeps them interesting."

"Yeah . . ." Mary Ellen pushed a stray lock of hair behind her ear.

"Justine might be feeling as anxious as you are, about fitting back in after having been away for a whole year. Instead of worrying about all kinds of what-ifs, why don't you make some plans to welcome her back?" Dr. Bobowick suggested.

Mary Ellen brightened a little. "A party?"

"Well, they might be a little too tired from traveling for a huge celebration. How about just inviting them over for dinner? I wouldn't imagine Corrine would feel much like cooking the minute she got back."

"I could put up a sign on their porch, and balloons on the mailbox, and bake a welcome-back cake. Can we have your lemon chicken?" It was Justine's favorite "company" meal.

Her mother nodded. "Of course. Make a list of what we'll need in the way of groceries and decorations, and find out exactly when they're coming home."

Mary Ellen headed out of the study, but stopped in the doorway and turned back. "Mom?"

"What is it, dear?" her mother asked, now with a touch of impatience in her tone. "I really need to get these exams graded."

"What if the Kellys stop on the way home from the airport to eat? Or what if they pig out on the plane?"

"Send Justine an e-mail invitation, tell her to check with her parents, and to RSVP."

"But what if they're too jet-lagged? Or—"

"Mary Ellen, stop! You'll drive yourself crazy." Dr. Bobowick shook her head. "Worrying is like paying interest on a loan that may never come due."

Chapter 2

"It's three o'clock and they're not here yet!" Mary Ellen wandered back in the kitchen, after peering through the living-room window to the street for the umpteenth time. Justine had sent a brief response to the invitation.

Our flight gets in around noon the Friday before Labor Day. A limousine is picking us up at the airport. Dinner sounds great. Mom says thanks. C-ya Friday. Love, J.

"Shouldn't they be here by now? The airport's only an hour away."

Dr. Bobowick looked up from the cutting board where she was slicing lemons, scallions, and ginger root for the

10

lemon chicken. "Justine said the flight was due around noon?"

Mary Ellen nodded and reached over her mother's arm to grab a piece of lemon, and put it in her mouth, puckering as the tart juice tingled her taste buds.

"They have to get all their baggage, then go through customs, and probably rent a car," Dr. Bobowick said.

"No, a limousine is picking them up," Mary Ellen told her. "Like rock stars. Can you believe it?"

Her mother smiled. "That sounds like Mr. Kelly's style. Anyway, all those European flights get in at the same time, so it may take awhile to clear customs."

At the sound of a car pulling in the driveway, Mary Ellen leapt toward the door and onto the back porch. Her eager expression fell. Not a limousine, just her grandmother's red Mustang pulling in. Gram hopped out of the driver's seat, wearing a pink-and-green sweatsuit, a matching headband stretched around her curly, gray-blond hair, and pink aerobic sneakers.

"Don't look so happy to see me!" she said.

"Sorry." Mary Ellen smiled, and gave her a kiss on the cheek as she came up the steps. "I thought you were the Kellys getting home from France." She opened the screen door and followed Gram inside.

"Whatever you're cooking up there smells scrumptious, Laura," Gram said to Dr. Bobowick.

"Lemon chicken, and I'm making plenty. You're welcome to stay, Mother."

"Thanks, dear, but not tonight," Gram said. "I'm all sweaty from my Jazzercise class. I have to run home and shower and get gussied up for company, and I just dropped in to borrow your vacuum cleaner. Mine had a tussle with a wad of dental floss, courtesy of my dear grandson and the monster trap he made the other day in my living room."

"Oh, Mother, I'm sorry," Dr. Bobowick exclaimed. "I'll pay to have it fixed."

Mary Ellen's grandmother waved away the apology. "Don't be silly, Laura," she said. "It was a very good monster trap. It just happened to snag my Hoover instead of a monster." Her blue eyes twinkled. She looked at the clock and clucked her tongue. "I do have to move along here, though."

"Mary Ellen, could you—" her mother started to ask.

"Get the vacuum cleaner for your grandmother?" Mary Ellen finished her mother's sentence for her. "And put it in the car? Of course. My pleasure."

"It's so nice to have a daughter who can read my mind," Dr. Bobowick said with a smile. "Saves my brain a lot of mileage. Not to mention my mouth."

Grinning, Mary Ellen went to retrieve the vacuum cleaner. After her grandmother left, she stood looking at the Kellys' empty house for a minute, then shook her head, in a kind of amazement that nearly a year had passed since she last saw Justine. The house, without the Alexanders in it, looked like a stage set, waiting for the actors and actresses to show up for a season premiere of a new TV show that was a spinoff of one of last year's. She wondered if Justine would snag the role of international jet-setting star, leaving Mary Ellen a boring bit part. *Stop it!* she told herself. Shaking off the nagging worries, she headed back to the house.

"Could you grab me a stick of margarine, please, dear?" Dr. Bobowick asked as Mary Ellen came into the kitchen.

Mary Ellen opened the refrigerator and smiled at the sight of the cake she'd spent all morning baking. It was devil's food with vanilla butter cream frosting, the layers stacked up into a model of the Eiffel Tower. She'd started with the biggest layer on the bottom, getting smaller and smaller until the cake was roughly the right shape, and held together with toothpicks. Then she'd frosted it and drawn in the grillwork with a tube of decorating gel, copying from a picture in the encyclopedia. The cake was so tall, Mary Ellen had had to take out one of the refrigerator shelves to make room for it. As she opened the dairy compartment to retrieve the margarine, Nicky scooted into the kitchen and zipped around behind her. She caught his grimy paw as he reached to swipe a fingerful of frosting.

"Oh no, you don't," she said. "Everything has to be perfect."

"I just want one lick," he pleaded.

"No," she said firmly. "No licks." Turning him around by the shoulders, Mary Ellen steered him toward the back door. "You have to wait till tonight, and then you'll get a whole piece."

He shrugged away from her, scowling. "I don't wanna go outside. There's nothing to do."

"Sure there is," Mary Ellen said. "You can ride your bike, or practice your soccer kicks with your net, or play on the swings—"

"It's no fun by myself," Nicky said mournfully.

Mary Ellen looked at him sympathetically. She might not miss the twins, but Nicky was going to. "I've got an idea," she said. "Why don't you go be the lookout for the Kellys? Wait near the mailbox and watch for a great big black car."

"Okay!" Nicky's face brightened, and he took off.

Dr. Bobowick finished the chicken, put it in the oven, and rinsed her hands. "Would you watch Nicky for a few minutes, sweetie? I'm going to shoot to the market and pick up a few things for Corrine—coffee, bread, milk, juice—so she doesn't have to worry about rushing out for groceries first thing tomorrow morning. I'm sure she'll have her hands full settling back in." She looked around the kitchen, frowning as if trying to remember something. Mary Ellen saw her eyes light on the salad bowl. "Oh. And could you—"

"Wash the lettuce. Yep."

Her mother smiled again, grabbed her purse from the counter, and scooted out the back door. Two minutes later, Nicky blared the news of the Kellys' arrival.

"THEY'RE HERE!!" he hollered from the driveway. "IN A GREAT BIG BLACK CAR!! I THINK IT'S THE BAT-MOBILE!!!"

Laughing, Mary Ellen dashed out the kitchen door, drying her wet hands on her shorts, and cut through the hedge to the Alexanders'—*correction, now Kellys' again*—driveway. A black stretch limousine was idling near the sidewalk, while a blue-uniformed driver had the trunk open and was taking pieces of luggage out and lining them up next to the car. Mrs. Kelly was already up on the front porch with her keys out, unlocking the door, and Olivia, wearing black jeans, a black top, black sneakers, a black beret, and black nail polish, with the sun glinting off her nose ring, was standing holding her arms out to Nicky.

"YAY!!! LIVIE'S BACK!!" Nicky jumped up as Olivia stooped down to scoop him up.

"Nicky! *Comment vas-tu, mon petit chouchou?*" she said, hugging him.

"Huh?" Nicky wrinkled his nose.

"I said, 'How are you, sweetie-pie,' or as the French would say, 'my little cream puff'?" Olivia translated. She gave Mary Ellen a grin and a wave, as Justine climbed out of the back seat of the limo.

A pang of anxiety fluttered in Mary Ellen's stomach. Then she and Justine were standing face to face, about a foot apart.

"Your hair!" Mary Ellen exclaimed.

The top layer of Justine's blonde hair was short and curly, like a wig over the rest which was long now, and wavy. Her outfit was a really loose cotton print top over a longish green skirt. And she was wearing a ton of makeup. She looked *so* different! Older.

"You like it?" she asked, patting the side of her hair lightly.

Mary Ellen detected a note of uncertainty in her voice,

and nodded vigorously. "I—I love it. It's like a whole new you."

"Yours, too," Justine said somewhat awkwardly. "Your hair, I mean. I really like it. It looks great short."

The two girls stood staring speechlessly for a long pause. Then something kicked in for Mary Ellen, a rush of the old familiarity.

"But it's YOU!" she shouted. "You're back! You're really back! I can't believe it!" The frozen moment broke, and suddenly they were hugging each other and laughing.

Justine stood back after a minute, and looked first at her own house, then the Bobowicks'.

"I can't believe it either. I know it's the same—my brain recognizes it—but it's like . . . remember how you said you felt when you got the cast off your leg?"

Mary Ellen nodded. "I knew it was my leg and it had been there the whole time, but still it felt new."

Having unlocked the house, Mrs. Kelly was back again, telling the limo driver where to put the luggage. When she finished, she stepped over and gave Mary Ellen a hug. "Thank you so much, dear. For the sign and the balloons—it's so thoughtful of you and your mother."

"She's at the store now, getting you a few groceries, and dinner's cooking, and—"

Mary Ellen stopped in mid-sentence. Something didn't seem right. Mrs. Kelly was holding her lips in a stiff smile, and both Justine and Olivia's expressions had gone somber. Something seemed . . . missing.

"Mrs. Kelly, you want these hanging bags in the master bedroom closet?" the driver asked.

Pressing her lips tightly together, Mrs. Kelly gave a jerky nod. She looked like she was about to say something but the words were stuck in her throat. Her chin started to tremble, and Mary Ellen could see tears well up in her eyes as she turned abruptly and walked toward the house again.

All of a sudden, Mary Ellen identified the missing some-thing. Justine's father!

"Where's your dad?" she whispered to Justine. "Is he coming later?"

Olivia gave Nicky a quick kiss on the cheek, then set him down, grabbed a bag from the sidewalk, and followed her mother.

Justine looked toward the house, where Mrs. Kelly was running up the front steps. Her shoulders sagged and she shook her head. "He's not coming," she said flatly. "At all. He's staying in Paris. With his girlfriend."

Mary Ellen's jaw dropped. Justine's father had a *girl-friend*??

Justine sketched the bare bones of the story as they set the table, while Mrs. Kelly had a glass of wine with Mary Ellen's parents in the living room.

"Secretary."

"How did you find out?" Mary Ellen whispered.

"Olivia saw them, that's how. In the Cafe de L'Etoile. She had a date a few nights after Mom's cooking school graduation, and that's where they went, and that's what she saw."

"Was she sure?" Mary Ellen couldn't believe it. "I mean, maybe it was just business, or something."

Justine snorted. "They were holding hands and making goo-goo eyes at each other."

Mary Ellen raised her eyebrows, not knowing what to say. She finished spooning the rice into a serving dish, grabbed a potholder to set the hot dish on, and nodded to-ward the dining room.

"Dinner's served," she called out to the grown-ups.

Justine whispered one last thing just before the adults came into the dining room. "Anyway, Olivia told him the next day, to give him a chance to explain, and he admitted everything. Word of warning—don't even mention his name in front of my mother. She either goes ballistic or falls apart."

The whole dinner was about the unpartiest party Mary Ellen had ever been to. Mrs. Kelly kept going back and forth from zoning out and looking sad, to putting on a brave smile and trying to talk cheerfully about how wonderful it felt to be back in the United States, and weren't Justine and Mary Ellen excited about going to junior high, and what a delicious dinner it was. But hanging in the air was the awkward topic everyone was afraid to touch.

Everyone except Nicky.

"Are you going to get a new Mr. Kelly if the old one isn't coming back?" Nicky asked during dessert and coffee.

"Nicky!" Dr. Bobowick exclaimed.

But it was too late. Mrs. Kelly excused herself and ran from the dining room, while Justine and Olivia both sat there looking helpless.

"I'll go over," Dr. Bobowick said, rising from the table as they heard the back door open and close. "Peter, could you get Nicky in the shower when he finishes his cake?"

"Sure thing," Mary Ellen's father said. Nicky looked up at him, realizing, Mary Ellen could see, that he'd definitely said the wrong thing. Mr. Bobowick reached over and ruffled his hair.

"Shower time, my man."

The distraction worked, and Nicky's worried expression was replaced by enthusiasm. "Can I bring my new SuperSprayer water gun in the shower?"

"Why not?" Mr. Bobowick said. "Meet me upstairs." He picked up his plate and went into the kitchen.

"Yay!!" Nicky ran to get his water gun from his swing fort.

"'Why not?'" Mary Ellen giggled. "He'll see why not. He'll be wetter than Nicky when the shower's done." But Justine and Olivia didn't smile.

Mary Ellen sighed. "I'm really so sorry for you guys.

What a terrible thing." The thought of her parents splitting up made her shudder.

"Hey, the way I see it, it's his loss," Olivia said. She stood and started clearing the table, while Justine reached over to the cake, cut herself another square, and took a bite.

"I don't think that's the way Mom sees it," she mumbled through a mouthful of devil's food.

"What's she going to do?" Mary Ellen asked. She started clearing the table with Olivia.

"I don't know." Justine polished off the piece of cake. "She doesn't have to work—I mean for the money, or anything."

"She's a woman in her prime!" Olivia declared. "The whole world is her oyster. She's bought into the whole patriarchal myth that she's helpless without a man. She needs to get in touch with the wild woman archetype inside her."

"I think that's what she was doing when she threw all Daddy's clothes out the window into the courtyard." Justine stacked the rest of the plates and carried them into the kitchen.

Mary Ellen followed her, carrying the cake. Setting it on the counter, she grabbed the tin foil from a drawer, pulled out a long sheet, tore it off, and started to wrap what was left of her cake-creation.

"Ooo—wait one sec," Justine said. She lifted the edge of foil, cut another chunk of Eiffel Tower, and popped it into her mouth. Mary Ellen raised her eyebrows. Justine hadn't buttered her roll at dinner, saying butter wasn't allowed on her diet. She was curious what kind of diet excluded butter, but allowed three pieces of chocolate cake. Justine noticed her expression.

"It's hormonal, I think. I get these chocolate cravings. But I'll subtract breakfast tomorrow. Anyhow, that's why God made baggy clothes—for us fat people."

"You're not fat," Mary Ellen said.

"Okay, pleasingly plump. That's what my father calls it."

"Why would you take *his* word for anything, Justine?" Olivia said as she made a second trip with dirty dishes.

"Good point," Justine said, and she reached for one more piece of cake as Mary Ellen covered it with foil.

Chapter 3

"Look at that!" Justine pointed to several dark smudges shaped like small partial footprints on the pale yellow wall, halfway between one of her twin beds and the bedroom ceiling. "What the heck were those Alexander kids anyhow, junior spidermen or something? How could footprints get up there?"

"Standing on their heads on the bed," Mary Ellen replied instantly. "Nicky does it all the time."

Frowning, Justine ripped a paper towel off the roll she'd been using to dust, and kneeling on the bed, sprayed the grimy spots with spray cleaner, and scrubbed the wall. Then she hung a poster of Sabrina Kelsey, the British supermodel, on the wall.

"Doesn't she have an incredible body?" Justine asked.

"I think she looks like she needs a triple chocolate milkshake," Mary Ellen commented. "I mean she's pretty, but she's even skinnier than me!"

"You're both lucky," Justine said.

Mary Ellen just shrugged and took the last few books from a box she was unpacking and stacked them on the bottom bookcase shelf. A moving truck had brought the furniture that the Kellys had put in storage for a year, along with boxes and boxes of their stuff. She and Justine had spent all Saturday morning putting things away. Now Mary Ellen picked up the two empty cardboard book boxes and stacked them on top of others in the corner next to the closet.

"What's in that last box?" Justine pointed.

Mary Ellen tore off the packing tape and opened the flap. "Shoes," she reported.

"Ugh. That means we have to move all those empty boxes to get near the closet." Justine wiped her forehead on her sleeve. "Okay, I'll start bringing them down to the basement."

"Why don't we just stick them in the hall, finish the last box, and then I'll help bring them down," Mary Ellen suggested.

"Okay, good idea."

Mary Ellen started moving the empties out into the hall. As soon as she'd cleared enough away, Justine moved in with the box of shoes, and started tossing them willy-nilly into the closet.

Mary Ellen stared. *Justine? The biggest neat freak she knew?*

"Where's that shoe bag organizer you used to have for the inside of your closet door?" Mary Ellen asked.

"Dunno." Justine shrugged. "Maybe it got packed in one of the other boxes. I can't remember, things were so confusing and we moved so fast last fall. It doesn't matter, though. Okay," she said, after tossing the last pair of sandals in, and closing the closet door. "Done." She turned and slowly surveyed the whole room.

"Just like it always was," Mary Ellen said.

Justine shook her head, frowning. "No."

"No?"

"Uh uh. It's not the same. It doesn't *feel* the same."

Mary Ellen bit her lip, not sure what to say. "Think it's because of—you know—your father?"

"Him not being here might be part of it, I guess," Justine said. "But when you think about it, Olivia was right. *'Plus ca change . . . '* Same difference. He was never here all that much. I mean, like home for dinner every night and stuff. He was always pretty much of a workaholic, so that part won't really be that different. It's something else. I don't know what."

"Well, maybe it seems different because you're different," Mary Ellen suggested.

Justine closed the closet door and looked at herself in the full-length mirror. Mary Ellen saw her frown in the reflection. "I guess that could be," Justine said. "I don't really know how, though. I mean, if you live with yourself every day, you don't notice you're different the way someone else who hasn't seen you for a year would. Do you think I'm different?"

Again, Mary Ellen wasn't quite sure what to say. Justine didn't really look much different, except for her hair, and the extra makeup. Mary Ellen couldn't really tell if the diet was having an effect, because she'd only seen Justine wearing baggy clothes so far. Mrs. Kelly's car pulling in the driveway saved her from having to answer.

"Oh good! She's back from getting the car from my aunt's house. She was going to stop by Dexter on the way home and register me. Come on, let's go see if we have any of the same classes." Justine headed for the door, scooping up the dirty paper towels and spray cleaner on the way. Mary Ellen followed, bounding down the stairs after her.

There were four canvas ShopBest Supermarket grocery bags on the floor, and Olivia was coming through the door with four more. Justine looked at them curiously. "Did you *buy* all those tote bags?"

Mrs. Kelly nodded, but didn't seem like she was really paying attention.

"Do you have any idea how wasteful it is to use paper grocery bags?" Olivia said. "Even recycled ones? And plastic . . ." she shuddered. "Forget it."

"It looks kind of weird, though," Justine said, wrinkling her nose. "I mean, are you going to use those all the time?"

"Yes, she is." Olivia answered for her mother. "It's the new Ms. Corrine Kelly. Responsible matriarch and citizen of the world. Right, Mom?"

"Yes," Mrs. Kelly said absently. She was holding four large potatoes in her hands, and looking at them strangely, as if all their eyes had just blinked at her. "Oh, now look at that," Mrs. Kelly said suddenly. "I went and bought four baking potatoes and we only need three." Her face went from looking confused to looking like it was about to crumple. "Excuse me, Mary Ellen. I'm sorry—I just—" She turned and ran out of the room, just like she had the night before.

"This," Olivia announced, "is beginning to border on the absurd. I just spent an hour giving her a pep talk and she unravels over a potato."

"That's not a very nice thing to say, Olivia," Justine said. "She really needs our support, you know."

"What she needs is a sledge hammer and a rock pile to get out some of her anger, and then she needs to start living her life. Living well is the best revenge." Olivia picked up the four potatoes from the counter, put three of them in the drawer bin, then coolly took the remaining one, chopped it in quarters, and stuffed it down the garbage disposal. She flipped the disposal switch and the sound of raw potatoes being ground to smashed potatoes, then flushed down the pipes, filled the room. Dusting her hands off when the potato disposal operation was complete, she nodded sharply, then strode out of the room.

Mary Ellen looked at Justine, her eyebrows raised.

"Since this whole thing happened, Olivia's been a little . . . hostile," Justine said.

Glancing at the sink, Mary Ellen gulped. "I guess *so!*"

Justine picked up her mother's purse from the counter and rooted through it. "Found it!" She pulled out an envelope like the one Mary Ellen's schedule had come in.

"Open it, quick!" Mary Ellen said. "Who do you have for homeroom?"

"Let's see . . ." Justine ran her finger down the printout. "Homeroom 103, Teacher: Mr. Gumble."

"Yay! Same as me." Mary Ellen crowded next to Justine's elbow and scanned the schedule. "Math and science are different." She frowned. "So is foreign language. I'm in first-year French."

"You're probably in the honors sections for math and science, and they put me in French II," Justine said. "How 'bout English and History?"

Mary Ellen found them on the list. "Yep! Same. Phys. Ed., too. And here's that same weird DTBDDTBY thing—Wednesday, fourth period, APR, with Ms. Coville. It has to be a misprint, but I can't imagine what it's for."

"Hmmm. What's missing?" She studied the schedule. "Health class maybe?"

"Could be," Mary Ellen said. "Or maybe it stands for something. You know, like what we do in letters, with initials. Hmmm . . . Data That Bores Dull Dummies To Big Yawns?"

"How 'bout Dopey Teenagers Being Double-Dared To Belch Yodels?" Justine suggested.

The two broke into giggles.

"I guess we'll find out on the first day. Speaking of which, we need to plan our attack. Come on." Justine headed back toward the stairs. "What are you going to wear?" she asked over her shoulder. "Have you decided yet?"

"Just jeans and maybe this new shirt I got—it's really pretty, dark blue cotton with long sleeves and peachy colored roses on it," Mary Ellen answered, following Justine into her room again..

"What about shoes? Accessories?"

"My new ones. Just ordinary casual ones," Mary Ellen said. "And I have my old blue backpack. What about you?"

"Don't know yet. I have to do some research."

"Research? On what to wear to school?"

"Yes, research. *You're* the scientific one. You should know how important research is. "

"Well, yeah, but not about clothes." Mary Ellen sat down on the bed as Justine grabbed a stack of magazines from her desk, then plopped down on the bed and sank back, leaning against the wall.

"It *is* important!" Justine went on. "The first day in a new school can make you or break you. I don't want to end up in the sludge."

"What sludge?"

"The masses—the mob—the generic American junior-high student. Here. Start researching. Jeans are fine, and the shirt sounds pretty. But accessories are key. You need to think shoes, purse, hair things—"

"I do?"

Justine nodded emphatically. "Mom said she'd drop Olivia and me off at the mall this afternoon. Want to come?"

"I'll have to ask, but I think it'll be okay."

"Okay, research time. Here, you scout this one for accessories. That's where you stand out from the mall clones." She handed Mary Ellen the Fall Fashion Issue of *Glamour*, and picked up *Cosmopolitan* for herself. "I'll check this one out for general trends."

"But if everyone sees the same stuff, and goes out and

buys it, won't that automatically turn them all into mall clones?"

"Not necessarily," Justine said, flipping through the pages. "You have to spot the trend first, catch it right on the cutting edge. Then you'll be one of the trendsetters, not the followers."

"I don't have time for this kind of research," Mary Ellen said. "I'd rather read *Modern Marine Aquarium* or *National Geographic*." She paged through *Glamour* quickly, shook her head, dropped the magazine on the floor, and reached over to pick up another one from the stack next to Justine.

"I really hate these magazines," Mary Ellen said, shaking her head again. "Look at this. 'Fourteen Flab-Fighting Tips From Super-Models'; 'Willpower—The Secret Ingredient To Make Your Diet Work.' "

"I wish I'd read that one before I tasted your chocolate cake," Justine said.

"An ad for Miracle Munch," Mary Ellen went on. "Drop ten pounds in ten days—guaranteed or your money back. They've got pages and pages of models who look like they've been fed on nothing but Melba Toast and water for months, showing us what we're supposed to look like, then they toss this in, to be politically correct or something. 'One Young Woman's Story—The Confessions of a Diet Junkie.' Why don't they make up their minds?" She flipped through the rest of the magazine in disgust, but stopped short when an ad caught her eye. "Look at *this*!!"

Justine leaned over and read out loud. " 'ShapeShifters: Improve your figure without the expense or the risk of cosmetic surgery. Thousands of women customers swear satisfaction from ShapeShifters Bosom Enhancers. Different sizes allow you to custom contour your figure to its ideal proportions.' "

Mary Ellen wrinkled her nose and pointed at the photograph, which showed the product packed in a special carrying case. "They look like someone crossed Silly Putty with grapefruit halves, and stuck 'em in Baggies."

"What are they made out of?" Justine asked.

Mary Ellen scanned the ad. "Some kind of silicone gel. In special plastic bags, like I said. Can you imagine *wearing* them? Still . . ." She looked down at her T-shirt, then at Justine, then back at the ad. $119.99. That would really cut into her baby-sitting profits. Laughing, she closed the magazine.

Justine tossed *Cosmo* aside and dug through the pile for another magazine.

" 'Choose Your New Image,' " she read out loud off the cover, then flipped to the article. "Hmmm. 'Baby Doll, Glamour Girl, Tough'N'Tender, or Sassy Sexy?' Which one do you think is me, Mary Ellen?"

Mary Ellen glanced over as Justine turned the pages. "None of them are you. None of them are even them. Look— not one pimple, not one stray hair, and they all have perfect teeth. They're illusions created by computer-enhanced photography. I saw a special on it. They take out every single imperfection pixel by pixel. And anyway, all the stuff in here is too old for us." She held up a two-page spread with all formal wear. "Are we going to be wearing black tie getups to Dexter? Highly unlikely."

"Okay, try this then." Justine tossed over the Back To School Issue of *YM*, and picked through the pile until she found the latest issue of *Seventeen*. She opened it at random, and frowned over the picture of a pale waif with spiky, flame-colored hair, leaning back against a guy with a matching hairdo, a black T-shirt, and designer jeans; the girl model was looking coyly over her shoulder at the guy, his face frozen in a pout, pretending not to notice her existence. "I could do that with the top of my hair—it's short enough. I'd only have to dye it . . ."

Mary Ellen leaned over to take a closer look. "Dye your hair the color of a radioactive tangerine? Would your mother let you?"

"Well, if I did it without asking, what could she say? It'd be too late then. She'd probably wig out though. This might not be the best time in the world to spring too many drastic changes on her."

"Forget it. I give up," Mary Ellen said, tossing the magazine onto Justine's pillow. "I'll be sludge. Thirty-two triple-A sludge. So sue me."

Justine laughed, too, but she shook her head. "You'll never be sludge, Mary Ellen. You can always hang out with the brains, anyway. Brains are outside sludge. Jocks are outside sludge. Artists and musicians are outside sludge. Even clods are outside sludge. But I'm lucky when I pull a B average, I don't play sports, I can't draw a stick figure to save my life, I'm tone deaf, and I'm not a complete clod. Not that I'd want to be. But what that leaves is generic. So I *have* to plan my image."

"You are not generic!" Mary Ellen sputtered. "That's ridiculous."

"I have no special talents. I—"

"Of course you do!" Mary Ellen felt herself getting angry.

"Name one," Justine challenged.

"Well . . . you . . ."

"See? I told you."

"Wait, I was just getting my thoughts organized. Organization!! You've always been a really organized person. That's a *huge* talent. And you can speak French now, too. You could be—you could be the executive director of a French corporation!"

"Follow in my father's footsteps?" Justine said, a touch of sarcasm coming through in her voice. "I don't think so."

"Oh, Justine. I'm sorry—I forgot . . ."

Justine waved the apology away. "It's okay."

"Well anyhow, your absolute top talent is being a best friend," Mary Ellen declared. "And anyone as smart as me would never choose a generic best friend. So there."

Chapter 4

"I just don't know," Justine said slowly, glancing down at the small, slanted mirror on the rug of Robertson's shoe department, twisting first her left ankle to get a side view of a pointy-toed, low-heeled black suede boot, then her right, in a caramel-colored moccasin with sturdy soles, and a fan-shaped pattern of teardrop cutouts over the toe.

"I like that one," Mary Ellen said, pointing to Justine's right foot. "It looks a lot more comfortable than the other one, too."

Justine frowned. "Yeah, but they're all over the place. I bet half the kids in school will be wearing them, or something like them."

"Maybe," Mary Ellen admitted. "They are kind of like

the ones I got, except for the color. Mine are burgundy." She sat back in the beige tweed square chair in the middle of the row, glancing at the seats to the right and left of her, both of which were stacked high with shoeboxes. They'd been here for an hour! This after three hours going back and forth between boutiques and clothing stores in the mall, while Justine coordinated every single item to go in her wardrobe with the proper accessory, down to socks, stockings, earrings and even underwear.

"Are you guys ready yet?" Olivia strolled up carrying three of the ShopBest tote bags stuffed to maximum capacity, and collapsed into a seat in the row opposite Mary Ellen. "I swear, I've been through every single store and jewelry vendor in this mall with a fine-tooth comb. Not *one* of them has anything *close* to what I'm looking for."

"You must have found something!" Justine pointed to the bags.

"Oh, clothes, yeah. That was easy. Two pairs of black Levis, two pairs of black leggings, four black shirts, a black fake leather skirt, a *gorg*eous black chenille sweater, and I cleaned them out of black undies in Penelope's Boudoir. But no one had any sterling silver uroboros earrings."

"Sterling silver uro-*who*-bus?" Mary Ellen asked.

"Uroboros," Olivia said. "A dragon swallowing his own tail. One of Jung's symbols for wholeness." She pulled a little sketch out of her pocket. "This. I dreamed it last night, that I had a pair of hoop earrings like this. Do you know what that means?"

Mary Ellen shook her head.

"It's a major breakthrough dream! Totally significant. It means my psyche is integrating."

"Congratulations," Justine said dryly. "Whatever the heck *that* means."

"Anyway," Olivia continued, "I guess I'll have to go to Center Jewelers in town and have them specially made."

"Won't that cost a lot?" Mary Ellen asked.

Olivia shrugged. "My father's opened his pockets wide. It's a guilt thing."

"Olivia!" Justine said. "How can you say a thing like that?" She kicked the moccasin off, and slipped her foot into a dark tan clog. "That is totally crass."

Olivia shrugged. "It's true. And the sooner you accept things the way they are, the better off you'll be. And so will Mother. I've already processed it. I'm fine."

"You go around every day looking like you're on your way to a funeral, and you think that's fine?" Justine put her hands on her hips and glared at her sister.

"It's not completely inappropriate," Olivia retorted coolly. "Everyone on the planet should be in mourning. Do you know that every single second, a football field-sized chunk of the rainforest is destroyed? Do you realize how many species have gone extinct as a result?"

"That's true," Mary Ellen commented, though she didn't think Olivia's choice of black jeans instead of blue jeans was going to make a whole lot of difference.

"So what are *we* supposed to do about it?" Justine asked, shooting Mary Ellen a *"thanks a lot"* look.

"Fast food chains are the biggest market for beef, and one of the biggest threats to the rainforest is ranchers who want grazing land for cattle. So you could start by boycotting Happy Heifer instead of ordering two double cheeseburgers for one thing." They'd had a snack at the mall's food court after the first hour of boutique browsing.

Mary Ellen watched Justine go beet red.

"I didn't have any breakfast," she mumbled. "And I only had a salad for lunch."

"That wasn't the point—" Olivia started to say, but Justine cut her off.

"Oh, just shut up, already. I have enough problems figuring out which pair of school shoes to buy, without worrying about the problems of South American cattle ranchers."

Olivia shrugged coolly. "Fine. Be an ostrich about everything. I'm going out to the car to listen to my new tape—*Song of the Gray Wolf*. Hurry up and make up your mind about the shoes. There's a poetry reading at The Coffee Cave tonight at 9:00, and I want to figure out what I'm going to wear."

"How 'bout something black?" Mary Ellen couldn't resist saying.

"Cute, Mary Ellen," Olivia said, but she cracked a little smile, then started to walk away. At the edge of the shoe department, she looked back at Justine and said casually, "If you buy leather shoes, I hope you say a prayer to the spirit of the animal whose skin you're wearing, who gave up its life for the vanity of your feet."

"I wish the species of know-it-all older sisters would go extinct," Justine said through clenched teeth, shaking the mate to the clog at Olivia's back. "She in*fur*iates me."

Mary Ellen couldn't help giggling. "She's kind of funny, you have to admit."

"You should try living with her on a day-to-day basis. You wouldn't find it so amusing." But she relaxed a little. "Anyhow, I've made up my mind." Justine took off both shoes, put her sneakers back on, and dug to the bottom of one stack of shoeboxes, pulling out the box of brown lace-up boots, the very first pair she'd tried on. "These. I'm positive."

Mary Ellen breathed a sigh of relief.

"You know," Justine said as they were finally headed toward the exit, "There are people who make a lot of money doing this for other people who don't have time. Maybe my mother could do something like that to keep her busy. I inherited all my shopping ability from her."

"That's something I'd *never* do. It's bad enough shopping for myself! Takes way too much—What?" Mary Ellen said abruptly as Justine grabbed her arm and yanked her behind a special-purchase sale rack of wool blazers, then pulled her down to a crouching position.

"Look over there."

"Over where?" Mary Ellen tried to stand up, but Justine yanked her down again. "I can't see what you're talking about," Mary Ellen complained.

Justine made a space between some of the blazers. "Look now," she said. "Can you see who that is?" She pointed toward the men's sportswear department, where a tall kid with longish curly black hair was standing in front of a three-way mirror, trying on a brown leather bomber jacket, while a woman standing next to him was holding a small boy who was struggling to escape. "*Is that Jason Hodges?*" she whispered.

Mary Ellen caught a glimpse of the kid's face as he turned sideways to check out the jacket.

"Please hurry and decide, Jason," they heard the woman say. "Andy's getting rambunctious."

"Yeah, it's him," Mary Ellen confirmed. "What's the big deal?" Frowning at Justine's weird reaction, she started to stand up again.

"Shhhh!" Justine hissed. "And get down." She let the coats fall back together.

"Justine, this is insane!"

"Just wait, okay? Wait till they leave," Justine pleaded. As she started to part a space between the blazers to spy again, the rack started tipping backward.

"Help!" Mary Ellen yelped, grabbing a fistful of wool, but it was too late.

The rack kept going, almost in slow motion, and landed on the floor, leaving the two girls exposed and surrounded by a mound of fallen blazers.

Customers gathered to gawk, and nearby salespeople hurried to lift the mess of cloth and metal off them, anxiously asking if they were all right. Mary Ellen caught Jason's eye as she struggled free of the wreckage. He grinned

and gave her a thumbs-up. The manager of the sportswear department, who'd scurried over, looked at the heap of merchandise, and heaved an irritated sigh.

"Miss Perkins, get one of the stockboys to help you sort that mess out. And go over to men's accessories and tell them I need a lint remover kit." He turned to Justine and Mary Ellen, who were standing now. "No harm done, you girls are all right? Sure you are. Good. Good."

Mary Ellen could see the manager was trying to hide his annoyance behind a show of concern, but it was obvious he just wanted the two of them to leave by the closest exit.

"Come back again soon," he said, as he herded them in the direction of the doors. "Thank you for shopping at Robertson's." He mopped his brow and hustled back to his department.

"Hey, Bobowick!" Jason called from the checkout counter, where his mother was paying for the jacket. "Gonna try out for cheerleaders this year? I hear they're looking for a token klutz."

Mary Ellen stuck her tongue out at Jason. "This one wasn't—" she started to call back, "*my* fault," but Justine whispered a panic-stricken, "Shut *up!*" in her ear.

"Hey, Kelly, welcome back. I've heard the expression, 'Shop Till You Drop,' but I don't think that's what it means!"

Justine turned crimson and didn't say a word. As soon as they got outside, she leaned against the brick wall near the pay phone, and closed her eyes.

"This," she said, "is *terrible*."

"Well, it could have been worse." Mary Ellen shrugged. "It's not like it happened in the crystal and fine china department, or anything."

"That's not what I mean," Justine said. There was a tragic expression on her face.

"What then?" Mary Ellen asked.

Justine opened her eyes. "I think I'm smitten," she whispered.

Smitten? As in, in love? Mary Ellen was bewildered. *How could—who—*As the thought dawned on her, she shook her head slowly. "No . . . you don't mean . . . Jason? Jason Brace-Face Hodges?"

Justine nodded tragically.

"Jason—who called you Justeeny-Weenie in kindergarten, who put a live frog in your lunchbox in third grade, and Tabasco sauce in your orange soda at the fifth grade picnic—Hodges?" Mary Ellen stuck her hand out and felt Justine's forehead.

Justine nodded helplessly.

"That's not smitten," Mary Ellen declared. "That's delirious."

Olivia pulled up in the car and honked. "What *took* you guys so long?" she asked as they slid into the backseat.

"Justine had a short psychotic episode," Mary Ellen said. "But she's snapping out of it, right?" She poked Justine. Justine didn't answer.

Chapter 5

"That's what you're wearing?" Mary Ellen asked, as Justine came into the Bobowicks' kitchen wearing a long denim skirt and a loose, long-sleeved white sweater. "Maybe I should change." She looked down at her cutoff shorts and T-shirt.

"No, you look fine," Justine said. "I decided I'm going with the long flowy skirt look this season."

"Where's your towel? The invitation said to bring your own towel and swimming stuff." Mary Ellen had hers rolled up, and her bathing suit was on under her clothes. Ben Aldrich's going-away barbecue was within walking distance, three blocks away at his grandparents' house, where he and his family had lived for the year. They'd come back east from California last August, when his father lost his job.

His father had finally found a new job in Massachusetts. Boston wasn't as far away as California, but it was still too far, Mary Ellen thought.

"I'm not bringing a towel because I'm not going swimming," Justine said.

"Why not? It's so hot. You're going to die of heat prostration in those clothes."

"No I won't," Justine said. "It's a cotton knit, so it's not hot."

Mary Ellen could see little beads of sweat near Justine's forehead, so she knew that was a lie. But she could also see the stubborn set to Justine's chin. It was useless to argue with her in that mood; besides which, if Justine decided to change her clothes, it would be another half an hour before they'd get there.

Almost all the kids from last year's sixth grade class were there by the time Mary Ellen and Justine walked into the backyard. About half of them were in the pool, and the other half were on the deck. On the picnic table were some gifts. Mary Ellen frowned. She hadn't thought people were going to bring presents. Glancing at the pile, she saw a calligraphied poem in a cheap picture frame on top. Scanning the lines, she grinned.

Friends may come
and friends may go
but one thing you
should always know
you've left your stamp
upon our hearts
we'll think of you
though we're apart.
May luck and sunshine
follow you
and happiness
in all you do.

You take the cake
and all the frostin'
Hope you do real well
In Boston.

Only one person in the world could have written poetry that bad. Amy Colter.

"Hey, Mary Ellen. Justine, welcome back!" Kevin Middendorf said in his squeaky voice. "Hey everybody, Justine's back from Paris!" A bunch of kids gave casual waves, but Mary Ellen could see Justine was mortified at the extra attention Kevin's announcement had caused.

"It's the Clod Couple in person," Jason said with a grin. "Wreck any more department store displays lately?"

"Highly amusing, Tinsel Teeth," Mary Ellen said dryly. "Remind me to put it on my list of laughs, right after stale knock knock jokes." But she smiled at him. Okay, she'd admit it, he *was* a lot better looking than he'd been last year. It was like he'd grown into himself over the summer. But he still had braces. And he was still Jason.

"Here, sit down. We're playing 'Choice.' " Ben moved over on the picnic table bench to make room for Mary Ellen and Justine. "Hi, Justine, I'm glad you got back before I left."

"Me, too," Justine said.

"What's Choice?" she asked Ben.

"A game Amy told us about. Just listen, you'll pick it up. It's easy," Ben told her.

"Okay, it's my turn to ask the Choice question," Jason was saying. He narrowed his eyes, looking around the circle of kids, stopping when he reached Mary Ellen, and grinning.

"Bobowick. Would you rather be buried up to your neck in Fancy Treat Gourmet Cat Food for eight hours, or tied to Kevin Peanut-butter-and-Pickle-Breath Middendorf, and hung from a ceiling fan for eight minutes?"

"Eeewww!" Mary Ellen wrinkled her nose, while everyone else laughed, including Kevin, who tried to snap his damp towel in Jason's direction but only managed to knock an almost-empty basket of tortilla chips onto the patio.

"Ooops," he said. "Sorry." He headed for the diving board end of the pool, while Mary Ellen looked at Jason and made a gagging face.

"Does it have to be cat food? Can't you make it tapioca pudding or something?" she asked.

Jason shook his head. "Nope. Those are your two choices. Take your pick, Bobowick." He snatched a mini-pretzel from the bowl on one of the small white plastic tables set around the patio and pool, and fired it at Mary Ellen's head.

"Watch me do a double axel, guys!" Kevin shouted from the diving board.

"That's an ice skating move, Kevin," Mary Ellen called out.

"Oh," he said. "Well then, watch me do a half nelson."

"That's a wrestling move," Ben yelled, laughing.

"Well, okay, watch me do a triple Middendorf flipple." Kevin pranced down to the end like a double-jointed grasshopper, then dove in, twisting his body like a contortionist before hitting the water with a splash.

"That looked more like a combination of cannonball, belly flop, and Wile E. Coyote falling off a cliff, Kevin," Mary Ellen called over when he surfaced, sputtering.

"Pretty good though, huh? An original move. What did-ya think, Justine?"

Justine rolled her eyes and shook her head. "It was original, all right."

"So what's your choice already, Mary Ellen?" Amy said in a bored tone. "If you don't hurry up and choose, you lose your turn." She stretched her leg out along the lounge chair she was hogging, and threw her shoulders back, sticking out the chest of her pink flowered bathing suit.

Showoff, Mary Ellen thought, hunching her shoulders a little, and folding her arms across her T-shirt. No use flaunting what you didn't have. But it was totally unfair for someone so obnoxious to have cleavage already. "No one said anything about a time limit, Amy."

"I thought of the game, so I make the rules," Amy said. "And the time limit's almost up. *Eewww! Kevin!!* Get away from me!"

"Eewww! Kevin! Get oouuwwtt!" Debra Hirsh, Amy's sidekick and one-person fan club, echoed.

Kevin had climbed out of the pool and was standing next to the patio, shaking his head back and forth like a dog shaking water off its fur. He grinned, gave one last shake, grabbed a dill pickle wedge from the platter on the picnic table, crunched off a big sloppy bite, and chomped away.

"Okay. I'll take the cat food," Mary Ellen said quickly. "No offense, Kevin—I just have a problem with pickles."

"Hey, dill pickles are really good for you," Kevin said, and stuffed the rest of it in his mouth. "The more garlic, the better, too. Garlic's a really healthy thing." He picked up a second pickle and ate half in one bite.

"I thought garlic was only good for keeping vampires away," Ben said.

"Then Kevin's breath would make Dracula pass out," Robbie Pellito put in.

Kevin just kept grinning and munching.

"So who's the next person? Are you going to give a choice sometime this century, Mary Ellen?" Amy asked.

Mary Ellen gritted her teeth. When she and Ben were planning this party after he found out his family was moving, they'd both wanted to leave Amy off the list. But Ben's mother said if most of the class was going to be invited, all of the class should be invited.

"Okay," Mary Ellen said, looking around, trying to decide who she wanted to pick as the chooser. Amy heaved a series of huge, exaggerated, exasperated sighs, and Mary

Ellen could see her watching the top of her bathing suit move up and down with each one. She saw Jason watching, too, then grinned as an inspiration seized her.

"Jason. Would you rather eat raw liver three times a day for three years, or listen to three minutes of Amy reading her poetry?" Mary Ellen sat back in satisfaction as Jason put his chin in his hands, like that naked thinker statue.

Now Amy glared at Mary Ellen while they all waited for Jason's answer. When he didn't respond right away, she reached over a pedicured foot and kicked him in the shoulder. "Ja-son!" She pulled a pout.

"Okay, okay." He moved out of kicking range. "That's a no-brainer, Bobowick. Pass the ketchup. Raw liver, *mmm-mmmm!*"

"I'll give you ketchup!" Amy shrieked. She grabbed the red squirt bottle from the table, aimed it at Jason, and squeezed. A goopy red string shot out, hitting him just above the ear. Jason jumped up and started wrestling the bottle away from Amy while she shrieked and giggled.

"I'll take that. Sorry kids, no food fights." Ben's mother intervened, holding out her hand for the ketchup, nicely, but firmly. She gave Jason a napkin, as Amy broke away and ran toward the pool, laughing and taunting him. Jason swiped the napkin across the side of his head, handed it back to Ben's mother, and raced in hot pursuit.

Mary Ellen snorted in disgust.

"I know what you mean," Ben said. "Choice. Would you rather watch Amy play Queen Bee to Jason's drone, or get a surprise?"

"I'd rather do anything than watch Amy," Mary Ellen said.

"Okay, come on." Ben stood up. "Go around to the front door. I'll meet you there in three minutes. Don't tell anyone." As she stood to follow Ben's instructions, Ben's father, stationed at the grill, announced loudly, "First round of burgers and dogs ready."

As kids swarmed toward the grill, Mary Ellen slipped around the side of the house to the front yard, where Ben was coming down the front porch steps, holding a medium-sized brown paper bag, the top closed and clutched in his fist.

"Is that the surprise? For me? What is it?" Mary Ellen asked, meeting him in the middle of the grass.

"You'll see," he said mysteriously. "If I tell you, it won't be a surprise. Come on." He headed across the lawn to the sidewalk. Mary Ellen jogged a few steps to catch up with him. A whiff of something citrusy wafted past her nose, like the lime aftershave her father used. Ben's hair, still wet from the pool, was combed, she noticed.

"You mean leave the party? Where are we going? I should tell Justine—"

"Your house," he told her. "And we won't be long."

"How come?" she started to say, but Ben reached for her hand and gave it a tug. And he didn't let go!

The late August evening was quiet, except for the raspy hum of cicadas, and a slight swishing sound coming from the paper bag, as they walked the three blocks to Mary Ellen's house.

"No one's home?" Ben asked as they walked up the Bobowicks' driveway.

"My parents and Nicky are over at Gram's house for dinner," Mary Ellen told him.

"Can we get inside? Is the house locked?" Now there was a note of anxiety in Ben's voice.

"I have my key." She pulled her house key on its tiny rubber dolphin keychain out of her front pocket.

"Good." He sounded relieved. Whatever was in the bag swished again.

"My mother has an ironclad rule about no water balloons in the house," Mary Ellen warned him, unlocking the back door, opening it, and flicking the light switch on as she went in.

"It's not a water balloon," Ben told her. He passed her and headed toward the front hall and up the stairs. *She and Ben? Alone in her house? Upstairs, where the bedrooms were??* They'd been up in her room together before, but never when her mother wasn't home. *What was he thinking?* But her curiosity got the better of her, and she followed him all the way to her room.

"Okay, close your eyes and hold out your hands," Ben said.

Tense with suspense, Mary Ellen squeezed her eyes shut and thrust her hands out.

"Don't drop it," she heard Ben warn, along with the rustle of the paper bag being opened. Then she felt a cold, plastic, pillow-shaped shifting-liquid weight in her hands.

"Now you can open them."

Mary Ellen's eyes blinked open, then blinked again, as she squealed in delight. "It's Bozo!" Inside a plastic Ziploc bag filled with clear water, a three-inch tropical fish, bright crimson with bands of white, was darting around its confined carrying quarters. The biggest clownfish from Ben's small saltwater tank, and his favorite fish!

"You're giving Bozo to me?"

Ben nodded, grinning, and reddening under his summer tan. "Yeah. I'm going to get a bigger setup when we move into our new place. I gave the damsels back to the fish store. But I wanted you to have Bozo. Better get him in the tank quick."

Mary Ellen walked over to her marine aquarium, lifted the lid to the tank, carefully unzipped the plastic bag, and gently poured, letting Bozo slide into the tank on the tiny waterfall. Immediately the clownfish dove for the bottom. Her five damselfish and the yellow tang began flashing agitatedly through the water and around the rock caves, sensing an intruder.

"They'll get used to him," Ben said.

Mary Ellen looked at Ben. She was *really* going to miss him. He was the first boy she'd ever been real friends with. "Are you sure you want to give him to me? You could probably transport him to Boston okay."

Ben shook his head. "I know you'll take good care of him. Plus, it'll give me an excuse to come over, whenever we visit my grandparents."

"You don't need an excuse," Mary Ellen said.

"So tell me about the kiss now! You promised you'd tell me the whole thing," Justine said, combing the tangles out of her wet hair. The two girls were sitting in Mary Ellen's room, reviewing their back-to-school lists for the last time. It was the first time Justine was sleeping over in almost a year!

"Okay," Mary Ellen said, towel drying her hair. "I'm not sure it exactly counts as a 100 percent kiss, though. I mean, he *kind of* kissed me."

"What do you mean, '*kind of*'?" Justine reached into the bag of Reese's bite-sized peanut butter cups she'd brought over, then held it out to Mary Ellen. "What's a *kind-of* kiss? Was there lip-to-lip contact?"

Mary Ellen shook her head. "I'm so stuffed I couldn't eat even one Reese's piece," she said. "Well, not exactly lip-to-lip. Actually, more like, um, nose to chin. He *kind of* took me by surprise, so I *kind of* jerked my head a little, so he *kind of* ended up bumping the side of my chin with his nose." She shrugged sheepishly, and Justine burst out laughing.

Mary Ellen was glad, because Justine had been furious that Mary Ellen had ditched her at the party, almost too mad to sleep over. She and Ben had been away long enough for people to notice, and tease them both when they got back.

"I say that still counts as your official first one, even if it wasn't 100 percent. It's the intention, not where the kiss lands that counts," Justine said now. "You two weren't the only ones who disappeared, you know," she added glumly.

"Jason and Amy?" Mary Ellen guessed from her expression.

"Yeah."

"Well, look at it this way. They *kind of* deserve each other. They're both so conceited, they can take turns holding mirrors up for each other. Especially Jason, now that his hair's long. He thinks he's—who was that muscle-man guy in the Bible who had all his strength in his hair, and lost it when his girlfriend gave him a buzz cut?"

"Samson," Justine said with a sigh. "You get kissed and I get dissed."

"Well . . ." Mary Ellen tried to think of something to say to cheer her up. "Kevin seemed really happy to see you," she said, half joking.

"That's not even close to being funny, Mary Ellen." She stood up, put the comb on Mary Ellen's dresser, and stared into Mary Ellen's mirror, frowning. "I know what would make me look better," she said.

"What?" Mary Ellen asked.

"One of those total head ski masks with the eye holes."

"Cut it out!" Mary Ellen frowned.

"Cut what out?" Justine looked defensive all of a sudden.

"I mean, stop saying stuff like that. Sheesh, with friends like yourself, who needs enemies?" Mary Ellen forced a little laugh, but it was beginning to bother her. That was like the fifth putdown Justine had aimed at herself in the past half hour.

"Okay. I take it back."

Mary Ellen nodded. "That's better."

"A mummy's wrapping would do just as well." She gave Mary Ellen a self-mocking smile in the mirror.

Chapter 6

"I can't believe it's raining on the first day of school," Justine said glumly, as the two girls huddled together under Mary Ellen's umbrella at their bus stop on the corner of the street. "I spent half an hour blow drying my hair so it'd be straighter and now it's going to friz into a Brillo pad. You were smart to get yours cut short."

"Yeah, it's so easy." Mary Ellen shook her head from side to side. "But if you don't like yours that way, it's easy enough to fix. I mean, I can't automatically make mine long—but you can cut yours. How come you bothered to get a permanent, anyway, if you have to spend half an hour getting it straight again?"

"I don't know. Seemed like a good idea at the time. I

wish it would grow out, though. A lot of kids had their hair cut this way in Paris, but I haven't seen one single person with this 'do since I got back." A rumbling engine made them both turn their heads as the yellow school bus swung around the corner. Quickly Justine took a small mirror out of the side pocket in her backpack, peering into it anxiously. "I should have worn a hat!"

"Then you'd have to worry about hat hair," Mary Ellen pointed out. "Don't worry. You look fine."

The bus braked to a slow screeching halt in front of them, red lights blinking, stop sign out, holding up all the traffic behind it and in front of it. The doors smacked open, and Mary Ellen started up the steps, with Justine right behind her.

"Good morning, girls!" A woman beamed at them from the driver's seat. "My name's Tina. Welcome aboard. Please find seats as quickly as possible. Don't want to be late your first day of school!"

About three quarters of the seats were taken. Mary Ellen spotted the last remaining empty double seat close to the rear of the bus, and advanced down the aisle. Amy and Debra, the last two people Mary Ellen would have chosen to sit near, were in the seat right behind it. When she was two seats away, Amy stood and dropped her backpack onto the empty seat.

"Sorry, this is saved," she said. "Jason and Robbie are at the second-to-the-last stop. I promised I'd save them seats." She sat there with a simpering smirk on her face, as if daring Mary Ellen to challenge her.

"You can't save seats on the bus," Mary Ellen said.

"Watch me," Amy retorted. She slid off the seat she was in, and into the one in front of it. "It's saved."

"It's saved," Debra repeated, nodding for emphasis.

"Is there a weird echo in here?" Mary Ellen said, cupping her hand next to her ear and pretending to listen hard. "Come on Justine, let's go sit in a less *noisy* part of the bus."

"Find a place, girls," Tina called out. "You're holding up the parade!"

"Hey guys, over here. Here's two seats." Mary Ellen recognized Kevin's voice even before she turned around. He was sitting in the middle of the bus, with an empty place next to him. Marcia Palumbo was in a single, too, across the aisle.

Shaking her head in disgust at Amy, Mary Ellen turned around, but Justine was blocking her way. "I don't want to sit next to him," she whispered urgently.

"It's not worth getting into a fight with—" Mary Ellen started to say.

"METER'S RUNNING LADIES! FIND SOME SEATS!" Tina bellowed.

Justine reluctantly shuffled toward the front of the bus, taking the seat next to Marcia and leaving Mary Ellen to sit next to Kevin.

"Love your hair, by the way, Justine," Amy called out loudly as the bus lurched forward with a loud rumble. "Did you get your small appliances mixed up this morning and use the blender instead of the blow dryer?"

"Hey, guys," Kevin said leaning in front of Mary Ellen, his jaw working up and down as he chewed a huge wad of green gum. "Ready for a running start?"

Justine gave him a stiff smile. Her face was still red from Amy's comment.

"Hear from Ben yet?" Kevin winked at Mary Ellen, then blew an enormous bubble, which popped as he tried to suck it back in, spreading a tissue-thin sticky green film over his chin.

Mary Ellen rolled her eyes, but couldn't help smiling. Kevin grinned good-naturedly as he started picking off sticky spots. The bus swung around another corner and stopped again.

"Uh uh. He's going to e-mail me when he gets online in Boston," Mary Ellen told him.

Ten minutes later, the bus pulled up to Jason's and Robbie's stop. They got on and swaggered toward the rear.

"Right here, guys," Mary Ellen heard Amy call, at the same time seeing Justine slink down in her seat, as Jason passed. The bus lumbered on again as soon as Jason and Robbie sat down. After one last stop to pick up some kids Mary Ellen didn't know, Tina bellowed a warning.

"Hang on to your seats, kids, we're the express bus now, next stop, Dexter Junior High."

The aisle turned into a melee as the bus screeched to a halt in the Dexter parking lot, in front of the main entrance. Kids jumped up and jostled to get off. Mary Ellen got squashed forward, while Justine struggled to break into the line behind her. A girl they didn't know had dropped her purse upside down next to the bus driver's seat, spilling the contents all over the floor.

"Hold up, everyone," Tina the Bus Driver yelled. "Mishap."

"I think I'd rather walk than endure this torture every morning," Justine said to Mary Ellen.

"Did you ever play Pig Pile?" Kevin said loudly from behind them.

"What's Pig Pile," Mary Ellen asked over her shoulder.

"It's when you have a whole bunch of kids, and somebody yells 'Pig Pile on Whoever,' and everyone else jumps on whoever," Kevin said, grunting good-naturedly as he got shoved from the rear. "Me and my cousins play it when they visit on holidays. Sort of a family tradition. Anyhow, this reminds me of it."

"That is the dopiest family tradition I've ever heard of, Kevin," Justine snapped. "And would you stop pushing? What do you want me to do, go over the people in front of me?"

"Sorry," Kevin mumbled through his mouthful of gum. "They're pushing me. Oooops!"

"Look *out,* Kevin!" Justine said, stumbling forward a step as he almost fell onto her.

Then the line started moving again. Outside the bus, Mary Ellen and Justine stood to one side, Justine touching up her lipstick with a little pocket mirror, while Mary Ellen just looked at the enormous brick building, and all the kids streaming toward the three entrances.

"I don't know if I'm ready for this," Justine said, slipping the mirror back in her purse.

Mary Ellen took a deep breath. "Well, ready or not, here we go."

"One-o-three." Mary Ellen read the number over the classroom door. "This is it."

Eighth-grade student council members with paper name tags had been stationed at all the entrances, at both ends of all the hallways, and near all the stairwells, to direct the traffic of incoming seventh graders and new students, and hand out copies of the school's floor plan.

The door to 103 was open. Mary Ellen went in, with Justine right behind her. The classroom was about half full. Sitting behind the teacher's desk was a youngish-looking, very thin man with red hair, a short goatee, and gold-framed glasses. Mr. Gumble, Mary Ellen presumed. From the decorations in the classroom, it looked like he was the music and drama teacher. On the desk in front of him were two metallic-enamelled black canisters about the size of two-pound coffee cans, and written on the blackboard behind him was his name, and a numbered list that said: 1.) Bell, 2.) School announcements, 3.) Attendance, 4.) Homeroom business, 5.) Free exchange of ideas time.

"Greetings," he called to them in a laid-back kind of voice, while waving a hand lazily. "Take any seats you like. Feel free to chat amongst yourselves until the bell rings. If you need a topic, consider this: How many surrealists does it take to change a light bulb?" Then he went back to reading his paperback book.

Mary Ellen and Justine looked at each other.

"How long do you think it's been since he escaped?" Justine murmured.

"Escaped?" Mary Ellen said, moving toward the center of the back of the classroom, where there were two empty seats next to each other, second to last in the third and fourth rows.

"Yeah. From the nut house."

Mary Ellen grinned, put her backpack on the floor next to her desk, and sat down. Kevin came in the door next, followed by Amy, Debra, Jason, and Robbie.

"Oh great," Justine said. "It's like a reunion from elementary. I thought Dexter was so big we'd be able to get away from them." She sat in the seat next to Mary Ellen as the homeroom teacher called out the same greeting to the others.

"Maybe they thought it would make it easier to adjust, if they kept some of the kids from the same elementary schools together," Mary Ellen said.

"What the heck is a surrcalist?" Jason called out to the teacher, as he and the others, except for Kevin, who'd sat right in front of Justine, took a group of seats near the window.

"A surrealist is an artist or writer who uses all kinds of subconscious stuff, like stuff from dreams, in their writing or their artwork, just the same as if it were real stuff," Kevin answered Jason's question. "And how many does it take, Mr. Gumble?"

The teacher smiled at him as if he was pretty amazed to find someone who could answer that question in his homeroom. "Tell you at the end of class," he promised.

By the time the bell rang, almost every seat in the class was taken, with Mr. Gumble's odd greeting given to each student who'd come in. As soon as it stopped, Mr. Gumble put his book away. He stood up, then pounded out a twenty-second rapid-fire drumbeat on the canisters which Mary Ellen now recognized as bongos.

"Welcome. This is your homeroom," he said. "This—" he pointed to the list on the blackboard, "is your daily homeroom agenda. Keep the seats you're in for now. I'll pass around a seating plan, and I'd be much obliged if you'd fill it in with your real names, not the names of your cartoon alter ego, your favorite movie star, etcetera etcetera etcetera. Okay, number one, bell. As soon as it rings, you're in your seats. Number two, announcements." He pointed at the loudspeaker box high on the wall next to the clock, and as if at his signal, it crackled with static, and a disembodied fuzzyish voice began to speak.

"Good morning, students. To our class of seventh graders, and to any new students, welcome to Dexter Junior High School. To our returning eighth graders, welcome back."

The box droned on for a few minutes about letters that would be sent home to parents, information about bus number changes, and the instruction to any students whose buses had failed to pick them up at the proper stops this morning to please come to the office at lunchtime.

"If the bus didn't pick them up, how would they be here to hear the announcement?" Kevin whispered.

"Their parents probably drove them," Justine said. She rolled her eyes, and Mary Ellen recognized her "How dumb can someone be?" look.

"If they get here too late to hear the announcement, they have to go to the office anyhow," Mary Ellen pointed out.

"Oh," Kevin said. "True."

Mary Ellen smiled. Kevin was incredibly smart about really complicated things, but sometimes amazingly dense about simple, common-sense things.

The morning announcements ended with the voice telling them all to "Have a good day and make at least one person smile."

"Number three, attendance, here we go." He read the list of students in alphabetical order. "All present and accounted for, good. I hate losing students on the first day. Number four, homeroom business. Today's homeroom business is lockers. I'll read your name, give you your locker assignment. All the lockers for this homeroom will be found on the wall directly outside this classroom. On your way out to stow whatever gear you want to stow, come up here, and pick a lock. Pun intended. If you have trouble with the combination, bring it to me and we'll figure it out."

Handing out the locker assignments took almost the whole rest of the homeroom period, and the bell for the end of the first module rang as the last kid came back in and sat down. Mr. Gumble did another brief bongo beat, then waved his hand lazily to say good-bye.

"Wait," Kevin called out loudly, over the noise of the exiting students. "How many surrealists does it take to change a light bulb?"

"Two," Mr. Gumble called back to him, and Mary Ellen saw the teacher grin. He had a nice smile. "One to hold the giraffe and the other to fill the bathtub with melting clocks."

Kevin laughed hysterically, while most of the other kids gave the teacher a hairy eyeball glance, and fled the classroom as quickly as they could.

"This is worse than the mystery meat they used to serve in elementary school." Mary Ellen said after one bite of the Welcome Luau Lunch. "It's so rubbery you could probably make tires out of it." She lifted the pink slab of what they were calling ham with her fork, watched the canned pineapple slice slowly slide off, and shook her head. "Look at that. They must have raided the art supply closet for the sauce. I swear it's glue." She took her paper napkin, laid it across her plate, unwrapped the layers of wrapping around a wedge of apple pie, and attacked it. "How do they expect us to run all over this place from class to class if we don't get decent food for fuel?"

"Makes it easier to stick to my diet, anyhow," Justine said. She hadn't touched hers either.

"Hi again, guys!" Kevin plopped himself down in the one empty chair at the end of their table. He opened a brown paper lunch bag, pulled out a white bread sandwich with dark tan, green-flecked filling, and took a humongous bite. A new rush of kids had just swarmed into the lunch lines, as the bell rang, signaling the start of the next twenty-minute module. "Can you believe those lines?" he said, chewing noisily. "Who'd be stupid enough to waste half a lunch module waiting in line for that slop, when they could bring nice fresh homemade—" He looked at Justine's and Mary Ellen's trays, then took another bite of his sandwich. "Ooops," he said through a mouthful, then grinned. "No offense."

"Nice fresh homemade slop?" Mary Ellen said pointedly, but she smiled. She scanned the cafeteria, looking for other familiar faces. None on this side of the double room. Judging from the way kids were huddled together at certain tables, it seemed that kids who'd gone to the same elementary school were grouped roughly into pockets. Kevin might be a clod, but at least he was familiar.

"What classes have you had so far?" he asked, poking the thin straw through the hole in the top of his box of Yoo Hoo, but squeezing the side of the box at the same time, so a little geyser of chocolate drink squirted up, splashing his glasses. "Ooops," he said again. He maneuvered the cuff of his rugby shirt over his knuckles, wiping the lenses with his shirt, while still sipping his drink and grinning his goofy grin.

"Earth science, social studies and French I," Mary Ellen said.

"Math, social studies and French II," Justine said. "I

can't believe they expect us to go from room 102 at one end of the school to room 327 three floors up at the other end in three minutes. What do they think we are, in training for a triathalon or something? I haven't been on time for one class yet."

"I think the trick is to try and weave through the middle of the halls," Mary Ellen said. "So you don't keep getting stuck behind kids opening their lockers. You have to hug the wall going up and down the stairs. I was on time for two out of three. How was your French class, anyway? Were you light-years ahead of everyone else?"

"Pretty much. It was *une pièce du gâteau*," Justine replied, while pulling out her little mirror again, and squinting into it.

"Huh?" Mary Ellen said.

Justine sighed discontentedly at the mirror, snapped it shut, and put it away. "A piece of cake," she translated. "How 'bout yours?"

"I think it's going to be a piece of cake in a different way," Mary Ellen said. "Madame Rénée's about eighty years old. She passed out our books, wrote some stuff on the board for us to copy, then put a language CD on for the whole rest of the class, one of those 'Repeat after me' things. Then she just sat there smiling while we mangled the language."

"The accent's harder than you think to get right," Justine warned.

"I get the feeling it's not going to matter much to Madame Rénée," Mary Ellen said, scraping the last bit of crumbs and apple off the small plate, then licking her plastic fork. "A few kids called out stuff while the CD was playing. She didn't even notice. Then on the way out of class, I looked back and saw her fiddling with her hearing aids. I think she was turning them back on!"

The bell for the end of the module sounded.

"Get ready for the stampede." Mary Ellen gathered her books with one hand, picked up her tray with the other, and worked her way to the nearest set of trash cans, where there was a sign for paper trash, food trash, and bottles and cans. A group of kids came over, barged in and dumped the contents of their trays in one of the cans, without bothering to separate anything. Mary Ellen watched them walk away, frowning. "This is bad," she said.

"What is?" Justine asked, coming up behind her, and dumping her trash unseparated just like the others.

"All this trash," Mary Ellen said. "I bet they could cut it down by half. At least stuff like paper napkins. I mean, who needs more than one?"

Justine looked pointedly over at Kevin, who was pushing the whole second half of his sandwich in his mouth, and struggling to stand up, with a big peanut butter glob on his lip. "They have to keep it sanitary, too. I mean, you wouldn't want them recycling plastic wrap, would you?"

"Of course not," Mary Ellen said. "But they could use less to begin with, like only wrapping the sandwiches once instead of a triple layer." She looked at Kevin, who was now juggling his tray while hoisting his overflowing backpack onto his shoulder. He finally made it over to where they were standing. "Don't you have another twenty minutes?" she asked him.

Cheeks bulging and jaw moving up and down frantically, Kevin shook his head. "Mmm hhmmf mmmfffll fmmmmfoooofer fffffllsssss."

"Hoom floomfle foofer floss?" Mary Ellen repeated. "What foreign language are you taking, Kevin?"

He shook his head vigorously. "I said, I had a special computer class," he said after he'd swallowed the mouthful. "I only get a twenty-minute lunch on A, C, and E days."

"Well, recycling's not high on my list of priorities for today, anyhow," Justine said. "Besides which, it's bad enough I have to listen to Olivia always spouting off about her causes. Don't *you* go getting all radical on me."

"I think you're right, Mary Ellen. I think it should be

on everyone's priority list," Kevin put in.

"Well, that's reason enough for me to keep it off *my* list, Kevin," Justine said snottily.

Across the mob of kids coming in and kids going out, Mary Ellen spotted Amy and Debra hanging back to talk to Jason and Robbie. So far she'd been lucky enough not to have Amy in any of her classes other than homeroom. Maybe her luck would hold. Carrying her books in front of her like a shield, shoulders hunched over, Mary Ellen bull-dozed out of the crowd and pushed open the double fire doors to the stairwell.

"Where are you guys going now?" Kevin called, strug-gling to keep up as a fresh herd of bodies swept between him and the two girls on the other side of the fire door. He edged his way through, while Mary Ellen and Justine waited with the pool of students waiting to go upstairs.

"APR," Justine answered him. "Second floor. And we're not guys, Kevin, in case you haven't noticed."

"Hey, me, too!" Mary Ellen heard him squeak as she started up the stairs.

"Oh, thrills," Justine said. She gave Mary Ellen a push in the back. "Hurry up, before he makes himself our ca-boose."

At the top of the stairs, Mary Ellen broke into a jog in what she thought was the right direction for the All-Purpose Room, though she felt a little bad about deliber-ately ditching Kevin.

"Hey, wait up!" Kevin said. "What do your schedules say this class is? There's a misprint on mine."

Mary Ellen stopped short and turned around. "A mis-print on yours? Ours, too," she started to say but Justine plowed into her.

"Come on," she whispered urgently. "If we walk in with him, he'll probably sit next to us. We get stuck with him today, we're probably stuck with him for the year." Justine turned to Kevin. "We have to make a pit stop. Seeya there.

Bye." Grabbing Mary Ellen's arm, she yanked her into the girls' room.

As the door was shutting behind them, Mary Ellen caught a glimpse of a slightly baffled and possibly hurt look on Kevin's face. She hoped he hadn't heard what Justine said, but suspected he had.

"What did you do that for?" she asked Justine.

"Because the whole year depends on how things shake out the first few days." Justine was looking in the mirror, frowning and poking at her chin. "If I get a zit the first week of school, I will—"

"What do you mean, shake out?" Mary Ellen started feeling the old irritation that used to surface whenever Justine got too bossy.

"I mean if we let Kevin Middendorf attach himself to us, we'll be committing social suicide."

"That's crazy," Mary Ellen scoffed. "Who would care?"

Justine pulled a lipstick from her purse, ran it over her lips, blotted them with a piece of paper towel from the dispenser, then turned and looked at Mary Ellen very seriously.

"Mary Ellen, the first few weeks of junior high are when everyone gets stratified into layers. And once you're stuck in one, that's it. Do you want to wind up in the pickles-and-peanut-butter-sandwich layer?"

"Well, it's better than the sludge layer," Mary Ellen said, trying to joke, but Justine wasn't laughing. The bell cut the discussion off. "Come on—now we're late. Besides which I'm dying to find out what class this misprint is. Aren't you?"

Justine shrugged. "It'll be whatever it is. And whatever it is, it's not like we have a choice." But she followed Mary Ellen out into the hall, which was almost empty, and ran with her toward the All-Purpose Room, where Amy, Debra, and Jason were converging on the doorway from the opposite direction. Justine started into the classroom first, just

as Debra, Jason, and Amy cut in front of Mary Ellen.

"Uh, Justine," Mary Ellen heard Amy say. "Is that some new kind of barrette, or what?"

"What barrette? I'm not wearing a barrette." Justine turned back, feeling the top of her head.

"Not there. In the back." Amy whispered something to Jason, and they both snickered, then breezed past Justine, who was looking frantic. "Mary Ellen, what are they . . ." She turned her head from side to side, looking back over her shoulder. Mary Ellen saw a flash of pale green about halfway down the back of her head. She dragged Justine back a step from the doorway.

"Hold still," she said, and gingerly touched what looked like a small green plastic floret of cauliflower.

"Ouch!" Justine yelped. "What . . ."

Gum! Mary Ellen thought back to Kevin's "ooops" when they were getting off the bus that morning. She gave a sharp tug. "Sorry," she said as Justine shrieked again. She held up the gum, with several long, wavy strands of blonde hair attached to it. "It must have happened when we were getting off the bus this morning, when Kevin bumped into you."

"You mean I've been walking around with Kevin-contaminated gum in my hair all day? I am going to *annihilate* that little jerk!"

Chapter 7

Mary Ellen, grimacing, went in first, and dropped the hardened, hairy gum wad into the trash basket by the door. The desks, most of which were filled, were arranged in a circle around the perimeter of the room. Amy, Debra, and Jason darted for three together, leaving only two empty seats—one on either side of Kevin.

"I'd rather sit on a chair of nails than sit next to him," Justine said fiercely, under her breath.

Mary Ellen was beginning to get a little tired of the whole "where to sit" deal. She did a quick scan. No other options!

"Kevin, could you move over so Justine and I can sit next to each other?" Mary Ellen asked quickly.

"Sure, no problem." He sounded nervous as he picked up his books and moved over, while darting glances at Justine, who looked so mad Mary Ellen could almost see the smoke coming out of her ears. Mary Ellen quickly slid into the desk next to him, leaving the other for Justine. "Is she really mad?" he added in a whisper.

"Why didn't you at least *tell* her?" Mary Ellen said.

"Tell her what?" Kevin said, holding his palms up helplessly.

"About the gum in her hair."

"Ohhhhhhhhh," Kevin said. "So that's where it wound up. It fell out of my mouth when I tripped, but I—hey, Justine, I'm really, *really* sorry," he said.

Justine glared at him fiercely. "Don't speak to me. Don't get near me. Don't even look at me, or you're hamburger!! Got it?" She folded her arms and gazed stiffly at the front of the room.

Kevin looked at Mary Ellen, then slumped in his seat. Mary Ellen could see that it really bothered him, and she felt kind of bad. Kevin was Kevin. Weird and sometimes pesty, but never mean.

At that moment, a short flash of brilliant color swept into the room, and a surprisingly loud and operatic voice, coming from such a small person, sang out, "WELCOME ALL!"

In front of the classroom, a very petite and pretty woman stood. Her brown hair fell in long, tumbling curls, with the beginnings of some gray, but her face looked fairly young. Her eyes were darker than black coffee. But the most striking thing about her appearance was her outfit. She was wearing bright green rubber gardening clogs, black-and-white striped tights like Raggedy Ann's legs, a short tangerine skirt, into which was tucked a rainbow-colored, large print, plaid blouse. She stood there in front of the blackboard in the APR in silence. But it wasn't a grouchy teacher silence, Mary Ellen could tell. It was more like a little kid on the verge of bursting to tell them all The-Best-Secret-Ever-In-The-Whole-Universe silence.

Amy leaned over to Jason, whispering loud enough for Mary Ellen to hear. "That plaid blouse is so loud I need earplugs!"

"I AM MS. BONNIE COVILLE!" the teacher announced, as dramatically as if she were saying, "I Have Just Discovered The Meaning Of Life!"

All traces of whispers died down, while kids exchanged glances. Without warning, Ms. Coville pirouetted past a table with teachers' supplies on it, snatching up a piece of fat red sidewalk chalk along the way. She wrote in huge letters on the board: D T B D D T B Y !!!!!

On the last exclamation point, the red chalk snapped and both halves went flying out of her hand. It didn't seem to faze her one bit. She grabbed the pointer from the ledge, flourishing it like a magician's wand, and pointing to each letter as she belted out the words like an opera singer.

"Dare To Be Different!!!! Dare To Be Yourself!!! There is no misprint on your course schedules. Dee-tee Bee-dee Dee-tee Bee Why—This is your social development class. And it is about YOU!!"

Now the room was so quiet you could have heard a marshmallow drop. Mary Ellen looked at Justine, who was shrinking back in her seat as if Ms. Coville had some kind of enthusiasm plague, and it might be contagious. Jason was snickering openly, along with a bunch of other kids.

"You're embarrassed!" Ms. Coville said. A beaming smile broke out on her face. "We'll fix that. There's only one way to fail this course," she went on. "And that is, not to try. Class participation is 75 percent of your grade. Assignments are the remaining 25 percent. Now, everybody up!"

Ms. Coville gestured for them to rise with her hands. With what seemed to be unanimous reluctance, all the kids stood.

"How can someone so little have such a big voice?"

Kevin said to Mary Ellen out of the side of his mouth.

"GOOD! GOOOOOD!!!" She took a moment to beam at them all. "Take three deep breaths . . . Inhale . . . Exhale. Good good! Inhale . . . Exhale." Her voice rose an octave on "inhale," and descended on "exhale." "One more time. Inhale . . . Exhale. Excellent. Now, repeat after me: Say it loud. I'm ME and I'm proud."

Amidst mostly mumbles, Mary Ellen heard Kevin squeaking enthusiastically.

"Tsk, tsk," Ms. Coville said. "That will never do. Pump up the volume, people! Individuality is a psychic muscle that requires exercise. Each class, we will begin with this affirmation. So get used to it. Think of it as warm-up calisthenics for your psyches. Now, again—SAY IT LOUD, I'M ME AND I'M PROUD!"

This time there was some sheepish laughter, but a few more voices joined in. Mary Ellen heard Jason crack, in a stage whisper, "This one's a few cans shy of a six pack."

Ms. Coville whirled toward him with the pointer. "A VERY colorful metaphor. You have the gift of wit. Wonderful!!"

Jason did a double take at the teacher's reaction.

"Use it to spread laughter," she added, her voice dropping into seriousness, "not to skewer fellow human beings." She looked at him for a moment, and to Mary Ellen's amazement, Jason nodded. Then, her brilliant smile back in place, Ms. Coville strode back to the front of the circle.

"This is your first pop quiz, people! Five times fast, and no mumbling. Anyone who fails to execute this exercise will receive their first F! Now, SAY IT LOUD. I'M ME AND I'M PROUD." The windows rattled with the volume. By the end of the fifth go around, faces were flushed, kids were laughing, but everyone, even Amy and Debra, was shouting, "SAY IT LOUD. I'M ME AND I'M PROUD!" Everyone except Justine. She was mouthing the words, but there was no sound coming out.

"Superlative!!!" Ms. Coville applauded them vigorously. "You all get an A for your first quiz grade. Now take your seats." Desks scratched the floor as kids bumped and jostled back into their places.

Ms. Coville stood silent again, perfectly still. Justine nudged Mary Ellen's arm with her elbow, and Mary Ellen looked over. On a corner of a page in her notebook, she'd written, "If she was any loonier, she'd have feathers." Mary Ellen gave her a quick smile and a nod. When she looked back at Ms. Coville, the pointer was aimed at her.

"Don't shoot!" she yelped, putting her hands up without even thinking. The whole class cracked up, including the teacher.

"Okay, people," Ms. Coville said. Finally, she was speaking in something that came close to a normal teacher's voice. "This is a class designed to assist you in self-discovery and self-celebration. We will get to know each other. We will get to know ourselves. We will learn to be free to be our best selves. We will start with the fundamentals. The ABC of You And Me. State your name, then a word beginning with your assigned letter, which describes you, or some facet of you. I'll demonstrate. Ms. Bonnie Coville—letter *U*. Unsquelchable! See? Easy as ABC. Now, I would like one volunteer to begin with letter *A*."

Everyone froze. Ms. Coville walked slowly to the center of the circle, held the pointer out straight, closed her eyes, and spun around slowly. When she stopped, the pointer was aimed at Kevin. "A volunteer! Step right up, please." She beamed her smile at him.

Grinning, Kevin stood and scuffed over to where the teacher stood. She handed him the pointer. "Your name, your letter *A* self-descriptive word, then you get to choose the next volunteer!"

"I'm Kevin Middendorf. Umm . . . aaaahhh . . . maybe . . ." His face scrunched up in thought. "I've got it! Adorable!" Half the class went into hysterics, and Kevin laughed with them. Mary Ellen was surprised to find herself feeling kind of proud of him for carrying off this crazy teacher's assignment with such good-natured humor. He held out the pointer and spun around. When he stopped, it was aimed at Jason, who hopped right up and went to the middle of the circle.

"Jason Hodges," he said. "And I'm Baaaa-d to the Bone!"

"Bad as in good, I take it," Ms. Coville said, smiling. "Choose the next victim—I mean—" she chuckled. "The next volunteer!"

Jason turned, stopping with the pointer aimed squarely at Amy.

"No fair, he peeked!" Amy protested. But she stood up, pouting coyly, and went and took the pointer from Jason's hand, pretending to whack him with it as he walked back to his seat.

"I'm Amy Colter," she said, and paused like she had to think really hard, then hooked into the perfect word. "*C*. Cool, of Course." She twirled daintily, choosing some kid from another school. The ABC game went on, kid after kid. Justine's letter was *O*. She blushed furiously, stammering and stuttering when she was in the middle, and finally came up with "Open-minded." Mary Ellen got *S*, and promptly said, "Scientific." Marcia Palumbo was last, with *Z*.

"My name's Marcia Palumbo and I just *knew* I was going to get one of the hard letters like *Q* or *Z*." She stood in the center of the desk circle, grimacing and scrunching her face up so her cheeks looked like a chipmunk's stuffed with acorns. She scratched her head, bit her lip, and shuffled back and forth from one foot to the other.

"I can't think of anything," she whined.

"How about lay-*zee*," Mary Ellen heard Debra whisper to Amy. "I slept over at her house once and she *paid* me to do her chores."

"Or zoned-out," Amy whispered back.

"To tear each other down is not the purpose of this class." Ms. Coville had bounced into the middle next to Marcia and grabbed the pointer, and was now aiming it back and forth between Amy and Debra. "Marcia, I would say you were *zealous* in your efforts to find a Z word just now." She patted her on the shoulder, and took the pointer back. "You may be seated. Amy and Debra, since you obviously wanted to help Marcia with this exercise, I will provide you with the opportunity. Each of you will write out the entire alphabet before we meet next week, and assign a positive word describing Marcia to them all." Ms. Coville beamed as if she'd just handed them each a box of gift-wrapped candy instead of extra homework. The look of outraged disgust on Amy's face made Mary Ellen's day.

"Question," Ms. Coville went on. "Is how we perceive ourselves as important as how we would like to be perceived by others? It should be *more* important. Think about this: with whom, throughout the course of your life, will you be spending the most time? You. Yourself. So start now to be the person with whom you would most enjoy spending every waking and sleeping minute for perhaps as long as the next eighty years." She picked up a piece of chalk, tossed it in the air, caught it behind her back, and flourished it in front of the blackboard. "Your assignment for next week: Know thyself! ID cards." She handed a stack of blank, four-by-six-inch index cards to the person closest to where she was standing, indicating that they should pass them around the circle.

Glancing at the clock as she reached for her assignment pad to copy what Ms. Coville was writing off the board, Mary Ellen was amazed to see the three module class was almost over!

"Be creative," Ms. Coville said when she'd finished writing out the homework requirements. "This is my ID card." She held up an index card. "On the front, I've placed my totem animal, the tortoise. How does the tortoise represent me? It dives deeply into the waters of the unconscious and brings to the air and daylight of consciousness materials through which I become aware of who I am."

As the bell rang, Ms. Coville's voice rang out over it. "Due next week. And for your own comfort, these are private assignments. You won't be required to read them, or share them, and no one will see them but me." She bounced over to the doorway, and said good-bye to each student by name as they filed out.

"Shwew!" Justine eased out of the hallway traffic after they went through the firedoor, and slumped back against the tan cinderblock wall. "What planet did she come from?"

"Really," Mary Ellen agreed. "But I like her. Can you believe she memorized every single name of every kid in the class the first day?" She pulled out her schedule, which was worn and ripping on the creases already after only one day, and checked for her next class. "I have a twenty-minute study hall now, in the library. That's this floor, on the other side of the building." She eased into the flow of traffic going in that direction. "Then English, then last period the gym to get school ID pictures taken."

"Me, too," Justine said, consulting her own schedule as they moved along with the throng headed in that direction. "No, I didn't like her. She's one of those nosy do-gooders, I can tell. And what was all that 'We' stuff? She have a hamster in her pocket or something?"

Mary Ellen didn't answer. But she glanced at Justine out of the corner of her eye. She seemed to be thinking about something. Mary Ellen bit her lip. It was something she'd noticed when it was Justine's turn to play the ABC game. She'd thought a word had popped into Justine's head immediately, but it was something she hadn't wanted to say in front of the whole class.

"Justine?" she said, as they walked through the wide central hall that connected the east wing of the school with the west wing, where the library was.

"What?"

"Was *open-minded* the first thing you thought of?"

Justine shook her head, and chuckled, but it wasn't a happy chuckle. "*Obese* was the first word I thought of. But I wasn't about to say it in front of Amy and Jason. Or anyone in the class for that matter. Not that I have to. It's pretty obvious."

"Justine, you are *not* obese!" Mary Ellen stopped and stared at her. "You said you lost nine pounds on your diet."

"Well, I gained back ten," she said glumly.

"Well, you grew, too, I think. Look, you're getter closer to being as tall as me." She stood up straight next to Justine, who moved away, shaking her head.

"Would you *mind* not broadcasting this to the entire world?" She scrunched down behind her books.

"Sorry," Mary Ellen said. "But you don't really think—"

"I think I don't want to talk about it anymore, okay?" Justine stepped into the library, pointed to the No Talking sign at the entrance, then headed for the far corner of the room.

Chapter 8

Mary Ellen spread her books out on the kitchen table, opened her assignment note pad, and groaned. B-day was going to be her toughest day on the schedule, with every one of her academic courses meeting. Here it was, only the second day of class, and she had homework in *every single subject*. In Earth Science, the class had already been assigned a term paper—"Choose one of the environmental problems caused by human beings that confront the world today; research the causes and possible solutions; imagine there is an international legislature to address these issues; and write a proposed bill to correct the problem you've selected." They had three months to do it, and it only had to be six to eight pages, but still—*the second day of class??*

"You're doing your homework down here?" Dr. Bobowick asked, coming into the kitchen. "After that major excavation we did to get your desk cleared off and your room clean for school?"

"I think that's the problem," Mary Ellen said. "I can't concentrate up there. It's too neat. It's like—it paralyzes my brain or something."

Her mother smiled. "I know what you mean. Like Gramps always used to say, 'Clutter—"

" 'Is a sign of the creative mind,' " Mary Ellen finished the sentence for her.

"Right. However, it does impede efficiency. All right, notebook, copy of the grant proposal for the Henderson Foundation, purse, keys, sweater . . ." Dr. Bobowick took inventory of the items she was carrying. "That's all, I think. Peter," she called out to Mary Ellen's father, who was reading the newspaper in the den, "don't forget, as soon as the videotape is over, Nicky needs to shower and get to bed. I hope I'll be home by nine, but I have a feeling this meeting's going to run late, because of the grant project for the new science building."

"Wait! Don't leave me defenseless this time," Mr. Bobowick hurried into the room as Dr. Bobowick started out the door. "Where are the secret weapons? I couldn't find them the other night and he tortured me."

Dr. Bobowick turned and rummaged among the papers on the kitchen desk. "They were right here this afternoon."

"I think he left them in the swing fort," Mary Ellen said. *Go Dog Go*, which Nicky knew by heart, frontward, backward, and upside down, and Dizzy his stuffed lizard, were the two crucial ingredients to a smooth bedtime for her little brother. "I'll run out and get them," she offered. Anything to postpone the mountain of homework she had to tackle.

"Thank you, honey. And Peter, don't let him—"

"I know, I know—have too much chocolate ice cream, give his sister's fish a bubble bath, jump on the bed, play with stapleguns, chainsaws, machine guns, or your sewing scissors. Go to your meeting, sweetheart. It's all under control." Mary Ellen's father shooed her mother toward the door, then headed back toward the den while Mary Ellen went out to retrieve Nicky's bedtime ritual gear.

As Dr. Bobowick backed out of the driveway, Justine popped her head out of her bedroom window.

"Did you start your homework yet?" she called.

Mary Ellen looked up. "Uh uh. But I wanted to ask if you'd help me with my French."

"Bien sur," Justine answered.

"Bean sewer? I don't think we've gotten that far yet."

Justine laughed at her pronunciation. "Good thing Madame Rénée's hard of hearing. Anyhow, it means 'of course.' I've been working for an hour already and barely made a dent," Justine said. "Want to do homework together? Maybe if we race each other, we'll get it done faster."

Mary Ellen nodded. "Your house or mine?"

"Yours," Justine said emphatically. She disappeared inside and was out a moment later with her stack of books. She and Mary Ellen converged on the Bobowicks' back porch.

"Any excuse to get out of there," Justine said. "It's more depressing than a morgue." She followed Mary Ellen inside, and dropped her books on the kitchen table. "Do you think it's going to be like this every night?"

"I hope not," Mary Ellen said. "But think about it—when we only had one teacher last year, she knew what homework she gave in different subjects, so if she loaded it on in one subject, she lightened it up in another. None of these guys knows what the other one's doing."

"What's the good news, Justine?" Mr. Bobowick came into the kitchen, with Nicky at his heels.

Justine shook her head. "None that I know of, Mr. Bobowick. Unless you want to count my mother having only three meltdowns today, the last one of which wound up as three broken dinner plates, so there were fewer dishes to do."

Mary Ellen's father looked at her sympathetically. "It's going to take time. Did you ever hear the story of the king's ring?"

Justine shook her head.

"A young king came to the throne after his father, the old king, died."

"Why did his father die?" Nicky asked. Mary Ellen saw his forehead wrinkle with worry.

"Well," Mr. Bobowick said, "he'd lived a very long and good life and was very old—"

"As old as you?" Nicky broke in, his worried look getting worse.

"Much, much, much older," his father said reassuringly.

"Nicky, let Daddy tell the story," Mary Ellen said. "Go ahead, Dad."

"Okay. So the new king summoned the court wizard to the throne and said, 'This is a time of great sorrow with the death of my father. But it's also a time of rejoicing, in coming to the throne to do what I've been preparing all my life to do. Give me wisdom, oh Wizard—' "

"What's wisdom?" Nicky interrupted again. "Is it where the wizard lives?"

"Huh?" Mr. Bobowick looked puzzled by the question.

"Well if a king lives in a kingdom, does a wizard live in a wizzdom?"

Mary Ellen and Justine laughed, and Mr. Bobowick smiled.

"Good guess, Nicky. Wisdom is something a wise person has inside. If someone's wise, they know a lot about a lot of things."

"There's a kid in my class who knows a lot about a lot of things," Nicky said. "His name is—"

"Nicky, please let Dad finish so Justine and I can do our homework, okay?"

Mr. Bobowick shook his head, as if nudging his train of thought back on the track. "So the young king said, 'Oh Wise Wizard, give me something that will guide me through times of both sorrow and joy.' The wizard pulled out a golden ring, uttered an engraving spell over it, and handed it to the young king, who looked at it, smiled as a tear came into his eye, and put it on his finger."

"What did it say?" Mary Ellen and Justine asked together.

"It said, 'This, too, shall pass.'"

Justine gave him a small smile. "Thanks, Mr. Bobowick. I'll pass it along to my mother if I can catch her in the right mood."

"Okay Nicko, we've got our orders from Commander-in-Chief, Mom. Bedtime. Let's go."

"Fly me," Nicky said, holding his arms out to his father.

Mr. Bobowick stooped down and hoisted him into take-off position. "Look, up in the sky, it's a bird, it's a plane—no—it's . . . Super Nicky and he's super sticky and super grimy!"

"No, Nicky the Power Pilot," Nicky said.

"I stand corrected. Nicky the Power Pilot." He flew Nicky out of the kitchen making a whooshing, windy sound.

"Your father's so nice," Justine said, sounding sad.

Mary Ellen nodded, feeling almost guilty to be so lucky. "Yours is too, Justine—it's just—" her voice trailed off. She didn't know quite what to say.

Justine shook her head. "How can someone *be* nice if they don't *act* nice? What he did was the farthest thing from nice I can imagine. 'This too shall pass,'" she repeated. "I like that. It's kind of comforting."

Mary Ellen smiled, then looked at the stacks of books and notebooks. "We better dig in, or *we're* not going to pass—any of our subjects. I'll race you through Vocab-Builder," she said, pulling out the yellow covered workbook. "On your mark, get set—"

"NOOOOOOOOOOOooooooooooooooo!!!!!" A bloodcurdling scream sounded from the upstairs hall. Mary Ellen dropped her pen. "What—?"

The screams continued.

"Nicky?" Justine said.

Mary Ellen bolted from the table so fast her chair fell over backward, and raced upstairs.

Stopping at the top, Mary Ellen looked down the hallway, where Mr. Bobowick was standing frozen, looking totally bewildered, holding Nicky, who had his body stretched stiffly sideways across the doorway to the bathroom, clutching the doorsill.

"I don't WAAAAANNNNNNAAAAaaaa!!!" he howled, his face scrunched up red, and panic-stricken.

"What's wrong?" Justine asked, coming up behind Mary Ellen.

"I have no idea," Mr. Bobowick responded. "We were on glide slope for landing in the shower, and—"

Nicky took a deep breath and belted out another yell. "I'M NOT GOING INTO THE BLOODY SHOWER OF DOOM!!"

Mary Ellen and her father exchanged baffled looks.

"The *what?*" Mary Ellen said.

Mr. Bobowick lowered Nicky to the floor, and he made a beeline toward his sister, tackling her around the knees, so she had to grab the banister to keep her balance.

"The Bloody Shower of Doom?" Justine repeated.

"What video was he watching before?" Mary Ellen asked her father.

Mr. Bobowick shrugged helplessly. "The Power Pilots. It's not Shirley Temple, but I don't think there were any Bloody Showers of Doom in it."

"Nicky, you love showers," Mary Ellen said cajolingly. She could feel him shaking. "You can use the purple squirt soap, okay? And I'll go find your SuperSprayer, and you can wash the shower stall after you—"

"I'm not going into the BLOODY SHOWER OF DOOM!" Nicky put his head up for a minute, yelled the words quickly, then burrowed back into Mary Ellen's stomach.

"Nicky, look at me," Mary Ellen said. Slowly Nicky lifted his face, and Mary Ellen could see there was genuine terror in his eyes. "What is the Bloody Shower of Doom?" An inspiration seized her. "Were you playing a scary game with Timmy and Tommy before they left?" The Bloody Shower of Doom sounded like something the twins might have cooked up.

Nicky shook his head again.

"Well, where did you hear about it?" she probed.

"Alex Michael Thomson Widdle the Forf told me," he whispered. "He said if I went in, first all the water would turn into blood, and then the Doom Man would reach up from the drain, and grab me by the foot and drag me down into the Doom Room."

"The Doom Room?" Mr. Bobowick asked helplessly. "Has there been some redecorating going on that I haven't noticed? Nicky, the living room is right underneath the bathroom. There is no Doom Room in this house."

Mary Ellen bit her lip, trying not to smile, because Nicky was obviously taking the Bloody Shower of Doom very seriously.

"How 'bout a plain old bath?" she suggested.

He shook his head vigorously. "The drain," he said. "The Doom Man will still get me."

Mr. Bobowick was frowning. "Who is this Alex Thomson Michael Fiddle and how does he know so much about our shower?"

"Alex Michael Thomson Widdle the Forf," Nicky corrected. "He's in my class."

"Nicky, look, some kids just make up stories," Justine said. "That's all that stuff is—a bunch of lies."

"Come on, Nicko, let's show that old Fiddle Faddle kid,

whoever he is, that we're not afraid of any old Bloody Shower—"

"NOOOOOOOOOOOOOOOOOO!" Nicky cut him off.

"Okay, okay," Mr. Bobowick backed off. "Calm down." He frowned down at Mary Ellen. "He's filthy—"

"How 'bout the kitchen sink?" Justine suggested. "It's got the spray attachment and Nicky's small enough to fit. Would that be okay, Nicky?"

Nicky nodded.

Mr. Bobowick threw up his hands. "I give up. Okay, Nicko, let's hit the sink. Mary Ellen, remind me to have your mother write a note to Nicky's teacher, about this Michael Johnson Riddle—"

"Alex Michael Thomson Widdle the Forf," Nicky said, nodding his head ominously at each syllable.

Chapter 9

"I swear, they don't even care if we get scoliosis from carrying all these books back and forth," Mary Ellen said as she came into the kitchen the next morning, with her backpack stuffed so full the zipper wouldn't close. "It's inhuman. It's . . . cruel and unusual punishment, and the only crime I committed was being a kid."

"Well, you'll have the weekend to rest your spine," her mother said unsympathetically. Mary Ellen raised her eyebrows. That kind of remark wasn't her mother's style at all. She looked at her closely. Her eyes had dark circles under them, and she looked like she hadn't slept well.

"Did your meeting go really late last night? I was awake till eleven and you still weren't home. What's the scoop?"

Dr. Bobowick nodded. "Very late. And the scoop is that the feud between the dean and Harvey Kettleman escalated to the point that Harvey resigned. On the spot. Which leaves the task of coordinating the Alumni and Foundation Heads reception for the new Science Building to me."

"Why you?" Mary Ellen asked.

"In a word, tenure, my dear. The dean volunteered me to take over, and without tenure, I don't really have the leverage to decline the kinds of offers that are really impositions in disguise. Like teaching an extra class of freshmen, and taking over for this reception. For which, by the way, none of the arrangements have been made. Harvey hadn't even hired a caterer. And it's only two weeks away!"

"Will you be able to pull it off?" Mary Ellen asked.

"I guess I'll have to. Nicky, you're still in your pajamas!" Dr. Bobowick exclaimed as Nicky wandered into the kitchen. "Your clothes are laid on your bed, I have an early class to teach this morning, Mary Ellen has to leave in ten minutes to catch the bus, Daddy has to leave in—" she glanced at the stove clock—"thirteen minutes to catch his train. What were you *doing* in your room all that time?"

"I was watching my ants," Nicky said. "They don't have to go to kindergarten. Why do I have to go?"

Mr. Bobowick, who'd appeared in the doorway to the kitchen just in time to hear Nicky's question, gave him a sympathetic nod. He dropped his shoes on the floor, and tugged at his tie with one hand, while trying to slip his right foot into his loafer as it kept skidding forward.

"Your ants don't go to kindergarten because they have to stay home and do their job of being ants, Nicko," he said. "They have to carry crumbs and build tunnels. My job is to be a stockbroker, Mommy's job is to be a biology teacher, Mary Ellen's job is to be a seventh grader, and your job is to be a kindergartner. Now run upstairs and see how fast you can get those clothes on."

"Ants don't have to wear clothes to do their job. Why do I have to?" Nicky asked, still not moving.

"Well, because . . ." Mr. Bobowick paused with his foot hovering over the uncooperative shoe, frowning as he pondered a response. Then his face lit up. "Because your ant farm is nice and warm inside. To them, it's always warm weather, like when we went to Disneyworld. Now go on up and—"

"How come we had to wear clothes to Disneyworld then?"

"Because—well, because—" Mr. Bobowick looked at his wife. "He's got a point. How come, Laura?"

"You're a *huge* help, Peter!" Dr. Bobowick said in exasperation. "Nicky, we wear clothes because it's our cultural norm. Now go conform to it and get dressed."

"If you think about it, Mom, that's not a very good reason," Mary Ellen put in. "I mean, we're supposed to be individuals, right? If someone would rather wear pajamas to school, I think it should be allowed. Or even no clothes. I mean, isn't it part of freedom of expression?"

Dr. Bobowick rolled her eyes. "I don't have time for a debate on the dividing line between an individual's freedom versus the common good of society as it pertains to fashion. There's plenty of scope for personal expression within the general cultural precept that we wear clothing, as evidenced by the fact that you're wearing striped socks with plaid sneakers, my dear, which in my day and age, would have been considered the gauchest of the gauche. End of this discussion for now, or we're all going to be late. Nicky, upstairs! Peter, could you supervise please, in a timely fashion? I have to pack my briefcase." Dr. Bobowick darted into her study, while Mr. Bobowick steered Nicky by the shoulders, as he sagged back against him, resisting.

"Come on, Nicko, sometimes a man's gotta do what a man's gotta do."

"I don't understand it," Mary Ellen's mother said, hurrying back into the kitchen. "Yesterday he had his turn at the finger paint easel, and his teacher seems lovely."

Mary Ellen shrugged. "Maybe he's just figured out that he's stuck in school for the next thirteen to seventeen years. They trick you into thinking it's fun the first couple of days, then the next thing you know, they hand you those fat red pencils and dotted line paper and it's work."

Dr. Bobowick shook her head. "I think there's something else bothering him."

"Did Daddy tell you about the Bloody Shower of Doom?" Mary Ellen asked.

"The *what?*"

"Bloody Shower of—"

"Yes, Doom. I heard what you said. But where on earth—"

Mary Ellen sketched the details of the bathtime scene the night before.

Dr. Bobowick looked flabbergasted. "But Nicky's always loved taking showers."

A knock at the back door sounded, followed by Justine's voice. "Ready Mary Ellen? Bus'll be here soon."

"Yep." Mary Ellen picked up her backpack, holding it in front of her so the bulging contents wouldn't spill out. "I know," she said to her mother. "But not anymore. Bye, Mom."

"A Doom Room in my house. That's all I need." Mary Ellen's mother just stood there shaking her head. Mary Ellen gave her a quick peck on the cheek as she brushed past her toward the door.

Justine was waiting at the bottom of the porch steps, wearing dark sunglasses. Mary Ellen looked up at the overcast sky and frowned.

"Is there something I'm missing?" she asked.

"What do you mean?" Justine said. "Come on, we have about three minutes to get to the bus stop." She started walking briskly down the driveway.

"I mean, the chance of any sunlight getting through this cloud cover is about the same as Nicky getting through to China in the tunnel he started in your backyard. Why are you wearing sunglasses?"

"The eyes are the windows to the soul. I don't want anybody spying on my soul."

"Anybody in particular, like, maybe, Jason Hodges?"

"Don't say that out loud!" Justine said. "If anyone finds out, I'll die."

" Don't you think Jason'll be a lot more likely to notice you if you're wearing black sunglasses on a drizzly gray day? Besides which, he'll think you're a complete nutcase."

Justine paused as the bus rumbled around the corner and began heading up the street.

"You've got a point. Okay." She took them off and slipped them into the side pocket of her backpack.

The bus screeched to a rumbling halt and the doors clattered open.

"Good morning, ladies," Tina bellowed. "Find some seats, gotta stay on schedule."

"I wish we were one of the earlier stops so we could get good seats," Justine muttered. She slid into an empty seat next to Shane Daly, while Mary Ellen sat across the aisle next to Kevin. Amy and Debra were two seats in front of them, each saving the empty seat next to them.

"Yeah," Mary Ellen said. "But this way we get to sleep in twenty minutes longer than the kids who get picked up first."

"Hey, Mary Ellen! Hi, Justine," Kevin greeted them cheerfully.

Justine didn't reply, she just slouched low in her seat. Mary Ellen set her backpack on her lap and worked on rearranging her books and binders so she could at least get the zipper closed.

When Jason and Robbie climbed on board, they went straight for the two waiting seats. Kevin was looking back and forth from Mary Ellen to Justine, who'd slumped even lower in her seat as she eyed Jason and Amy. He frowned for a second, then leaned across Mary Ellen and tapped Justine on the arm.

"Hey, Justine!" he said. "You decide on your topic for the earth science report yet?"

Justine shook her head and looked the other way, out the window. Kevin leaned back and looked at Mary Ellen, who gave him a helpless shrug.

"Well, how 'bout you, Mary Ellen?"

"Something about the Brazilian rainforest, I think," Mary Ellen said absently, watching Amy and Jason flirt with each other, and the reaction Justine was having. "The problems caused by building hydroelectric power plants on the Amazon and its tributaries."

"I'm doing mine on cattle flatulence," Kevin said cheerfully.

Now Mary Ellen's attention was caught. She turned to stare at him. "Excuse me?"

"Yep. Cattle flatulence," Kevin said loudly enough that all the kids in the surrounding seats tuned in. "It's a huge problem. See, what happens is, fast food places spring up, creating a demand for more hamburgers, which means there needs to be more beef, which means there needs to be more cattle. The more cattle they breed, the more grass and hay they eat, the more methane gas they produce, and it gets into the atmosphere."

"Clouds of cow farts," Robbie said, snickering. "Trust Middendorf to be on the case."

"Not cow farts. The majority of bovine methane comes from cattle belches," Kevin corrected. "Like this:" He inhaled and belched out the beginning of "Row, Row, Row Your Boat."

"*Eeeeewwww!* Kevin, that is absolutely disgusting," Amy squealed.

"Hey, a hidden talent." Jason egged him on. "Play it again, Kev."

"Are you planning on doing a live exhibit like Mary Ellen did with her fruit flies last year?" Debra said snidely.

"No, not a science report. You should save that for the talent show," Robbie said. "Kevin Middendorf and his Quartet of Belching Cattle." He, Jason, Debra, and Amy cracked up.

"Go ahead and laugh. Nero fiddled while Rome burned," Kevin said. "But I'm telling you, it's a serious situation. Methane happens to be the second-largest contributor to the gases that make the greenhouse effect."

Mary Ellen grinned across the aisle at Justine. "He *is* funny, you have to admit," she said.

"Right. About as funny as a screen door on a submarine." Justine shook her head. "He and Olivia would make a good match."

"I've got the solution to the problem of bovine methane, Kevin," Mary Ellen said. "Mix in Maalox with the cattle feed. Presto! No more gassy cattle."

Jason turned around, nodding and laughing. "Hey, good one, Bobowick. Maybe you'll actually be a decent scientist someday."

Mary Ellen grinned, then looked over at Justine. To her astonishment, Justine was glaring at her.

"What?" Mary Ellen said. "What's the matter?"

Folding her arms across the front of her oversized cotton sweater, Justine humphed without a further word of explanation, then turned her head and stared icily past Shane and out the window as the bus pulled into Dexter's parking lot.

It took until the end of homeroom before Justine would tell her what was wrong.

"You know I have a crush on him. You were hogging all

the attention. He probably thinks I'm a huge bore by comparison."

"I was not!" Mary Ellen protested as the bell rang. "I don't want his attention. You can have it for all I care." *Sheesh! Moody was one thing, but this was getting ridiculous.* Being stressed out from family problems was understandable. But when you started splashing it all over the whole world, especially your friends who didn't do anything, it got annoying pretty fast. Mary Ellen was beginning to get a little tired of having to walk on eggshells around Justine.

The frown on Justine's face turned to a look of uncertainty, and then resignation. "I'm sorry. And I know. Anyhow, Amy's pretty much cornered the market on him. So it doesn't really matter." She looked down at her schedule and frowned. "Uh oh, did you see what we have first today?"

"Yeah, Phys. Ed.," Mary Ellen said. She stood and picked up her books.

"Phys. Ed. with Ms. Dart," Justine corrected in an ominous tone. "Olivia nicknamed her The Poison Dart. She said she makes Attila the Hun look like the tooth fairy. We better not be late."

Making their way hastily through the crowded corridors, they followed the flow of girls into the gym. It looked like at least five or more regular-sized classes were combined into the one gym class. A perky looking young woman in a green warm-up suit, with a silver whistle on a string around her neck, was directing everyone over to a section of the bleachers, gesturing with both hands, one of which held a thick stack of papers, the other a clipboard. "This way, women. Take a seat and settle down."

"She doesn't look that bad," Mary Ellen said.

"I'm not sure that's her," Justine answered. "Olivia said she was like an Amazon woman. She was on the women's Olympic basketball team twelve years ago. This one doesn't look big enough. Or old enough."

As the bell rang for the start of the module, a very tall

woman with blondish silver hair so short it was almost a crewcut, and wearing a black warm-up suit with gold and purple trim, strode in from a door at the far end of the gym. She had a clipboard and a silver whistle, too, and as she approached the bleachers, where kids were still climbing and settling in, she gave three sharp blasts.

"Sit," she barked.

The green-suited woman trotted behind her like a puppy as she paced back and forth.

"Wow! And I thought I was tall," Mary Ellen whispered to Justine, looking up in amazement. They'd squeezed into a spot in the third bleacher row, right in front of Amy and Debra.

"I wonder if she needs extra oxygen up there," Justine answered, out of the side of her mouth.

"I'm Ms. Dart, and that's how I expect to be addressed. This is my teaching assistant Ms. Musanti." At the end of each sentence, she gave a sharp nod of her head, then passed a hand over one side of her hair. "With such a large class, the only way to accomplish the goals of this curriculum is to use the time efficiently. To that end, I expect prompt and complete cooperation." She stopped, gave a crisp nod to Ms. Musanti, who immediately handed the stack of stapled papers to the last girl in the front bleacher row, with a gesture that she was to pass them down.

"The top sheet of the papers you're receiving now is the list of required gear for Phys. Ed.," Ms. Dart said crisply. "Anyone showing up for class without the proper attire and equipment will be counted as absent for that day. Anyone who falls short of the number of Phys. Ed. classes required for the passing of this course will have to repeat it during summer sessions, in order to have enough credits to graduate junior high. With regards to my attendance policy, if you're thinking of cutting this class, think again. The first unexcused absence will earn you one detention. The second unexcused absence will earn you two detentions. And so on.

Culpability accrues with interest." Now she stopped, put her hands on her hips, and scanned the class. "Are we clear on this, women?"

Weak and scattered murmurs of assent rippled through the bleachers.

"Excuse me? I said, 'ARE WE CLEAR ON THIS, WOMEN?' The correct response is, 'Yes, Ms. Dart. We're clear on this.'"

"Oh no, not another radical one," Justine groaned. "Where do they *find* these people?"

"Do you have something you'd like to share with the class?" Ms. Dart snapped suddenly, her gaze focused on Justine.

Mary Ellen felt Justine shrink back, and saw her turn scarlet as she shook her head.

"When I speak, I expect the courtesy of attentive listening." Then she went on barking out information. There wasn't a whisper in the bleachers, only the sound of sheets of paper shuffling as Ms. Dart went over the list of rules and regulations and requirements.

"You'll be divided into squads, both for activities and sports, and for order in the locker room. This is due both to the size of the class, and to one of the curriculum goals, which is to foster team cooperation and spirit. Ms. Musanti?"

Like a well-trained robot, Ms. Musanti held her clipboard in front of her and started reading. "Each squad will be comprised of eight women. Roll call will be taken by squad. You'll have ten minutes of the first module to change into your gear, and report to the gym. Demerits *will* be issued for tardiness in reporting for roll call. Three demerits merit one detention," she said, then smiled as if her little play on words might get a round of applause for cleverness. She stopped speaking and looked expectantly at her boss.

"The human body is a machine that must be kept well-tuned and well-maintained in order to perform optimally,"

Ms. Dart said. "In line with proper body care is proper hygiene. To this end, showers at the end of each gym class are required for each student." She turned and nodded again to Ms. Musanti, who consulted her clipboard again and started speaking as if Ms. Dart had pulled a string in her back, like one of those talking dolls.

"You'll have the entire last module to shower and change back into your school clothes. The order of squads for shower call will alternate by the week. No late passes will be issued for your next class, should you fail to shower and change in the allotted time."

"Any questions so far?" Ms. Dart asked. No one raised a hand. "Good. I expect the best effort and cooperation of each student for one reason: I want you to expect your best from yourselves. As your names are called, assemble on the blue line." She pointed to one of the wide tape lines that went around the perimeter of the gym floor. "Ms. Musanti?"

Right on cue again, Ms. Musanti began reeling off names for each squad. Justine got put into B squad. She made a sad face at Mary Ellen as she got up to go stand with her squad. Debra and Marcia were in B squad, too. When Ms. Musanti got to C squad, Mary Ellen's name was first. "Ms. Bobowick. Ms. Colter. Ms. Daly. Ms. Jennings. Ms. Manasevit. Ms. Palmer—"

Great. Mary Ellen stood unenthusiastically. Sharing the same squad with Amy was about as exciting a prospect as having all her molars yanked out with rusty pliers. As she went to step over the bleacher, the front of her shin scraped the edge of the bleacher seat in front of her, barking it sharply, and making her stumble forward. While one hand went to cover the sharp pain on her leg, the other flailed wildly so she could regain her balance, in the process whacking Amy on the side of her head.

"OUCH!" Amy yelled indignantly.

"What's the problem?" Ms. Dart snapped, looking up from her clipboard.

"Sorry," Mary Ellen mumbled humbly. "I tripped." She winced, still rubbing her shin. Injury number one for the school year.

"She smacked me in the head is the problem," Amy said.

Ms. Dart looked at Amy, then at Mary Ellen, then back to Amy who was standing there smugly, waiting for Mary Ellen to get taken apart by the teacher.

"Your name," she said crisply to Mary Ellen.

"Mary Ellen Bobowick," she said, and gulped.

"Get with your squad, Ms. Bobowick. And pay attention. Most of the accidents that happen in gym classes are due to inattention." Her tone of voice was surprisingly mild.

Relieved, Mary Ellen stepped up onto the next bleacher, carefully watching her feet.

"Your name," she heard Ms. Dart say again.

"Amy Colter," Amy said in a haughty tone of voice.

"Toughen up, Ms. Colter. This isn't the sandbox in nursery school. I don't have the time or the patience for petty bickering."

Standing with her squad, facing the bleachers, Mary Ellen caught Amy giving her a look of concentrated spite. She smiled broadly.

Chapter 10

"We're here!" Nicky announced, charging past Mary Ellen into the Kellys' kitchen. Their parents followed right behind.

"So I see," Mrs. Kelly said with a smile. "And right on time for the first course." She slipped her apron on, lifted a plate covered with small one-person-sized quiches, and waved the Bobowicks in front of her, into the dining room. She set the dish down on one corner of the table. "Just pass it around and serve yourselves. I'll go get the bread."

"Your mom went to so much trouble," Mary Ellen said to Justine as they took seats on one side of the table. "I mean, it's only us!"

"It's not trouble to her. She loves doing it—especially

for anyone who appreciates it at least enough to show up on time," Justine said.

"Wow, this is like a fancy restaurant!" Nicky said, as he climbed onto the dining room chair Olivia held out for him. "Mrs. Alexander always had clothes to fold on the table."

The Kelly's dining room table was set with a creamy lace tablecloth over a dark red one. All the dishes and glasses on the table were fine china, but with a variety of patterns from different sets. The candle holders, napkins, napkin rings, and even the silverware settings didn't match either, but somehow, the total effect was that everything complemented everything else, and it all looked good together.

Mary Ellen had brought over half-a-dozen zucchinis from their garden earlier in the afternoon, and Mrs. Kelly had hollowed them out so they looked like little green canoes and stuffed them with what looked and smelled like turkey stuffing. The salad contained several different kinds of lettuce, with a ring of radishes carved like roses laid around the edge of the dark wooden salad bowl. Over on the sideboard were covered sterling silver serving dishes, with little candles underneath them to keep them warm. And dessert was displayed under a glass-domed cake keeper, thin pale brown pancakes draped over an upside-down bowl, next to a crystal pitcher of orange glaze.

As they passed the salad around the table, Mrs. Kelly went over to the sideboard, and took the lid off one of the serving dishes. A lemony-buttery fragrance filled the room as she dished out thin pieces of battered, sautéed veal onto plates, adding thin slices of lemon and tiny green capers as garnish.

"None for me, thanks, Mother." Olivia held her hand up.

"I'll take her share, Mrs. Kelly," Mary Ellen said. "It smells out of this world."

"Well, out of this country, maybe. Veal Française." Mrs.

Kelly smiled and put an extra piece on Mary Ellen's plate.

"Go ahead and enjoy, Mary Ellen, carnivores don't bother me," Olivia said cheerfully. "Live and let live, I always say. But no slaughtered—"

Mrs. Kelly cut her off. "Olivia! We have guests who don't share your gastronomic politics, and who would *like* to enjoy their dinner!" Her voice had more oomph in it than Mary Ellen had heard since they'd moved back.

Even Olivia looked surprised at her mother having voiced such a strong objection. She shrugged agreeably, then smiled. "I'll take a double order of rice pilaf if there's enough."

Mary Ellen's father chuckled. "Olivia, I admire you for living by your principles. At this moment, I'm glad I don't share them, because I think this spread would push me right off the vegetarian wagon." He pushed his salad plate aside and went right for the veal.

For a few minutes, the conversation stopped and only the sound of appreciative chewing could be heard.

"Yes, thanks," Dr. Bobowick said with a nod, as Mrs. Kelly handed her a basket full of golden brown rolls.

"They look like little chef's hats," Mary Ellen commented. "Or inflated mushrooms."

"Les petites brioches," Justine said through a mouthful. "Loaded with butter. They are absolutely *killer* calorie-wise. I can't resist them, though."

"It's incredible, Corrine, I don't know how you manage to do all this!" Dr. Bobowick waved a hand to encompass the whole dining room. "Especially when you've only been back for a week."

"What amazes me is that everything tastes as good as it looks," Mary Ellen commented, rubbing her hand on her full stomach. "You know how sometimes, like at the diner, you go for a piece of cake that looks fantastic, but then when you take a bite, it tastes like everything went into the outside, instead of flavor on the inside."

Mrs. Kelly smiled, a little ruefully. "My sole talent—gracious homemaker. That and two-fifty will buy me a cup of cappuccino, I'm afraid."

"Mother!! You're *doing* it again!" Olivia said, glaring at Mrs. Kelly with exasperation.

"What did I do now?" Mrs. Kelly winced a little.

"Mary Ellen gave you a compliment, and you turned it around into saying something negative about yourself! It's—it's—" she sputtered, looking for the right word. "It's—self-deprecating." She said the word with a flourish and gave a vehement nod. "Not to mention rude. I mean, it's contradicting a guest."

"I'm sorry," Mrs. Kelly said sheepishly.

"And that's another thing!" Olivia rolled her eyes. "You're always saying you're sorry for the least little thing. Stop being sorry you're yourself. *Be proud* of it."

Mary Ellen and Justine looked at each other, and Mary Ellen knew they were both thinking the same thing. Now Mrs. Kelly looked embarrassed. Justine patted her mother's hand, and smiled.

"Be careful Mom, or Olivia will boss you into coming to school and taking that stupid Dare To Be Yourself course."

"I think I'm stuffed," Nicky announced. "But I want another green canoe."

"You never eat zucchini at our house, Nicky," Mary Ellen commented, surprised.

"That's because Mommy doesn't make them into boats."

"Now that is true genius, Corrine, to cook zucchini that would prompt a five year-old die-hard squash hater to ask for seconds! But Nicky, take a few minutes to digest," Dr. Bobowick said. "Give your stomach time to get the message to your brain about how much food is in there already."

"You might want to save a little room for dessert, Nicky," Olivia whispered. "Crepes suzette—pancakes with yummy orange sauce, real special gourmet stuff."

"Oh, I always have room in the dessert part in my stomach."

"Gourmet stuff," Mary Ellen said loudly. An idea had just popped into her head. Everyone turned and looked at her questioningly.

"What, honey?" her mother asked.

"Well, I was just thinking," she said, then hesitated. Maybe it was a dumb idea, besides being none of her business. She looked doubtfully at Mrs. Kelly. But Mrs. Kelly gave her an encouraging nod.

"I was thinking, Mom—you have to arrange for all the catering for that big thing at the University and you only have a week left, and the caterers you've called already are all booked. And Mrs. Kelly can do this stuff practically with her eyes closed, and it would help you out a lot, and maybe it might be good, you know, something to do—"

Mrs. Kelly was already shaking her head as if getting ready to declare her unworthiness, but Mary Ellen could see Dr. Bobowick thought it was an interesting, and possibly a really good, idea.

"Mary Ellen, that is absolutely brilliant!" Olivia said.

"Corrine, this dinner outclasses the last one of those shindigs by a light year," Mary Ellen's father said. "This could be a way for you to use your immense culinary talents, and do a favor for a friend at the same time."

"Mom, he's right," Justine put in. "And I *know* you could do it. You could do it with both oven mitts tied behind your back."

"What do you think, Corrine?" Dr. Bobowick asked. "I don't want to push you into doing something you don't feel up to doing, but I would be eternally grateful."

Mrs. Kelly frowned slightly, as if calculating something in her head. "What's the anticipated head count, Laura?"

"About a hundred and fifty," Dr. Bobowick said quickly. "The reception is from five to eight, spanning the dinner hours, so my instructions were to arrange for hors d'oeuvres hearty enough to count for a light supper, and then dessert and coffee. I have the budget sheets back at the house."

"Let's see, thin sliced, chilled beef tenderloin on sliced baguette rounds with a horseradish spread could work, and miniature quiches, and maybe curried chicken in little puff pastry pockets . . ." Mary Ellen could almost see the wheels turning in Mrs. Kelly's brain, and for the first time since they'd gotten home from Paris, she looked almost happy.

"Mother, this could be the start of a gourmet catering career for you!" Olivia's eyes were alight with enthusiasm. "Once you get established, you could market your own line of frozen gourmet foods—or get your own show on the local cable station, or both! And then—"

Mrs. Kelly cut her off, holding up her hand in mock terror. "I think that's thinking a little too big for me, sweetheart!"

"But why?" Olivia stood up, grabbed a brioche from the basket and held it up. "This is a chef-d'oeuvre!"

"What unit is that in French I?" Mary Ellen whispered to Justine.

"Probably seven or eight. It means 'masterpiece,'" Justine told her.

"I've got your first ad campaign," Olivia went on excitedly. "'For hor's d'oeuvres that are chefs-d'oeuvres, call Corrine! Corrine's Gourmet Cuisine.'"

"Olivia, I think you have a future in marketing," Mr. Bobowick said with a chuckle.

"Only if I believe in the product," she said, then looked at her mother. "Mom, at least try, okay? Just give it a try. Your product is top shelf. You know I wouldn't lie to you."

Mrs. Kelly looked around the table at all the expectant faces. "Corrine's Gourmet Cuisine . . . it does have kind of a ring to it," she murmured, then smiled, hesitantly at first, but then more confidently. "Let me sleep on it overnight, Laura. I don't want to commit and then leave you stranded. Send me over the budget sheets tonight, and I'll see if I can

98

come up with a menu that will work. I'll let you know first thing tomorrow."

"Wonderful!" Dr. Bobowick said.

"Superlative!" Olivia was beaming. Then she clapped her hand over her mouth, as if an even more brilliant idea had hit her. "Dr. Bobowick, what about servers and stuff? Don't caterers usually have their own staff?"

"Yes, as a matter of fact. I hadn't even thought about that part of it. Would that be something you'd—" Dr. Bobowick started to say.

"Yes! I accept the position. Minimum wage, plus tips, plus permission to sample all the goodies!" Olivia said. "And how about Justine and Mary Ellen? Isn't there some law that says you can work for a family business if you're underage?"

The two mothers exchanged raised-eyebrow looks, then Mrs. Kelly, smiling, spoke.

"Would you be interested in some part-time work, girls? "

"Yes!" Mary Ellen and Justine said in unison.

Chapter 11

The morning bell was ringing just as Mary Ellen and Justine slid into their desks in homeroom. Justine's cheeks were flushed with the heat of the day that promised to be a scorcher.

"You're going to roast!" Mary Ellen had said when she first saw Justine's outfit, a long-sleeved, striped jersey and black jeans. She'd worn cool clothes on purpose, a denim skirt and a short-sleeved blouse, and sandals with no socks.

"So I'll sweat off a few pounds. It'll make up for eating those crepes suzette Sunday, and the Napoleons yesterday that my mother was experimenting with for the Dickerson dinner thing."

As the drone of the morning announcements over the loudspeaker stopped, Mr. Gumble beat out a reggae rhythm on his bongos. The murmurs subsided. "All right folks, let's get down to business. Hope you've all been thinking about candidates for homeroom representative to student government. The floor is open to nominations."

Debra Hirsh leapt to her feet. "I nominate Amy Colter," she said loudly, then looked down at Amy.

"I swear, I don't think Debra could sneeze without looking at Amy to see if she did it right," Justine whispered.

"Anyone second the nomination?" Mr. Gumble asked.

"Not," Justine whispered loudly. Mary Ellen rolled her eyes as she saw Debra poke a girl she didn't know, but who looked liked she'd been cast from the same cutesy cheerleader mold. The girl called out, "I second the nomination."

Mr. Gumble wrote Amy's name on the board, then turned around. A few kids were whispering back and forth, but no one else put forth a nomination. He looked up and down the rows, giving small nods of encouragement to every student whose eye he caught, but no one spoke up.

"Come on folks, Amy can't run against herself," Mr. Gumble said in his wry tone of voice. "Just think how terrible she'd feel if she ran against herself and lost."

The kids laughed.

Justine poked Mary Ellen in the back and, leaning forward, whispered, "You should run, Mary Ellen. If Amy wins, she'll probably lobby for designer gym suits and Godiva chocolate milk."

Kevin spoke up before Mary Ellen had a chance to answer. "I nominate Justine Kelly."

Mary Ellen saw him look at Justine hopefully, then watched his face fall as she glared at him.

"I decline the nomination, Mr. Gumble," she said loudly.

"Why'd you do that?" Mary Ellen whispered.

"For one thing," Justine whispered back, "because you have to stand up and give reports to the class about student government meetings, and no *way* am I going to stand up and make an idiot out of myself."

Mary Ellen frowned. Another change. Last year Justine wouldn't have thought twice about doing an oral report. In fact, she would have liked it.

"I nominate Mary Ellen Bobowick."

Hearing her name called, Mary Ellen spun around in her seat to see Jason grinning at her broadly, while Amy shot him dagger glances. Mary Ellen knew he'd done it just to bug Amy, which was reason enough to accept, she thought with a grin.

"I second the nomination," Justine called out.

"I third it," Kevin said excitedly.

"Well, it appears we have our two candidates then," Mr. Gumble said. "Will our nominees please stand?"

Mary Ellen stood up, glancing at her opponent, who was already beaming a phony campaign smile at all the kids.

"As class representatives," Mr. Gumble went on, "your duties will be to attend student council meetings once a week, take notes, and report to your homeroom, and to represent your classmates in bringing any matters or issues of concern to the attention of the student council. Okay." He punctuated his remarks with a short drumroll on the bongos. "You'll have three weeks to run your campaigns. Choose a campaign manager, and see me for a copy of the election rules—where signs and posters are allowed, and so on. Three weeks from today, the candidates will give their speeches outlining their platforms, and one month from today, the elections will be held. Okay, you have about five minutes of free chat time. If you need a topic, consider this: Why do we park in driveways, and drive on parkways?" He picked up his paperback and settled back in his seat.

"Want me to be your campaign manager, Mary Ellen? I've got a great graphics program on my computer at home—I can do really good posters," Kevin said eagerly. Mary Ellen looked at Justine, who gave a small grimace of distaste. But Mary Ellen didn't have the heart to turn Kevin's enthusiastic offer down.

"Well, I was going to ask Justine, Kevin, but if you want to help her, with posters and stuff, that would be great."

"Cool!" As the bell rang, Kevin stuck out his hand, grabbed Justine's, and pumped it. "I'll make a list and give it to you by the end of the day, partner. Later, dudes."

"We're *not* dudes, in case you didn't notice," Justine shouted after him crankily, then turned on Mary Ellen. "How could you do that to me?"

"Come on, Justine, he's not that bad. He'll lend energy to the campaign, anyhow. And I thought the extra help would be a good thing. Give him a chance. Maybe you'll warm up to him."

"I couldn't warm up to him if we were cremated together," Justine said. "But we can talk about it later. Did you see what we have first period today?"

Mary Ellen nodded.

"Ugh," Justine said. "What a way to start the day. We better hurry. If we're late, the Poison Dart will shoot us."

"Do you have everything on the list?" Mary Ellen asked two minutes later as they hurried into the girls' locker room, which was already bustling with kids rushing to get ready.

Justine nodded. "My locker row's back there—I'll see you out in the gym." She headed for the far side of the locker room, while Mary Ellen turned down row J, squeezing past the three girls who were already there, over to the cinder-block wall. She stood still for a couple of seconds, suddenly a little self-conscious about getting changed in front of strangers. She was no prude, and they *were* all girls, but still. . . . She turned toward the wall for at least a *little* privacy.

She pulled her gym shorts on under her skirt, which she let drop to the floor. That was easy. The T-shirt was a little harder. Mary Ellen managed to wrestle both her arms out of the sleeves of her blouse and into the sleeves of the T-shirt. With a combination of tugging, wiggling, and yanking, she got the T-shirt on as the blouse came off over her head. While she was stuffing her feet into socks and sneakers, Ms. Musanti gave two shrill warning toots on her whistle. Jamming her things into the small locker, Mary Ellen gave the lock a hasty twirl, keeping an eye out for Justine as she joined the stampede of kids heading out the locker room door.

"Line up by squads, women!" Ms. Musanti was directing from just inside the double fire doors to the gym.

As the squads began roughly sorting out, Mary Ellen was jostled toward the group of girls with Amy Colter at the center. She recognized some of the other faces assigned to her squad at the last gym class. Craning her neck, she looked around. Still no Justine. Where was she? The short girl next to her, Rebecca, Mary Ellen thought her name was, stumbled against her in the shuffle, in the process stepping on her untied sneaker lace.

"Aaagh!" She just managed to catch her balance by grabbing on to the nearest arm.

"Let *go* of me!!" Amy shook off Mary Ellen's arm and shoved her backward.

"What's the problem here, women?" Ms. Dart strode through the path that had magically parted in the crowd.

Regaining her footing, and crimson with embarrassment, Mary Ellen just shrugged.

"The problem is she's a terminal clod," Amy said, glaring. "She practically yanked my arm out of the socket!"

Ms. Dart stared at Amy sardonically, long enough for Amy to drop her gaze, then looked back and forth at the two of them for a moment. Pointing a finger at Amy, she barked, "You. Ms. Colter. New squad—B. You—Ms. Palumbo— you're in C squad now." She put a hand on each girl's shoulder and steered the switch. "This makes two strikes," she added, giving Amy and Mary Ellen both ominously neutral looks. "Three strikes . . ." she paused, "and you're out." She strode back to Ms. Musanti, and gave her a nod.

"Squads, in alphabetical order, fall in, straight rows. Arms out to your sides, two armlengths between you. Arms out to the front, two armlengths between rows."

The eight squads shuffled into uneven rows stretching across the gym.

"So I'm out, big deal," Mary Ellen heard Amy whisper to Debra from the row in front of hers. "At least I'm out of *her* squad." She jerked her head backward at Mary Ellen.

Debra giggled. "C for Clod. The Clod Squad."

"All right, now," Ms. Musanti was shouting. "Warm-up stretches. Shoulders back, chests out, spines straight, pelvises tucked . . . Good posture is the foundation of a strong skeletal system. Now, arms up and one and two and . . ."

In the scuffle with Amy, Mary Ellen had forgotten about Justine for the moment. But as she bent sideways to do waist stretches, she saw Justine sneak through the fire doors and start tiptoeing along the front of the gym next to the stage, behind both the gym teacher and her assistant. And she wasn't dressed in gym shorts and a T-shirt like all the others, she had on her full sweatsuit. Mary Ellen frowned. It was so hot, even Ms. Dart and Ms. Musanti were wearing shorts and T-shirts.

As if she had eyes in the back of her head, Ms. Dart suddenly spun around. Mary Ellen saw Justine freeze, like a deer caught in the glare of oncoming headlights.

"Latecomer, name please," she said crisply.

"Justine Kelly." Mary Ellen could hardly hear her voice. She was relieved on Justine's behalf that it had been loud enough for Ms. Dart to hear.

"Ms. Kelly, one demerit." She marked it on her clipboard. "Join your squad."

"Field hockey, ugh," Mary Ellen said as they were on their way back in from the field. "I'd rather take up mud-wrestling than play field hockey."

"With you and Amy out there on the same field together, it could happen," Justine joked, out of breath from the workout.

"Come on, women, move it, we're on a tight schedule here, chop chop to the showers. Squads A and F first, B and E second, C and D third." Ms. Musanti punctuated her orders with whistle toots. Amidst a chorus of groans, the herd of girls stepped up the pace to a slow trot.

"How could you get dressed so quick when it took you so long to change into your gym stuff?" Mary Ellen asked seventeen minutes later, as she scurried, her hair half wet from the shower cap that leaked around the edges, and frizzy, and caught up with Justine at the locker room doorway. "Shew! Two minutes to make next class." She shook her head.

"They can make us go in those stupid cubicles, but they can't force us to take showers. I stood on the side, ran the shower for ten seconds." She ran her hand through her hair, then frowned. "I never should have gotten that perm right before leaving Paris. It looks like I'm wearing a bird's nest on my head."

"Shoulders back, chests out . . ." Amy and Debra, with their newest groupie in tow, and imitating Ms. Musanti, elbowed their way roughly between Mary Ellen and Justine. "Clod Squad, move aside, the Bod Squad is coming through." They broke up into a fit of snide giggles out in the hall.

"If Amy's head gets any bigger, I swear, she's going to need her own zip code," Mary Ellen said to Justine.

"If I get any fatter, I'm going to need my own area code," Justine said glumly, tugging at the waistband of her jeans.

Mary Ellen opened her mouth to contradict Justine, then closed it and sighed. It wouldn't do any good, anyway. She was starting to get the feeling that the person she saw when she looked at Justine wasn't even close to the person Justine saw when she looked in the mirror.

* * *

"Hey guys, over here."

Mary Ellen and Justine, on their way to the end of the lunch line, looked at each other.

Justine groaned. "Not again!"

"I've been—"

"I know, saving us a place," Mary Ellen said. "Look Kevin, thanks, but kids'll get mad at us if we cut in line." She started to move away, but Kevin grabbed her arm, turning to the kid behind him in line. "You don't mind, do you? Campaign strategy for homeroom rep," he said importantly. The kid looked at him like he might be contagiously weird and stepped way back to make room.

"These are hamburgers?" Mary Ellen wrinkled her nose as she looked at the silver tray full of flat, grayish-brown patties. The serving woman held one that drooped floppily between the end of a pair of tongs in one latex-gloved hand, and an open, flimsy looking hamburger bun in the other. "Maybe Olivia's not so far off with her veggie burgers. This looks about as appetizing as ground rodent patties," she said to Justine. "I'll take the macaroni and cheese, please." As the woman dished her up a bowlful, she turned to Kevin and jokingly said, "Maybe we should make it number one on the platform agenda, 'No more gray hamburgers.' "

Kevin started to grin, then stopped. "Hey—wait a minute—that might not be a bad idea."

Mary Ellen shook her head. "I was only kidding, Kevin. I don't think a seventh-grade class representative is going to be able to do much about quality control in terms of the lunches."

"Not if it was just any old lunch. But hamburgers—that's where we start!"

"We start with hamburgers?" Mary Ellen said.

"Look. For one thing, the cattle ranchers are one of the biggest threats to the Amazonian rainforest." Kevin was getting more excited and louder by the second, drawing lots of stares.

Mary Ellen tried to shrink by hunching up her shoulders. Maybe Justine had been right about accepting Kevin's offer of assistance. *She* was the one who was going to have to get up and give the campaign speech. "Kevin, look, I'm very big on saving the rainforest, you know that, but I'm pretty sure those are made from regular old American beef. And anyway, even if it was imported, I have no idea how I'd find out—"

"Look—there's a whole bunch of bad things about hamburgers. Antibiotics in the feed. Greater potential for food poisoning contamination. But the biggest thing—methane! Whether it's South American or North American or New Zealand beef—they all add to the greenhouse gases."

Justine had moved ahead with only a styrofoam bowl of salad and one of green Jell-O on her tray, and Mary Ellen walked faster to catch up with her, sliding her tray on the metal counter, while Kevin waited for his macaroni.

"Mary Ellen, we're *never* going to get rid of him if you keep encouraging him, " Justine whispered.

She paid the cashier, waited for Mary Ellen, then moved quickly toward the middle aisle of the cafeteria, scanning for a table with a few empty seats. Five more minutes to the next module bell, so it was still crowded.

"If you don't mind," a familiar snotty voice said from behind them. "You're blocking the way." Amy bumped Mary Ellen with her tray. Before Mary Ellen had time to react, she'd pushed past them, with Jason and Robbie and Debra in her wake. She tossed a parting comment over her shoulder. "Nice sweater, by the way, Justine. But haven't you ever heard the fashion tip 'overweight people should never wear horizontal stripes'? It makes them look fatter."

Justine's face turned crimson, but she didn't say anything.

But Mary Ellen glared. "What is your problem, Amy?" She felt Justine tug her sleeve, and turned to her.

"Forget it Mary Ellen," Justine mumbled. "I don't want to make a scene, okay?"

Mary Ellen opened her mouth to argue, then shut it again. She didn't know why Amy had singled out Justine as her social-torture victim this year. She wasn't overweight as far as Mary Ellen could tell, through all the baggy clothes, anyhow. Even though *she* seemed to think she was.

But before Mary Ellen could respond to either Justine *or* Amy, Kevin piped in.

"Oh yeah? Who died and left you in charge of fashion? And by the way, Justine is not overweight." Kevin said indignantly. "I bet she's probably the perfect weight according to those charts they print on underwear packages."

Amy practically choked, laughing. "No. She's not overweight. She's just undertall."

Debra and Robbie were laughing hysterically, too. Justine started walking toward the back of the cafeteria. The others were laughing too hard to notice, but she caught Jason's eye. He was half smiling, but hanging his head a little, as if he felt guilty. Mary Ellen stared hard at him for a moment, then turned her back coolly.

Kevin caught up with Mary Ellen as she slid into the seat next to Justine.

"Don't pay any attention to Amy," he said to Justine. "She's lower than pond scum on the food chain."

Justine looked at him, furious. "*You* are lower than the bacteria that *feeds* on pond scum," she said through gritted teeth. "Don't defend me, don't ever mention underwear charts to me, don't talk to me, don't even come close enough to me to breathe my air!" She got up, grabbed her books, and took off, leaving her untouched lunch tray on the table.

Mary Ellen stared after her, too stunned by the outburst against Kevin to move.

"What'd I say?" he asked weakly. "How come she hates me so much?" He looked so upset Mary Ellen felt really bad.

She shrugged helplessly. "I don't think it's you she hates, Kevin," she said slowly, staring at Justine's back as she fled the cafeteria.

Chapter 12

For about the umpteenth time since she'd started doing her homework after dinner, Mary Ellen glanced at the clock over the stove. Eight-o-five, and Justine still hadn't called. Mary Ellen had knocked off her earth science in study hall that afternoon, leaving math, and a short story in their English anthology to read. *Done.* She put a check mark in her assignment pad next to those two items. Next on the list, a quickie French exercise in *le*s and *la*s, and then only the ID card for DTBD class. Stretching and yawning, Mary Ellen stood and walked over to the side window, peering at the Kellys' house, up to Justine's window, to see if the light was on yet. Negative.

Justine had disappeared from lunch, hadn't been in history class, and hadn't been on the afternoon bus. As soon as Mary Ellen got home, she'd called. Mrs. Kelly said Justine had called from school, sick, and wanting to come home. She was up in her room now, napping. She'd tell Justine to call her when she woke up.

"Honey, have you seen Dizzy? I've got *Go Dog Go*, but I can't find the reptile." Mr. Bobowick came into the kitchen, his shirt front sporting big wet spots from giving Nicky a shower. After five days of trying to get rid of his fears of the Bloody Shower of Doom while scrubbing him in the kitchen sink, they'd finally hit on a defensive maneuver that satisfied Nicky's fear of the Doom Man reaching up and grabbing his foot. Mr. Bobowick put a large, clear Pyrex bowl over the drain, and let Nicky take a quick shower with the shower curtain half open, while the water half filled the tub, and half splashed over the walls.

"Pyrex is to the Doom Man like kryptonite is to Superman, Nicko," his father had told him. "It makes him so weak he couldn't whip a wet noodle. No Doom Man can get through the Pyrex shield." He'd finally succeeded in convincing Nicky.

"He took Dizzy to show-and-tell at school today," Mary Ellen said. "Did you ask him if he's sure he didn't leave him in school?"

Her father shook his head. "Not exactly. But that sounds like there may be a connection. He said Dizzy ran away because he didn't like Nicky anymore now that he was in kindergarten."

Mary Ellen frowned. "I wonder if that kid's been picking on him again."

"Good thought," Mr. Bobowick said. "I'll go check it out."

He was back downstairs five minuets later, his expression grim.

"Bingo?" Mary Ellen said.

"Bingo," her father replied. "Good old Diddle Riddle the Forf told Nicky after show-and-tell that only babies and girls have stuffed animals. He brought in a 'real' plastic samurai sword that he got when he was fighting ninjas in Japan. He called your brother 'Baby Baby Stick your Head in Gravy' all afternoon until all the other kids were doing it, too. Oh—and he knows real karate, too, not just fake grandmother karate. I'd like to tell Nicky to kick Diddle Fiddle's butt right off the playground."

"What about Dizzy? Did you find out what happened to him?"

"No." Mr. Bobowick shrugged helplessly. "He keeps saying Dizzy ran away. You want to go up and give it the good sisterly try?"

Mary Ellen nodded and went up to Nicky's room, where he was lying in bed, propped up against his pillow, staring mournfully out the window. She sat on the edge of his bed.

"Can't get to sleep?" she asked.

"Uh uh," he said.

"I wonder if Dizzy's having trouble getting to sleep, wherever he is," Mary Ellen said casually. "I bet he has as much trouble getting to sleep without you as you do without him. I wonder where he is."

At that, Nicky's face grew worried. "I didn't think about that," he whispered.

"Do you know why Dizzy ran away?" Mary Ellen asked.

Nicky's face fell and a few tears leaked out of his eyes. "He ran away because he doesn't like me anymore."

Mary Ellen tried to figure out what to say next. "Nicky, you know Dizzy can't really run away, because he needs you to carry him, right?"

"Yeah," Nicky said. He swiped the tears off his face with the sleeve of his pajama top.

"And of course he still likes you. All the like you put into Dizzy comes back to you. That's the way it works with special stuffed animals. The special like can't go to anybody else. And it never goes away."

Nicky looked uncertain now, and the tears stopped. "I helped him run away," he admitted.

"Okay," Mary Ellen said patiently. "Where did you help him run away to?"

Nicky bit his lip. "I helped him run away to the garbage can in the garage."

Mary Ellen stood up. "Well, I'm going to go help him run back home. I'll be right back."

"What's the scoop?" her father asked as Mary Ellen came down to the kitchen.

"Dizzy 'ran away' to the garbage," Mary Ellen told him. "I'm going to rescue him."

Dr. Bobowick was pulling in the driveway as Mary Ellen was on her way back from the garage. She waited for her mother to park the car and watched as she slowly got out.

"Tired?"

Dr. Bobowick nodded. "Exhausted. 'If you want something done well, give the job to the busiest person you know,' the dean said to me tonight. His way of patting me on the back, I suppose, for all this extra fund-raising work for the department. What are you doing with Dizzy out here?" she asked, noticing what Mary Ellen was holding in her hand.

Mary Ellen told her mother Nicky's latest chapter of the Alex Michael Thomson Widdle the Forf saga as they walked toward the back door. She held Dizzy up under the back porch light. The floppy stuffed lizard was a little grungier than usual, but bore no serious new scars.

"I think he probably could use a bath himself, but he'd probably fall apart in the washing machine."

"Give him a light Lysol spray shower," Dr. Bobowick suggested. "I'm too tired to wash and dry him tonight."

Mary Ellen held the back door open for her mother, and followed her in, brandishing Dizzy for Mr. Bobowick's inspection.

"Hallelujah," Mr. Bobowick said in relief.

Mary Ellen went upstairs to deliver him personally, with a quick stop at the bathroom to give him a disinfectant shower.

"Dizzy!" Nicky cried. "Welcome home!" He held up his arms.

"Okay, now remember. What are you going to do next time that Alex Johnson Griddle kid—"

"Alex Michael Thom—" Nicky started to correct her.

"—son Widdle the Forf." Mary Ellen couldn't help smiling. "Anyway, what are you going to do the next time he starts saying anything that bothers you?" Mary Ellen asked.

"What?" Nicky said.

Mary Ellen plugged her ears with her index fingers. "This," she said.

Nicky smiled. Mary Ellen kissed him on the forehead, gave him an extra tuck-in, and went back to the kitchen, where her parents were debating.

"I'm not sure that's the best idea, Laura," Mr. Bobowick was saying slowly. "He has to learn to stand up to bullies. Remember the trouble he had with the twins the first few weeks? I think we should give it a little time, see if he can work it out for himself."

Mary Ellen could see that her mother didn't completely agree, but was going to defer to her dad's judgment on this one, at least for the time being. Gathering her stuff off the table, she decided to tackle the last assignment up in her room.

"MARY ELLEN BOBOWICK," she wrote on the top of the blank four-by-six-inch index card Ms. Coville had passed out in class last week, then turned it over, opened her assignment pad, and stared. A pictorial representation of who she was. She could dig through the family picture drawer, but she knew there weren't any recent pictures of her, and her last year's school picture looked like the photographer had caught her about two seconds before a sneeze, with the sun in her eyes. She got up from her desk, idly walked over to the fish tank and opened the lid. Bozo darted to the top.

"Sorry, Bozo, only me." She wondered if he missed his old tank and Ben. And she wondered if Ben was fitting right in in his new school. And if there were a lot of really gorgeous girls in his class. Sighing, she gave Bozo and the damsels their bedtime snack, a pinch of dried brine shrimp. The latest issue of *Modern Marine Aquarium*, on top of the shelf next to the tank, featured clownfish as the cover story. A totem for her ID card . . .

Clownfish. They were bright, color-wise. She was bright as far as brains went; she'd be stupid not to admit she had a pretty decent one. And kind of funny—maybe not a blatant comedian like Jason, but her sense of humor was okay. But she could pull back and blend into the crowd, the way clownfish hung out between the coral pink fingers of sea anemones. Ms. Coville had said the tortoise was her totem. Clownfish seemed like as good a totem as any for Mary Ellen. She snatched the magazine, opened to the article, carefully ripped out a small picture of a single clownfish and anemone, and set it aside, to trim the edges and rubber cement it, after she filled in the rest.

NAME YOU WOULD CHOOSE IF YOU CHANGED YOUR NAME. She chewed on the top of her pen, wondering how honest she should be with this personal info. Ms. Coville had promised no one else would see the cards, but still, they'd only had one class, so she qualified as a stranger. And a fairly strange stranger at that. A different name. Last year, when Jason mangled her name into a Hairy Melon and Smelly Ellen, she would have changed it to anything. She would have changed it to Rumpelstiltskin! But overall, she liked Mary Ellen. It felt like who she was. She wouldn't choose to change it. On the card, she wrote out the category, followed by a colon, then printed in all uppercase: NOT APPLICABLE.

Birthday was simple. Favorite color? She hadn't thought about that one in a while either, and was surprised to realize she didn't know. Scanning her room, she realized that there was more of green in it than any other color. Fine, green.

Favorite activity . . . Another tough one. Why was that so tough? If someone had asked her last year, or the year before, she would have said looking at stuff through her mother's microscope in the lab at Dickerson. But she wasn't sure that was true anymore. At least, she hadn't done it in a while. What did she like to do most these days? There was computer, but she wasn't into programming or anything, the way Kevin was. She liked it for what it did, but didn't need to know how it did it. And she liked hanging out with her friends, doing all kinds of things. That seemed like a reasonable answer.

Next category: Least favorite activity? She twiddled her pen in her fingers for a minute, then it came to her. Gym class.

Strongest personality traits. Hmmm . . . were brains considered personality traits? No, the products of brains might be, though. Intelligence. What else . . . Caring about people she was close to, which she condensed to 'loyal and considerate.' It sounded a little conceited, but since no one but Ms. Coville was going to see it, it didn't really matter. She added it to the list, paused, then, with a grin, wrote one more thing: modesty.

Strongest negative personality traits. No contest: Messy and disorganized.

Favorite food. That varied from year to year. But after Mrs. Kelly's dinner the other night, her new favorite food was definitely crepes suzette. The last two things were the hardest: "Complete the following sentences. IF I COULD BE ANYTHING OR ANYONE I WANTED, I WOULD BE___ and IF I COULD DO ANYTHING IN THE WORLD I WANTED, I WOULD___."

Leaning back in her chair, Mary Ellen scratched her head with her pen. Nothing popped immediately into her mind. She sifted through her brain, but the harder she tried to pull an answer out, the more it eluded her. Funny, again—last year she would have said marine biologist, and swimming with dolphins. But she wasn't sure that was true anymore. Or at least, not the whole of what she wanted to be or do. Those probably would have been Ben's answers, too, she thought.

Why was she thinking about him tonight? A sudden pang of missing him took her by surprise. She wondered if he'd gotten an e-mail address up in Boston yet. *You have his regular address,* her brain reminded her. *Yeah, but wouldn't it be too much like chasing after him to write a letter?* she countered. What if he didn't write back? She'd feel like an idiot. But if she waited for him to write first, she might find herself waiting for the next eighty years, if she lived that long! Mary Ellen shook her head to dislodge the dilemma from her brain. She didn't have to decide right now. But she did have to finish this assignment that had seemed so easy when Ms. Coville gave it in class, but turned out to be a lot harder than she'd thought it would.

She closed her eyes tightly and concentrated hard on pulling up an answer to fill in the blank. Then she opened her eyes and started scribbling on a piece of scrap paper, trying to get the answers to go from her subconscious straight through her pen to the page before she had a chance to think about it. When she'd scrawled two lines, she looked at what she'd written: "I'd be a marine biologist at the New England Aquarium in Boston, working with a special friend, and I'd do ocean and marine life research and write books like Jacques Cousteau." She tilted her head. Interesting, that part about the special friend that had snuck in there! She copied it neatly, stuck the ID card in her DTBD notebook, and put it in her backpack.

Glancing out her window, she saw Justine's bedroom

light was on, which meant she was awake. Why hadn't she called? Mary Ellen frowned. But 10:00 was too late to call. If Justine didn't come over to walk to the bus stop together, she'd knock on the Kellys' door on her way.

Chapter 13

"Come on in, Mary Ellen," Mrs. Kelly called cheerfully when Mary Ellen knocked. Justine hadn't shown up by T-minus ten minutes in the schoolbus countdown.

"Is Justine okay?" she asked, stepping into the kitchen. "Is she going to school today?"

Mrs. Kelly, sitting in the breakfast nook with several sheets of large paper laid out on the table, shook her head. "She said her stomach was still bothering her. She seemed fine last night at dinner, but this morning she said she was up during the night."

"Oh. Okay." Mary Ellen turned to go, but Mrs. Kelly called her back.

"Mary Ellen, could I have your opinion on something?"

Justine's mother pointed to the papers in front of her.

"Sure." Stepping over to the table, and looking over Mrs. Kelly's shoulder, Mary Ellen recognized a copy of the architect's rendering of Dickerson's new science building. It was in the style of most of the other Dickerson University buildings, a stately old-fashioned brick, with lots of classical looking columns. The new four-story science building had a domed middle section, and the main entrance had double columns two stories tall on either side of it; the side wings each had smaller entrances with single-story columns. On another sheet of paper was a much less detailed magic marker sketch of the same building, and under that, the edges of sheets of oversized graph paper poked out.

"They'll be unveiling the architect's model at the reception, and I thought it might be nice to unveil the dessert at the same time," Mrs. Kelly said. "Your mother seemed to love the idea."

"You mean dessert—?" Mary Ellen pointed to the simpler sketch.

"Yes! Actually, the Eiffel Tower cake you made for our welcome-home dinner gave me the idea." Mrs. Kelly was beaming with enthusiasm. "The building itself will be carrot cake, with a cream-cheese-based frosting tinted brick color, for the slate roof, I'll use licorice Necco Wafer tiles, edible flowers, and broccoli floret bushes for the landscaping, and the columns I'll make out of meringue. So the entire building will be edible!"

"That sounds like so much work!" Mary Ellen said.

Mrs. Kelly nodded. "But I've already begun making the patterns." She pulled out one of the graph paper sheets and held it up. It was covered with a hand-done blueprint of the different parts of the building, labeled in Mrs. Kelly's handwriting. "And I have the rest of the menu set, I think. The dishes and linens are on order from the rental place, and the flowers, and of course the liquor, and I've hired a bartender . . . let's see what else . . ." She consulted a clipboard with a yellow legal pad on it, and flipped over a few sheets covered with lists. "Oh! And waitress uniforms for you and Justine. Are you free tomorrow after school? I thought I'd run you two up to the mall."

Mary Ellen nodded. "What kind of uniforms?"

"White tuxedo shirts, black bow ties, black skirts and stockings—do you have a comfortable pair of black shoes?"

"My mom has black leather sneakers that'll fit. Would those be okay?"

"Fine." Mrs. Kelly nodded, then glanced at the clock. "You better run dear, so you don't miss the bus. Oh, and Mary Ellen, would you mind picking up Justine's homework assignments? I don't want her to get behind in anything so early in the year."

"Sure thing." Mary Ellen checked the clock herself. "A minute and a half. See you later, Mrs. Kelly—the cake idea sounds fantastic."

Outside, she could hear the muffled rumble of the bus approaching the corner. She broke into a run at the foot of the driveway, and just made it to the stop as the doors popped open.

Kevin was halfway back in the bus, sitting by himself in the seat next to Amy and Debra, who'd staked off the one in front of them for Jason and Robbie again. Kevin slid over, waving a stack of papers as Mary Ellen stumbled breathlessly down the aisle and sat down next to him.

"I was experimenting with my printshop program. Wanna see?" he asked eagerly. "And we have to come up with a slogan for you. Hey, where's my co-campaign manager?" He frowned slightly, and Mary Ellen thought she detected more than a touch of disappointment in his voice. Was Kevin working on a crush on Justine? *Uh oh.* For his sake, Mary Ellen hoped not. She was actually a little worried, because while Kevin might be a little dense to social nuances sometimes, he wasn't so oblivious that his feelings couldn't be hurt.

"She's out sick today," Mary Ellen told him

"Oh. Hey, maybe I'll call her tonight, to see how she's feeling. And, you know, talk to her about the campaign and all. Just, you know, call her. What d'ya think? Should I call her?"

Mary Ellen could hear him trying to sound nonchalant, and something in her wanted to protect him from what she suspected Justine's reaction might be. She shook her head vigorously.

"No, I wouldn't call her. Justine—uh—doesn't like talking on the phone much. And she'll probably be back in school tomorrow, so we can talk about the campaign at lunchtime. Let me take a good look at these." She took the stack of poster samples from his hand and pretended to pore over them intently, to distract Kevin from the topic of Justine, and the idea that Justine would be happy to be paired with him as co-anything.

"What are your key issues going to be?" Kevin was asking. "You don't want to have too many, because then it sounds like you're any old politician lying through his teeth with promises, just to get votes."

"Well, Justine and I were talking about some changes in the cafeteria—better recycling, less packaging," Mary Ellen said absently, as she paged through the different poster designs. Kevin had put a *lot* of work into them.

"That's a good one!" Kevin said excitedly. "Let's see, what'd be a good slogan? How about, 'Lunch may be tasteful, but over-packaging is wasteful.'"

Mary Ellen laughed. "I think calling the lunch they serve tasteful might be a gross exaggeration, if not a total lie." Then in a lower voice she said, "I'll leave the dopey poems to Amy's campaign. Did you see her signs?"

"Yeah, with her picture on them and everything. I don't have a scanner for my computer yet," he said glumly.

"Don't worry about it," Mary Ellen said, still talking low. "Anyone who'd vote for someone whose slogan is '*If you want a school that's cool / Vote for Amy—Don't be a fool!'* deserves what they get! Want these back for now?" She held up the papers.

Kevin shook his head. "Nah, you keep 'em. Just let me know which design you like the best, and I'll print out a whole bunch when we come up with the right slogan."

Mary Ellen leaned down and opened her backpack, which was on the floor beneath her feet. She had the stack of flyers half in when the bus lurched to a halt to pick up Jason and Robbie, sending the papers and half her books sliding across the aisle floor, and jolting her forward so she bumped her head.

"Ouch!" She sat up and gingerly felt underneath her bangs for the beginnings of a lump.

"Ooops! You okay?" Kevin asked.

Jason stooped down to pick up the papers, and handed them to Mary Ellen with a grin. "Anyone ever tell you you're a hazard to your own health, Bobowick?"

"You're hilarious, Jason," Mary Ellen said, still wincing from the pain. "Banging my head is up there on my list of laughs, right after tap dancing barefoot on thumbtacks."

"You couldn't tap dance to save your life, Mary Ellen," Amy said with a smirk. Then she looked up at Jason with her best toothpaste smile. "Here, Jason, I saved you and Robbie seats."

"Take your seats please, people, we're on a mission," Tina bellowed back.

"We're gonna back-of-the-bus-it today." Jason jerked his thumb toward the rear where the rowdiest of the guys were sitting. "Thanks, anyhow." He and Robbie moved down the aisle.

Mary Ellen couldn't help smirking. Amy scowled, then looked down at the floor. Mary Ellen followed her gaze. Leaning against the metal support of Amy's seat was a four-by-six-inch index card, with a colorful picture on front, sporting unmistakable, bright red splotches of clownfish.

"Give me that!" Mary Ellen lunged for it but Amy was quicker. She snatched, and turning her back as a shield against Mary Ellen's frantic attack, read out loud. " 'I'd be a marine biologist at the New England Aquarium in Boston, working with a special friend.' Mary Ellen wants to be a fish and jump in the tank with Flipper!"

"I do *not* want to be a fish, and Flipper isn't in the New England Aquarium, he's at the Miami Seaquarium, for your information." Her face almost as red as the clownfish's, Mary Ellen finally succeeded in grabbing her ID card back.

"If Mary Ellen and Flipper got married, that would make her a fishwife," Debra giggled.

Kevin spoke up defensively in Mary Ellen's behalf. "A fishwife isn't someone who marries a fish, in the first place, Debra, a fishwife is a woman with vulgar speaking habits who sells fish at a market, and in the second place, Flipper is a dolphin, not a fish, so if she DID marry him, she'd be a dolphin wife. So there." He gave Mary Ellen a nod as if he'd put Debra in her proper place, while Amy and Debra continued shrieking in hysterical laughter. Mary Ellen stuck the stupid ID card securely in her backpack, seething.

"So Kevin managed to put his foot in it and make things worse," Justine said, after Mary Ellen recounted the story that afternoon. "Typical. *Quel cretin.*"

"Kell kretan?"

"You don't pronounce those *n*'s at the end the same way you do in English," Justine coached. "It's a different sound. Stick your tongue behind your bottom teeth and try to smile with your mouth open and say 'ten' at the same time, without letting your tongue touch the roof of your mouth or your face move."

Mary Ellen tried it a few times. "Any language that makes your face do such weird things has got to have something wrong with it." She tried again.

"Better. You'll get it down." Justine turned the page of

her French II exercise book, and her pen started racing down the page as she filled in the answers.

"It's so much more work in French, remembering what's masculine and what's feminine," Mary Ellen complained. "I'll never memorize it all. There's no logic to it, and besides, what difference does it make, anyway, if a frying pan is feminine and a balloon is masculine? And who decides which is which? Do they have some kind of Bureau of Inanimate Object Gender Control?"

Justine shrugged. "I don't know. I never asked."

"What did it mean, anyway, what you said about Kevin?" Mary Ellen reached for a miniature eclair filled with mocha-flavored cream. Mrs. Kelly had set out a plate of fancy pastries as an afterschool snack, before racing off to do errands. "These are incredible, by the way. More experiments for the reception?"

Justine nodded. "Yeah, in case anyone doesn't like carrot cake. Keep them away from me. I think it's great my mother's cheered up and everything, but the catering business is full of occupational hazards." She pushed the plate across the breakfast nook table, then pulled it back, took a small strawberry tart, stuffed it in her mouth, and pushed it away again. "I swear," she said after swallowing, "It's bad enough trying to stay on a diet without your own mother sabotaging you. And I said, *quel cretin,* which means 'What an idiot.'"

"He's really not that bad, you know, Justine. I mean, at least he's nice."

"That's not the way you felt about him last year when he had a crush on you. You were the one who started calling him peanut-butter-and-pickle breath," Justine pointed out.

"True," Mary Ellen admitted. "But that was back in elementary school. I wouldn't do it now. I mean, I actually kind of like him. He has an interesting brain."

"Let him leave it to science, then, instead of working on ways to make me look like a fool in front of Jason. There.

Done." She closed her book and put it on top of the pile of homework she'd already finished. "What's next?"

Mary Ellen scrawled the last three *le*s and *la*s in front of their nouns and closed her workbook. "Just the DTBD assignment, but that's not due till next week. Here." She pushed her assignment pad over so Justine could copy it.

"Cultural Expectation Exposé," Justine read out loud. "Huh?"

"We have to do a five-minute oral presentation on some kind of cultural brainwashing that gets imposed on people and messes with the way they see themselves. Like music videos. Or mouthwash ads." She looked sideways at Justine. "I think I might know what I want to do, but I'm not sure. Hey, you still have any of your Debbies? My last one got dismembered when Nicky got a hold of her."

"Yours never stayed in very good shape for long, anyway," Justine said with a laugh. "But yeah, I still have two—Designer Debutante Debbie, and Aloha Hawaiian Debbie—the collector's editions, in their original boxes. They're up in the attic with my Madame Alexander dolls."

"Can I borrow one?" Mary Ellen asked, an idea beginning to take shape in her mind.

Justine looked at her suspiciously. "What for?"

"I don't want to tell, in case it doesn't work out," Mary Ellen said. "It might be a stupid idea."

"They're collector's items, now, you know. And even more valuable because I kept the original boxes. You won't shave her head if I lend you one, will you?"

Mary Ellen shook her head. "Nope. Promise. I'll return her in absolutely perfect collectable condition." Through the Kellys' window, Mary Ellen saw her father's car pull in the driveway, with Nicky in the passenger seat.

"I gotta go," she said, gathering up her books. "My mother's teaching till nine tonight, and I promised her I'd make dinner. Be thinking about a campaign slogan, okay? And dig up that Debbie for me." She headed for the door, then turned back. "You *are* coming to school tomorrow, right? I can't face that pack by myself."

"I'm coming," Justine assured her. "And my mother said she'd pick us up right from school to go for our waitress clothes, so we get to skip the bus ride home."

"I'm not going to wear a short one," Justine said stubbornly, handing the saleswoman outside the fitting room three short black skirts, then folding her arms across her chest. "I tried on a five, a seven, and a nine and they all looked terrible. None of them fit. I'm a non-size."

"Justine, this is very important to me, you know that," Mrs. Kelly said in a pleading tone. "Mary Ellen's mother is counting on me for professionalism, and that includes a professional-looking staff. I think shorter skirts are better—it's a more tailored look."

"Besides, I look like a total stringbean in long skirts. Somebody might stick me in a bowl of veggie dip," Mary Ellen said, trying to lighten things up a little. She didn't really care whether they wore long or short skirts, and she was getting a little impatient with the latest shopping-with-Justine ordeal.

"Well, it's better than looking like a penguin who's too fat to fit in its own skin in the short one," Justine snapped back. Mrs. Kelly passed a hand wearily over her eyes, finally shrugging her shoulders. "Okay. If it means that much to you, and if Mary Ellen doesn't mind, I'll get you both the long ones with the elastic waists. Here, run over to the hosiery dept and get some black pantyhose, while I pay for these." Mrs. Kelly handed Justine a twenty and the two girls started over to the other department. Mary Ellen glanced back over her shoulder and caught Mrs. Kelly's eye. She was staring at Justine with a worried frown on her face.

"Are Nicky's things together?" Gram was saying to Dr. Bobowick as Mary Ellen came into the kitchen, rustling her shopping bags. Her little brother was sleeping over at Gram's tonight. They were leaving early tomorrow for a trip to the city, to go to the museum with the dinosaur bones.

Dr. Bobowick nodded. "In his duffel bag, up in his room. Mary Ellen, would you mind—"

"I know, I know, running up to get them."

Dr. Bobowick walked over to the back door to call Nicky in from his swing fort.

"Nicky, come on. Gram's getting ready to go."

By the time Mary Ellen retrieved the duffel bag and came downstairs again, Nicky was coming in, dragging his feet, very uncharacteristically for him when the prospect of a sleepover and field trip with Gram was ahead of him.

"Do I hafta go?" he asked his mother.

Dr. Bobowick did a double take. "Is this Nicholas Bobowick who *loves* to go over Gram's and play with Nibbles and practice karate?"

"It's not real karate," Nicky said, looking down at his feet.

Mary Ellen, her mother, and her grandmother exchanged troubled glances.

"Says who it's not real karate?" Gram asked.

Now Nicky looked guilty. He didn't answer.

"Nicky, is there a reason you don't want to sleep over at Gram's tonight? Can you tell me what it is?" Dr. Bobowick asked gently.

He looked up at Gram, then fearfully at his mother, then burst into tears, and tackled her with a hug.

"Sweetheart, what's wrong?" Dr. Bobowick asked.

"I bet I know. Alex Michael Thomson Widdle the Forf," Mary Ellen said grimly. "Nicky, has that kid been saying stuff to you again?"

Nicky nodded, between sobs that sounded like hiccups. "He said that a bad magician was going to come and get my mother and put her into a box and saw her in half, and take both halves away, and I'll never see her again."

"This," Dr. Bobowick said grimly. "Is the last straw." She worked her way with Nicky over to one of the kitchen chairs, sat down, and pulled him onto her lap, while Mary Ellen and Gram watched somberly.

"Just who is this Alex-Mr.-Big-Long-Name child?" Gram asked.

"The bully in Nicky's kindergarten class," Mary Ellen told her. "He's been mean before, but this sounds like it's from a lousy horror movie. How could a kid that young say something so evil?"

"I don't know," Dr. Bobowick said, "But I am *going* to find out. It's most definitely time for a parent-teacher conference. Nicky, listen to me. No one is going to put me in any box. And no one is going to hurt me or cut me in half or take me anywhere. Do you know why?"

Nicky looked up. "Uh uh. Why?"

"Because I have a secret power," she told him. "And it protects me from any bad things any Alex Diddle Dumpling or anyone else might say to you."

"Alex Michael Thomson Widdle the Forf," Nicky corrected automatically. "What secret power? Can I have some?"

"You already do," his mother told him. "The power is that we all love each other—you and I and Daddy and Mary Ellen and Gram. We have a whole huge family of the strongest kind of power there is. Love power. Okay? Do you believe me?"

Mary Ellen watched as Nicky looked at his mother a little doubtfully for a second, then smiled, wiped his eyes with his sleeve, sniffed twice, and nodded.

"Humph," Gram said. "And one last thing, Mr. Nicholas Bobowick. You tell this so-called karate expert that you have taken Tae Kwon Do karate lessons from a real live white-belt."

"Is that higher than a black belt?" Nicky asked.

"I don't know if it's higher," Gram said, her eyes twinkling. "But it holds my karate duds closed just as well as a black belt."

Chapter 14

"What's this?" Justine picked up an envelope with what looked like a party invitation half out of it from the desk in Mary Ellen's kitchen. She turned it over and read silently.

Mary Ellen looked over from the counter, where she was tearing the lid off a just-delivered cardboard pizza carton to use it as a serving tray. Her parents were out, Nicky had gone to Gram's, and Justine was sleeping over. It seemed like such a luxury, she thought, having Justine back next door, so they could do sleepovers on the spur of the moment again.

"What's what?"

Justine looked up from the invitation in her hand.

"You're invited to Jason's birthday party?" Her expression looked really hurt.

"Yeah. Aren't you? I'm sure you are . . . Jason would never . . ." Mary Ellen knew Jason could be obnoxious, but she was pretty sure he would never invite her and leave Justine out.

"If Amy talked him into not inviting me, he would," Justine said.

"No way." Mary Ellen shook her head vigorously. "Amy hates my guts way more than yours. So if he invited me, you have to be invited, too. And besides—that just came today. Maybe yours got held up in the mail."

"You think?" Justine looked doubtful but hopeful at the same time.

"Definitely." Mary Ellen tried to reassure her. "Okay, chow's on. I got half pepperoni and half pepper and sausage, just like you like." She set out two cans of soda, two plates, two napkins, and a knife and fork for Justine, then carried the pizza over to the table and sat down. "Dig in."

Justine grabbed a piece of pepper and sausage, and took a huge bite. Mary Ellen stared. She'd never seen Justine eat pizza that way before. In all the years she'd known her, she always cut it up into bite-size pieces, because she hated the sloppy way the grease and cheese got all over her chin. Actually, it was kind of nice to see Justine had relaxed some of her old neatness standards. They took up so much extra time, for one thing. But still, it was kind of weird. Mary Ellen frowned slightly.

"What's the matter with you?" Justine asked, catching Mary Ellen's expression.

That's what I'd like to ask *you*, Mary Ellen thought. But she could tell by Justine's defensive tone of voice that it might spark an argument.

"Nothing," she said, keeping her voice neutral, and grabbing a slice from the pepperoni side of the pie, folded it in half and bit a huge hunk out. A long, greasy string of melted mozzarella slopped down, and she sucked it in, like drinking through a straw.

"Oh, by the way," Justine said, after they'd both eaten three pieces in near-record time. "Kevin left a message on our answering machine, saying he wanted to get flyers printed up this weekend. He actually wanted to come over to my house tomorrow to 'have a meeting.' Ugh. Can you believe it?"

Mary Ellen eyed the pizza in the box, took a reading on her appetite, and decided there was room for one more piece.

"I don't know where you put it all," Justine commented enviously. "Everything I eat goes straight to my thighs."

"I think I just burn it up," Mary Ellen said. "So did you call Kevin back?"

"No way! I swear, I think I'm allergic to him or something. I feel all itchy, like I'm about to break out in hives whenever he gets near me."

"But his feelings will be really hurt if you don't call him back."

"I can't help it. And I can't worry about his feelings. I've got enough problems worrying about my own feelings. And my mother's feelings. And my father's feelings. Do you know he keeps sending me e-mail?" Justine sighed.

Mary Ellen stared at her curiously for a moment. This was the first time Justine had made any real reference to how she felt about what was going on in her life. "What does he say in it?"

"Oh, stuff like how am I doing, and he doesn't want to lose his relationship with his daughters, and how is my mother holding up. As if he really cared." The last sentence came out with a bitterness Mary Ellen had never heard in Justine's voice before. "I haven't answered any of it anyway. I don't have anything to say to him. And if he wants to know how my mother is, he should come back here and ask her in person."

Mary Ellen didn't know how to react. "Well," she said awkwardly, "Don't worry anymore about Kevin, anyway. I'll call him back, and I'll try and be the buffer zone between you guys in school. If that's any help."

"Thanks." Justine smiled, kind of sadly, and Mary Ellen knew Justine understood the feelings behind what it was Mary Ellen couldn't put into words.

"That's what friends are for, right? Okay—like Gram always says, 'Don't sit and stew. Find something to do.' Let's clear up this stuff and get down to campaign business." She jumped up and started stuffing crumpled napkins into the empty pizza box, then stopped. "You know something? Here we are, supposedly this ecologically aware family and we're using paper napkins. Even your mom uses cloth ones."

"She just does it because she likes them better, I think," Justine said. She stood and put her hand over her stomach. "Ugh. I feel like I swallowed a bowling ball. Why did I eat so much?"

Mary Ellen didn't want to get started on *that* topic again, so she ignored the question, steering the conversation back to her campaign.

"Yeah, but it doesn't really matter what the reason is. The effect is the same. It saves paper, therefore it saves trees. Think about this: figure there are over fifteen hundred kids at Dexter. Figure at lunch every day, even if each kid uses only one napkin, and tons of kids grab a whole handful because they're too lazy to be careful about getting just one. What if we used cloth napkins in the cafeteria? I mean, it's possible—they do in fancy restaurants. And rental places rent table linens out, for parties and stuff, like your mom's using for the Dickerson thing."

"I don't know, Mary Ellen." Justine sounded skeptical. "I doubt you could talk the school into renting cloth napkins. That probably costs a lot."

"Maybe not. Maybe the school shouldn't rent from a linen service. I mean, if there was an initial investment, you know, money to buy the cloth napkins—wait—I have an even *better* idea! We get some fabric company to donate cloth in the school colors, we hook up with the home-ec classes when they're doing sewing, so they can hem them all—and wash and dry them right at school! What do you think?"

"I think you're coming down with a fever, Mary Ellen. First of all, there's no washer or dryer at school. Second of all, who's going to wash and dry them? Think about it—you're talking seventy-five hundred napkins a week." Justine got out the foil and started wrapping the extra pizza.

"You don't have to use that much," Mary Ellen said. "Pile two or three pieces on top of each other, and you use only half the tinfoil."

"Mary Ellen, don't turn into a fanatic on me, okay?" Justine rolled her eyes, but cut a shorter piece off the foil roll.

"I'm not being a fanatic. I'm being—what was Marcia's Z word from DTBD? I'm being zealous." She stuffed the pizza box into the trash compactor after putting the crusts into the bin for composting, then grabbed a piece of paper and a pencil off the kitchen desk. "Maybe we could get a washer and dryer donated. Or even buy them, with the money saved from not having to buy paper napkins. It probably wouldn't be all that much work for the cafeteria people to throw them in the wash."

"They'd all have to be folded, or at least spread out flat," Justine said. "Hey—maybe they could get kids to do that in detention!"

Mary Ellen grinned. "That's a great idea! All they do now is homework or make spitballs. We'll rehabilitate them! So—a slogan. Something to the point. Something . . . something with pow that says who I am and what I stand for."

Justine twiddled a strand of her hair, thinking. "Well, you're standing for conservation. And recycling. And not wasting. How about, 'Don't Waste—Resources OR Your

Vote!! Mary Ellen Bobowick for Student Council.' "

"That's not bad," Mary Ellen said. "You know what? I'm going to call Kevin and get his input. And I'll mention we're working together and that's why you didn't return his call."

"Don't mention anything about me being here now. He might want to talk to me or something."

"Justine, what is such a big—" deal she was about to say, but saw from Justine's expression she wasn't going to get a logical answer. "Okay, I won't." She shook her head. It wasn't worth an argument. Opening the kitchen drawer, she dragged out the phone book, and looked up Kevin's number. "There are only two Middendorfs, and one of them is on Platt Street which is off Elm which is Kevin's bus stop. This has to be it."

She punched out the numbers on the keypad. Kevin picked up on the second ring. Mary Ellen filled him in on the napkin idea, and waited for him to applaud the idea enthusiastically.

"What's the matter?" she asked, when he hesitated before responding. "Don't you think it's a good idea? *You* were the one who came up with that other slogan about wasteful and tasteful."

"I know, and it's an excellent idea," he said. "Really. But I've been thinking all afternoon, it might be kind of a big issue to run a homeroom campaign on. I think it's an idea that once you got elected, you could work through the student council, and get everyone's backing. I think you'd need that kind of support from the student body to push anything this big through the administration."

"I hadn't thought about that, but you're probably right." Mary Ellen was surprised at the practicality of Kevin's reaction. "Okay, well how can we pare it down for just the homeroom election, and still get across the idea of an environmental platform?"

"Well, Amy's probably gonna go with cute, or cool, or something like that. So what you want to do is show the contrast—that you're someone of substance. Maybe just plain old honesty is the best way to go. Something like, 'Vote for the one who'll represent YOU! Mary Ellen Bobowick for Student Government.' "

"That's not very catchy," Mary Ellen said, a little disappointed in the lack of flash.

"Not on the surface," he agreed. "But you'll have a chance to be more specific when you give your speech. That's where you need to concentrate on convincing kids. Make up a list—the issues that are important to you, but also make up a plan—like how you're going to find out what's important to them. Maybe a suggestion box in the classroom, or something. Or a questionnaire you could pass around. Hey, by the way, have you seen Justine? I called her before but she hasn't called me back."

Crossing her fingers and feeling guilty, Mary Ellen murmured something that sounded like a vaguely negatively inflected murmur.

"Well, just say hi for me. You know, if you see her over the weekend and all. I'll do up some flyers and bring them in on Monday for your final approval."

Mary Ellen thanked him and hung up, looking at Justine reproachfully. "He's really a nice person, you know, Justine."

"Would *you* want him to have the hots for *you?*" Justine asked pointedly.

Mary Ellen tried to picture it. She couldn't. Actually, she couldn't picture anyone having the hots for her. Ben had moved away before things even got to lukewarm!

"Well, I think you could handle it a little differently, is all. I mean, I don't think he's madly in love with you. I think he just wants to be your friend. Come on, my mom rented some videos. You can have dibs on choosing the first one." She headed toward the doorway to the living room. Justine followed, grabbing her overnight duffel bag from the floor next to the refrigerator, where she'd put it when she came in.

"No, you go ahead and pick whatever one you want," she said. "I think I'm going to run up and take my shower first. I'm totally beat . . . I'll probably fall asleep before the end anyway. Oh wait, by the way, here." She tugged the zipper open and handed Mary Ellen a boxed Designer Debutante Debbie. "Don't rip the box when you open it, okay?"

"Oh good! Don't worry, I'll guard every speck of cardboard with my life." She looked at Debbie's bright, painted smile, grinned, and handed her back to Justine. "Put her up on my desk, okay?"

"Mary Ellen, that is an *evil* smile," Justine said, her foot on the first step. "What *are* you planning on doing for your report anyhow?"

"You'll see. Your mother doing the patterns for the cake building gave me the idea."

"You're not going to have my Designer Debutante Debbie jump naked out of a cake or anything, are you?" Justine eyeballed her very suspiciously.

"Nope. Scout's honor." She held up her right hand with her fingers parted in the middle.

"That's not scout's honor. That's Mr. Spock's greeting, 'Live long and prosper.' "

"Well anyhow, I promise this Debbie will live long and prosper, if you call being all dressed up in stiff, scratchy clothes with your eyes painted open and stuck in a cardboard box prospering. Or living—even for a doll."

Justine shook her head, but she laughed, and headed up the stairs.

"The video's half over," Mary Ellen announced almost an hour later when Justine came into the den, wearing a floor-length nightgown and towel-drying her hair. "I swear, for someone who hates showers so much they're willing to risk the wrath of Dart, that sure was a long one." She shifted over on the couch to make room for Justine.

140

"That's okay. I've seen this movie already anyway."

"Did you have enough hot water?" Mary Ellen asked. "It usually runs out after—"

"Shhh—yes, plenty," Justine said, staring at the TV. "Watch—the good part's coming up."

"B and E squads first in the showers today, C and D second, and A and F last," Ms. Musanti hollered out cheerfully, after consulting her clipboard.

"Ugh," Justine grunted, jogging up alongside of Mary Ellen as the class filed noisily in through the gym, to the locker room. "I swear, gym class is one of those things that you *know* some cruelly warped and perverted individual who absolutely loathed adolescent females thought up."

"I bet she'd forget how to *breathe* if she didn't have it written down on that clipboard," Mary Ellen heard Amy say to Debra from behind, just before the two of them plowed forward and cut into the locker room in front of Mary Ellen and Justine.

"Bod Squad beats Clod Squad to the shower today," Debra said.

"I'm in B squad, too Debra," Justine said. "Give it a rest, will you?"

"It wouldn't be so bad, you know, if you didn't have that hot sweatsuit on, Justine," Mary Ellen said. "I mean, technically, it's still summer for another six days."

"Sweating is good for losing weight. Besides, I'd rather sweat to death than wear those stupid orange gym shorts in public," Justine retorted. "I tried them on and my butt looked like a pumpkin, I swear. At least the sweats are maroon."

Orange and maroon were the Dexter colors. They *were* the most revolting colored gym shorts Mary Ellen had ever seen. But as long as everyone else was stuck wearing them too, she didn't really care. At the beginning of class today, Mary Ellen had noticed Ms. Dart really scrutinizing Justine when she came in late, as usual, wearing full Phys. Ed. regalia on the hottest day they'd had since school started. "Another demerit, Ms. Kelly," Ms. Musanti had said, marking her clipboard, and nodding at Ms. Dart, who merely nodded back. "That makes three, which means you need to report to detention next Tuesday afternoon. Fall in with your squad." Justine had caught Mary Ellen's eye, and given her an "Oh well, what can you do?" shrug. Mary Ellen knew Justine wasn't crazy about getting changed in front of other people. But to almost *ask* for demerits. Mary Ellen couldn't figure it out. She couldn't figure out Ms. Dart's mild reaction, either.

As she turned into her locker row to grab her shower stuff now, and Justine waited at the end of the row, Ms. Dart walked up the center aisle of the locker room, stopping next to Justine.

"Ms. Kelly," she said.

Mary Ellen spun around in time to see Justine freeze, and shrink back against the end of the lockers. She opened her mouth as if to respond, but no words came out.

"Do you have an older sister named Olivia?" the gym teacher asked.

Justine, looking very confused now, just nodded.

"Tell her 'The Poison Dart' said hello." Then, to both the girls' astonishment, Ms. Dart smiled before walking away.

Mary Ellen and Justine exchanged baffled looks, but a blast of Ms. Musanti's whistle told them there wasn't time for an analysis right then. They hurried over to Justine's locker, where Justine took out her as-yet unused shower stuff.

"And you know," Mary Ellen said in a low voice, after checking to see if Ms. Musanti was within earshot. "You're going to get busted one of these days for skipping showers if you're not careful. Besides which I'd think you'd want to cool off. I mean, it's not like they're the Bloody Showers of Doom, or anything."

"The hot water makes those flimsy curtains fly around," Justine said. "I am *not* going to take off all my clothes in there."

"But there's doors that lock outside that," Mary Ellen said.

"The cracks on the sides of the door are too big," Justine said, her voice taking on that stubborn tone that meant she wouldn't back down.

Mary Ellen shrugged, and headed for the showers. If Justine wanted to risk wasting more afternoons at detention, she guessed it wasn't really any of her business, anyway.

As Justine disappeared into the one empty stall to fake taking a shower, Mary Ellen leaned back against the cinder block wall with the other kids who were waiting for the next round.

"Two more minutes, B and E squads. Move it along," Ms. Musanti said, pacing around the shower and locker rooms like a policewoman walking her beat. She checked her watch, then blew her whistle. "All right B and E squads, time's up! Out of the showers pronto."

The sound of all the showers being squeaked off simultaneously was followed by the sound of clothes rustling and girls grumbling. Justine came out, changed, and carrying her bundle of gym clothes, and gave Mary Ellen a smile as she passed by. Mary Ellen was lined up for the end of the shower stall, which stayed closed after all the other doors had opened and two damp squads had scurried for the sinks and mirrors while the last two sweaty waiting squads hurried into the steamy stalls.

Ms. Musanti came over, looked at Mary Ellen, then checked out the feet of whoever was still in there, and rapped sharply on the door. "Time's up, move out now, or you'll get the demerit."

"I'm coming—just wait—" It was Amy's voice, sounding slightly frantic.

143

"I don't think so," Ms. Musanti said sternly. "Out. Now."

The stall door opened and Amy stepped out, dressed, but with her shoelaces untied, and her clothes half falling off, clutching her towel and gym clothes to her chest. She glared at Mary Ellen with such hostility that Mary Ellen shrank back against the wall, then clomped off toward the locker room. *Now* what was Amy's gripe? Shrugging, she scooted into the vacated stall. She'd barely have time to turn the water on, turn around once, and turn it back off.

Undressing quickly, Mary Ellen hung her things on the hook, then she reached up and tilted the shower nozzle down so her hair wouldn't get wet. She didn't bother with soap or shampoo, just started doing a fast rinse. As Ms. Musanti's five-minutes-till-the-bell whistle pierced the noise of spraying water, Mary Ellen gave a last splash to her face, and groped to turn the shower off. This was a health hazard, she thought with annoyance, making kids move so fast on slick shower floors. If she made student council, maybe *that* was something she could lobby for— more leisurely after-gym showers! As she shuffled toward the curtain, her toe stepped on something wet and squishy.

"Aaagh!!" Pulling her foot up, Mary Ellen balanced precariously for a second, before stepping over the tiled ledge into the changing part of the stall, without even grabbing her towel in like she usually did first. Pulling the curtain aside, she peered back in and saw a small, crescent-shaped package, like a tiny, soft plastic pillow filled with some kind of milky beige liquid. It looked oddly familiar. . . . Where had she seen—the magazine ad!! ShapeShifters!!! Was *this* what Amy was searching for so frantically before? Using her gym sock as a glove, Mary Ellen picked it up gingerly and rolled it inside her sock, planning to stash it in her backpack. She wasn't sure what she was going to do with it yet. But it had to be good for *some*thing!

* * *

144

"Hey, guy-irls," Kevin said, catching Justine's look and correcting himself before she had a chance to, as he set his books down on the corner table. "It's your friendly neighborhood campaign-in-the-neck co-manager. Listen, I came up with a good gimmick, I think. Justine, Mary Ellen was talking about your sister eating veggie burgers. Could you get some to bring in and hand out pieces at lunchtime? It might be a good way to show you want to start with small changes—like going from gray burgers to veggie burgers, you know?"

"You mean like those people do in grocery stores when they're handing out coupons?" Mary Ellen asked, raising an eyebrow.

"Yeah, like that. You can say you're on a conservation and environmental as well as a health platform and—"

"It sounds pretty dumb to me, Kevin," Justine said. "No offense. But what if kids hated the samples? It might actually end up losing Mary Ellen votes."

Kevin immediately backed down. "Oh. I didn't think about that. Yeah, you're probably right. Okay. Well, anyhow, I printed up a bunch of posters. What do you think?" He handed Mary Ellen and Justine each three pieces of paper.

Mary Ellen studied them. On the first, there was a one-inch border of little blue-and-green earth globes. Centered at top, in plain block letters, were the words:

— 🌎 —
THINK GLOBALLY, VOTE LOCALLY!
MARY ELLEN BOBOWICK FOR STUDENT COUNCIL

The second, also with a globe border, said:

— 🌎 —
YOUR VOTE CAN MAKE A WORLD OF DIFFERENCE!
VOTE FOR MARY ELLEN BOBOWICK—HOMEROOM REPRESENTATIVE

And the last one, with a wider border of pointing fingers, said:

☞ ——— ☜
VOTE FOR THE ONE
WHO WILL REPRESENT YOU!!
M.E. BOBOWICK

"I couldn't fit your whole name on that one," Kevin apologized. "But combined with the other ones, it'll get your name around. What do you think?"

"I think they're great, Kevin." Mary Ellen smiled at him. "Thanks a lot."

He reddened and beamed with pleasure, setting the stack of flyers down on the edge of the table where they started to slip off. He made a grab for the papers, just catching them, but knocking his glasses off in the process. He made another grab, and this time his elbow caught the edge of his tray, which went clattering to the floor.

"Ooops!" he said, with a sheepish grin. He hopped out of his chair, squatting to pick up his coldcut combo and chocolate milk, both of which, fortunately, hadn't been opened yet.

"Very suave, Kevin," Amy was laughing at the next table. "You make a perfect campaign manager for Mary Ellen's Clod Squad campaign."

"You can run for the Bod Squad campaign," Jason teased Amy, reaching over and snapping the elastic back of her bra through her shirt.

"Jason!" she squealed. "Cut it out." But instead of leaning away from him, she leaned toward him, practically falling into his lap.

"Talk about throwing yourself at someone," Justine muttered.

"Yeah," Kevin said. "Talk about throwing, she makes

me want to throw up." He opened his mouth and stuck his finger in, making a gagging face.

At that, Justine grabbed her books and jumped up. "And you should *grow* up, Kevin," she said angrily, and walked quickly, almost running, toward the cafeteria exit.

Kevin's shoulders sagged. He looked at Mary Ellen. "What did I say wrong *this* time?" he asked weakly.

"I don't know, Kevin, " Mary Ellen said, not looking at him. She was looking at the front of Amy's blouse after she sat back up. Jason was looking at it, too. Something seemed to be missing. Mary Ellen grinned. It looked like Amy had been demoted from the B squad, bra-size wise, to the double-A squad.

Chapter 15

Mary Ellen sat in her seat in DTBD class, her project wrapped in dark green trash bags, twice as tall as her desk, and leaning against the wall. She couldn't *wait* to give her presentation. Justine had just started hers, on the hairdressing and beauty salon industry in the United States, titled, "Is It True Blondes Have More Fun?" She had a poster with graphs showing the amount of money spent on hair care products, and wigs for women *and* hair transplants and toupees for men.

"One of the most traumatic things for some men as they age is the loss of hair from male pattern baldness. A few movie stars have fought the stereotype, but more have given in to the myth that hairier is better." She looked at her chart, then gave a kind of bitter little laugh. "Take it from me, I've seen it first hand. Men wig out when they start losing their hair."

She sat back down, and Ms. Coville looked at her with what seemed to Mary Ellen to be an almost sympathetic expression. "Very good, Justine. What I especially liked about your presentation was the fact that you didn't confine this topic to the female gender, though that might have seemed the obvious thing to do. Empathy—being able to understand from another's point of view—is a wonderful trait."

Ms. Coville looked at Mary Ellen, whose presentation was last, and smiled enthusiastically.

"And now, Mary Ellen! Enlighten us please. I'm DYING to know what your presentation is."

Mary Ellen stood, took the large, flat package that was as tall as she was to the front of the room, and leaned it against Ms. Coville's desk, adjusting it so when she pulled off the top bag, the bottom one would drop and reveal the two parts of her exhibit.

"My project," Mary Ellen began, "is about the insidious image of the perfect female body that the toy manufacturing companies, Watrell Toys especially, start indoctrinating us girls with before we have a clue, as early as preschool." She pulled the top bag off, and slid the bottom one down, revealing two life-sized, nearly naked models of a five-foot six-inch female. On one was an enlarged photocopy of one of the most familiar faces in American toydom, the Debbie doll. Mary Ellen had traced two forms onto graph paper, then spent an evening at Dickerson with her mother, enlarging the outlines section by section on the copy machine. She'd copied the actual Debbie doll face from Justine's collector's designer box. Then she'd rubber-cemented the sections onto foam board, and cut out the outlines with an exacto knife. The whole project, once she'd gotten started, had taken a lot longer than she'd expected it would. But when she saw the reactions on the kids' faces, she was glad she'd done it.

"As you'll notice, there are some extreme differences in the proportions of the two bodies. This one—" she pointed to the generic female body, "I enlarged from a diagram in *The Human Body Source Book*. It's an average sixteen-year-old-girl's body and proportions."

"Hey Bobowick, how come you chickened out and put underwear on them?" Jason called out with a grin.

Mary Ellen had thought hard about that. She'd thought about total nudity, on the grounds that it was okay in museums; and she'd thought about something funny, like construction-paper fig leaves; in the end she'd decided to go with simple white sleeveless undershirts and underpants. She thought real underwear would give her foam board models more oomph than construction paper cutouts. Her mother had bought it at SaveMart, because there was no way Mary Ellen was going to show her *own* underwear to the class!

"Because I didn't want to lose the point of my report with sensationalism," she said to Jason. "It might seem funny, but it's really not." She stepped aside to let the class compare the two figures. "If Debbie were a real sixteen-year-old girl, her actual measurements would be 38-18-33, her liver would be squished up into her lungs, she'd probably have compressed vertebrae from her head being so big, and she'd be so crippled with bunions from those plastic high heels, she'd need a wheelchair to get around."

Everyone, including Ms. Coville, laughed, and Mary Ellen smiled too, then got serious. "Think about it, though. These dolls aren't made for sixteen-year-olds. The biggest part of the market for them is probably six-to-ten-year-olds. This is what is subliminally planted in their minds as what they're supposed to look like when they grow up. Only they don't imagine this—" she pointed to the Debbie enlargement, which looked so ridiculous it was almost alien. "They

get an image in their heads no regular person could live up to. And a lot of them will be miserable trying. My mother bought me a Debbie when I was seven. First I made her a duct tape space suit, then I glued her to an old record turntable, because I was playing astronaut training with her."

Justine laughed out loud. "It's true, she did."

"Did you launch her?" Jason asked.

Mary Ellen grinned and shook her head. "No, after that I played Amazon explorer. She got captured by an indigenous tribe of headhunters. So I chopped her hair off, then pulled her head off and colored it with green and black magic markers, to look like a shrunken head. Looking back now, I think that was a pretty healthy reaction."

Everyone laughed again.

"So, that's my report. Any questions?" This was the moment Mary Ellen had been waiting for. She held her breath and looked around. Kevin had his hand up. Good old Kevin. She grinned.

"What's that lump under Debbie's shirt?" he asked.

The whole class cracked up. Mary Ellen reached inside and pulled out the small, soft, plastic squishy sack that she'd taped to Debbie's chest.

"I'm glad you asked, Kevin." She stood in front of the class, deliberately not looking at Amy who was two desks away. "This is an item called a ShapeShifter. It's advertised in a lot of women's magazines and in the back of a lot of teenage magazines, too. They come in pairs and they cost $119.99 a set—in different sizes, too. They're advertised as 'figure improvers.'" She tossed it up and down in her hand a few times.

"Let's see," Robbie called out. "Pass it around so we can see."

Mary Ellen grinned, and obligingly handed it to the kid closest to her, Shane Daly, who touched it gingerly, squealed "Eeeewwww!," then passed it on.

"Oh—I wanted to say one other thing," Mary Ellen said

over the giggles and comments as the ShapeShifter went around the room. "Something like this can serve a legitimate purpose, as a prosthesis, for women who've had mastectomies. But the ad says they're worn by thousands of satisfied actresses and models. And I think that stinks. It's one thing to hold up a cultural ideal of beauty that's real. But when it's fake, it makes it really hard on regular people."

The ShapeShifter had reached Robbie, who tossed it to Jason like a beanbag. It went flying across the room a few more times, as Ms. Coville led a loud round of applause.

"Wonderful, Mary Ellen! Down with false idols. Excellent report."

As she went back to her seat, carrying the two foamboard figures, Mary Ellen finally allowed herself to sneak a glance at Amy, who was inspecting her thumbnail very closely, while Debra was nudging her, looking worried, and trying to get her attention. For a second, Mary Ellen felt like maybe she'd gone overboard.

"Hey, where'd you get it anyway, Bobowick? Did you pay 120 bucks for it? Or did you get a half-price discount for only one?" Jason asked, snickering.

Mary Ellen glanced at Amy again, and now, for the first time ever, saw real fear in her eyes. She looked back at Jason.

"One of my cousins who's in college is a theater major. She used them for a part in a play she was in, and let me borrow one for my report." She ad-libbed the fib right off the top of her head, and was glad, she wasn't sure why, when Jason dropped the issue without further comment.

"Wonderful, people, all of your reports. A very important step toward owning your own unique identity is to refuse to allow someone else, be it a Madison Avenue ad agency or a clique in school, to define it for you," Ms. Coville said. "Now, next class assignment: Live Under Your Own Hat!"

Though they were getting used to Ms. Coville's nutty approach, all the kids looked at each other. From underneath her desk, Ms. Coville pulled out a brown grocery bag. Sticking her hand inside, she pulled out a lopsided red-and-white striped Cat-in-the-Hat-type–top hat. It had theater tickets sticking out of the ribbon band, flowers growing out of the crown, a spring attached to a flat waving hand, a row of identical cutout paper doll silhouettes with a big circle with a slash drawn over it, a tiny plastic cello that looked like a Christmas tree ornament, and, hanging from the brim, one on either side to balance it, a pair of roller blades with a first aid kit taped to one, and an ace bandage taped to the other. She lifted it and stuck it on top of her head.

"Next class, a week from Monday, is HAT DAY!" She turned and started writing instructions on the board:

1. Choose your hat. Suggestions: baseball cap, ski cap, bike helmet, straw hat, derby, fedora, golf cap, beanie, mantilla.
2. Make a list of characteristics, interests, personality traits, special talents, hobbies, even bad habits that are uniquely YOU!
3. Think of a symbol that can convey each of the things listed under #2.
4. Think of an object to represent each symbol from the things listed under #3.
5. Gather your materials and decorate your hats.
6. HAVE FUN!!"

Still scribbling when the bell rang, Mary Ellen didn't notice Jason step alongside her and pick up her Debbie doll model.

"Can I have this dance?" he said, and started waltzing her around the room.

Mary Ellen grinned. "It's her pleasure. Don't step on

her poor feet though. Those permanent tiptoes have gotta be killer."

"So Jason," Amy sidled up next to him. "Want me to come to your party early and help set things up?"

Jason shrugged amiably. "If you want. There won't be much to do. I mean, we're not going to be setting up for musical chairs or pin the tail on the donkey, or anything."

"That's okay," she said coyly. "I'm sure we can find something to do." She took a step closer to him. He took a casual step back.

"Hey Bobowick, can I have this?"

Mary Ellen raised an eyebrow. "For what, party decorations?"

He grinned. "Yeah. Like, original artwork. Here, sign it for me." He handed her a pen.

Mary Ellen grinned back and signed across one leg. Jason waltzed her out of the room, with Robbie, cracking up, following him.

Amy glared at Mary Ellen, but more weakly than usual.

"Hey, I can't help his taste in women," Mary Ellen said.

Without a word, Amy turned and stalked out of the room. Debra paused to give a vicariously snotty sniff, then stalked after her.

"That was *perfect*!" Justine said. "Absolutely perfect."

Mary Ellen smiled modestly.

"It was an absolutely useless meeting," Dr. Bobowick said that night, shaking her head in disgust.

"Were Mr. and Mrs. Widdle there, too?" Mary Ellen asked, munching on a cheddar-basil bread twist that Mrs. Kelly had sent over for sampling.

"Mr. Widdle!" Mr. Bobowick snorted. "Mr. Alex Michael Thomson Widdle the Fird was there, in all his five-foot-two arrogance. It's no wonder the kid's a pint-sized basket case."

"Mrs. Widdle was too intimidated to say a word, and Nicky's teacher, while lovely and sweet, is young, and certainly no match for that grandiose ego," Dr. Bobowick said. "Miss Cane said that she couldn't understand why Nicky was so upset, because Alex is the smallest child in the class, and no, she hadn't noticed any fighting or bickering going on, but she would keep an eye on things."

Nicky wandered into the kitchen in his pajamas. "Did you go see Miss Cane?" he asked.

"We sure did, Nicko," Mr. Bobowick said. "And she said you're doing a super job in kindergarten."

"Is she going to kick Alex Michael Thomson Widdle the Forf out of school for being bad?" he asked.

Mary Ellen watched her father exchange a silent communication with her mother.

"Well, Nicko, it's like this," Mr. Bobowick said slowly. "Sometimes, you come up against situations in life and—"

"Knock, knock," Olivia said as she rapped lightly on the back door.

"Come on in, Livie," Mr. Bobowick called out. Mary Ellen could tell he was relieved at the momentary reprieve from an explanation that probably wasn't going to make Nicky feel any better.

"Here, Dr. B, the final list," Olivia said cheerfully. "Mom wants to know if you can look it over and see if there's anything she may have missed." She handed Dr. Bobowick a plastic binder, with about two-dozen typed pages inside. "I spent the afternoon showing her how to set up different files on the computer, you know, one for food lists and prices, one for recipes, another for the rental equipment and costs, a calendar, and a timetable. She's ready to go into business now!"

Opening the report, Dr. Bobowick scanned the first two pages. "Your mother," she said, "is an astounding woman. What she's pulled together in such a short time is nothing short of magic."

"Let her know that, will you please?" Olivia said earnestly. "She doesn't think she's any good."

"I will," Dr. Bobowick said. "I promise."

"Does your mother know magic, Livie?" Nicky asked hopefully.

"Well," Olivia said thoughtfully. "Kind of. Yes, she knows a certain kind of magic. But there's a lot of different kinds."

"Does she know the kind that can make a mean kid go away and never come back?" he asked.

"Ahhh." Olivia nodded. "That old Alex Widdle the Forf again, huh?" She looked at Mary Ellen's parents. "No luck with the teacher?" They both shook their heads. "May I?" she asked.

"Be our guest, Olivia," Mr. Bobowick said. "I'm plumb out of magic myself. I've tried the old sticks and stones will break your bones, but that didn't work."

"Not strong enough," Olivia said to Mr. Bobowick. "And not true, either. Words are pretty powerful." She squatted down on the floor so she was eye-level with Nicky. "He's been saying stuff to you, right Nicky?"

Nicky nodded.

Olivia nodded back. "Well," she said. "I happen to know a little bit of magic myself, just the kind you need when someone says bad stuff to you. It's a spell."

Nicky frowned now. "I don't know how to spell yet."

They all chuckled.

"You don't need to know how to spell," Olivia told him. "All you need to know is how to talk. I'm going to teach you my special spell. Whenever he says anything to you, all you have to say is this: 'Ob-al-ob-ex thob-a-fob-orf, gob-et ob-out ob-uv mob-I fob-ace.' Then you walk away. It takes all the power out of his words. "

He wrinkled his nose. "I can't say that. I can't remember."

"Yes you can," Olivia said. "Any little guy who can recite *Go Dog Go* from cover to cover can remember a little magic spell. Come on, I'll go upstairs with you and teach you till you know it by heart."

"Will it really work?" Nicky asked.

"Yep. You can't forget about the walking away part though." She stood up and held out her arms. Nicky jumped up into them.

"Yay! Livie's going to teach me magic."

Olivia winked at Mary Ellen and her parents, then took Nicky up to bed.

"What was that spell?" Mr. Bobowick asked.

Mary Ellen laughed. "It's Ob-talk—kind of like pig Latin. She said 'Alex the Forf, get out of my face.' "

Chapter 16

"Wow!" Mary Ellen stood with Justine, Olivia, Dr. Bobowick, and Mrs. Kelly at the entrance to the ballroom on the upper floor of the Dickerson College administration building, the center part of which had once been the mansion of a huge estate. An enormous chandelier with glass prisms hung from the center of the high, domed ceiling. A black grand piano stood in one corner, and around the room were groupings of expensive-looking couches, chairs, and coffee tables on oriental rugs. A university maintenance man was in the process of lighting a fire in the huge marble fireplace across the room.

Two long banquet tables were set up on either side of the fireplace. One was covered with a feast of finger food, a huge wicker cornucopia overflowing with cut vegetables, and baskets of different kinds of crackers and breadsticks. The other was set with wide silver serving trays placed over cans of Sterno in little silver containers, ready for the hot hors d'oeuvres that would be cooked in the service kitchen down the hall.

In the center of the room, next to a table with a large, cloth-covered rectangle on it, was a table with the scale-model carrot cake, which Mrs. Kelly had brought in piece by piece that morning, assembled, frosted, and decorated.

"I think maybe you did too stunning a job, Corrine," Dr. Bobowick said slowly.

"You do? Why?" Mrs. Kelly asked. "Is something wrong?"

Dr. Bobowick shook her head laughing. "No, nothing's wrong. I just meant when the foundation heads and rich alumni see this spread, they're going to figure Dickerson's loaded, and doesn't need their donations at all!"

"Oh." Mrs. Kelly smiled in relief.

"And I think it's a wonderful idea to unveil the dessert when we unveil the model," Dr. Bobowick said.

"I need to stop back home to get the draping cloth and frame I made." Mrs. Kelly clucked her tongue. "I ironed it and left it spread on the dining room table so it wouldn't crease."

"I'm going to run home and change now. Would you like me to pop over and get it?" Mary Ellen's mother asked.

Mrs. Kelly shook her head. "That's alright, Laura. You have enough to do to get ready. We're really all set here. I want to run to the store for some potpourri and little baskets to set in the ladies' room. The house is on the way."

Dr. Bobowick looked at her watch. "Okay, an hour and fifteen minutes till showtime. I'll be back by 4:30. I owe you a huge favor in return for this, Corrine." She gave Mrs. Kelly a quick hug and hurried off. Mrs. Kelly picked up her purse from a nearby coffee table and prepared to follow her out.

"Wait a second, Mom," Olivia said. "I have a present for you." She reached into the pocket of her long black skirt, and pulled out a stack of white business cards. "Here."

As Mrs. Kelly took them, Mary Ellen and Justine crowded in to read along with her. Inside an oval border of pink and green fleurs-de-lis, in large, bold, italic script were the words:

—— . ——

*Corrine's Gourmet Cuisine
Catering Extraordinaire*

Below that, in smaller, plainer lettering it read, 'Ms. Corrine Kelly—fine catering services for all occasions, private and corporate,' along with the Kellys' phone number.

"I thought putting *corporate* would be good. It sounds like money, you know? And I would have made more, but I did them in the computer lab at school, and I didn't have time."

"My goodness!" Mrs. Kelly exclaimed. "My own business cards!"

"Nothing like a business card to make a person feel empowered," Olivia went on. "There might be important rich people here, and if they like it and ask who did it, you can just give them your card."

"Thank you, sweetie. It's a wonderful gift and vote of confidence." She smiled at Olivia, then went back to efficient mode. "All right, now. I'm off to SaveMart. Olivia, you're in charge of putting the first batch of hot hors d'oeuvres into the oven, at 4:15 on the button, if I'm delayed. Set the timer for twenty minutes. They need to be out in those serving dishes by 4:45. And the dip for the vegetable crudité basket—it's in the—"

"I know, I know, Mom," Olivia said. "Red and green

hollowed-out cabbages in the fridge. They need to be out on the table by 4:45, too."

"Okay, then." Mrs. Kelly turned to Mary Ellen and Justine. "You two make sure cocktail napkins are placed around the room in strategic but discreet spots, and set out the brandy snifters with the floating candles. I'll light them when I get back." She looked around the room, and bit her lip, frowning.

"Not to worry, Mom," Olivia said. "Everything's under control." She gave her mother a gentle push toward the exit, while she headed toward the entrance to the service kitchen.

"Oh! One last thing," Mrs. Kelly exclaimed. She dug in her purse and came out with two covered pony-tail elastics. "Justine, there's a law that people serving food have to have their hair tied up somehow, if it's longer than shoulder length."

"Ugh," Justine said, making a face.

"Honey, please. Just stick it in braids or something. I have to go now."

"Want me to help you put it in braids?" Mary Ellen asked after Mrs. Kelly left.

"No. With the frizz from the perm, I'll end up looking like Pippi Longstocking. Maybe I'll do a French twist or something. Do you have any bobby pins?"

Mary Ellen lifted a lock of her short hair. "A bobby pin? For what? Maybe your mother can pick some up—Oh!" Mary Ellen interrupted herself abruptly.

"What?"

"I just thought of something! Your mother should take pictures of all this stuff before any of the people get here. You know, like for a portfolio, so she can show people what she can do."

"You're right," Justine said excitedly. "I wonder if I can catch her and tell her to bring the camera and get film at

SaveMart. And bobby pins, too. Her car was parked right out front—did she leave yet?"

Mary Ellen turned abruptly to run to the window, but the hem of her long skirt got caught under the heel of her black sneaker.

"Aaagh!" she yelped, jerking precariously toward the cake.

"Look out!" Justine shouted at the same time, sticking out her arm to save Mary Ellen from falling right into the display, but in the process, sweeping her hand across the west wing entrance. The two meringue columns went flying and the small entrance roof fell down onto the steps.

"Oh no!" Justine wailed. "Look what you made me do! I can't be*lieve* you, Mary Ellen. You really *do* belong on the Clod Squad!"

Mary Ellen looked from Justine's brick-tinted frosting-covered fingers to the columns that had cracked into meringue shards when they hit the floor. She felt her face getting hot.

"It wasn't *my* fault! *You* were the one who said we had to wear these stupid long skirts!"

The two girls looked at each other angrily for a second, then at the cake.

"It was an accident, anyhow," Mary Ellen whispered.

Justine let out a heavy sigh. "Well, it sure wasn't an on-purpose, I know that. But what are we going to do? My mother will have a flying cow when she sees it."

"Maybe we can fix it somehow," Mary Ellen said. "Spread the frosting a little thinner or—"

"Mary Ellen, it looks like a miniature wrecking ball just swung through. Look at that gouge! And what about the columns?" Justine pointed to the pieces of shattered meringue on the hardwood floor.

"Well, we *have* to do something," Mary Ellen said decisively. "Okay, go to the kitchen, make sure Olivia's tied up in there, and sneak some of that smoked salmon dip and the cream cheese horseradish spread out of the refrigerator. And a knife or spoon or something."

"What are you going to do?" Justine asked.

"The first thing I'm going to do is roll up the waistband of this stupid skirt!" Mary Ellen said. "Then I'm going to do some building renovations. Go get the stuff and *hurry!!*"

As Justine took off, Mary Ellen went over to the raw vegetable basket, and carefully took out eight of the biggest cut carrot sticks she could find. A minute later, Justine, out of breath and flushed, was back, with two stainless steel mixing bowls and a butter knife.

"Here," she huffed.

Mary Ellen took four of the carrot sticks. "Give me those pony-tail elastics."

Raising her eyebrows, but not arguing, Justine handed them over. Mary Ellen took one, and joined the carrots end to end, with a little overlapping. She measured it against the ones on the undamaged wing.

"Knife," she said, snapping out her hand like a surgeon. "And cream cheese spread." Justine pulled the plastic wrap off the bowl and held it out, as Mary Ellen dipped the knife in and began coating the carrots.

Ten minutes later, two carrot-core columns to hold up the little porch roof to the entrance had been installed, and the gouge in the building was filled in with pinkish smoked salmon spread, mixed with some of the frosting to darken the color.

"The columns are kind of bulgy in the middle," Justine said.

Mary Ellen stood back and looked at her handiwork critically. "They don't sparkle like the meringue ones, either," she said.

"How 'bout sprinkling some sugar on?" Justine suggested. "My mom got the really fine kind, granulated but not powdered, you know? It's over on the table with the coffee stuff."

"That might work." Mary Ellen nodded. "Okay, you go do that, while I go wash my hands."

"What are you guys *doing* out here?" Olivia called from the kitchen doorway down the hall. "I could use some help, okay? Come get these candles."

"Coming," Justine sang out, waving a hand. As soon as Olivia's back was turned, she shoved the bowls toward Mary Ellen. "Go hide these under the vanity in the ladies room. I'll grab some sugar, and throw it on the columns while I'm putting a candle over there."

"This has been a smashing success, Corrine." Dr. Bobowick was standing next to Mrs. Kelly behind the side-by-side model display, which had just been unveiled to a loud chorus of *ooohs* and *ahhhs*. Mrs. Kelly had been so rushed when she got back with the wooden dowel frame and the silk drapery, that she'd let Mary Ellen and Justine set it up, while she supervised all the last-minute things in the kitchen. Now the two of them, standing next to Mrs. Kelly, with their trays empty and ready to walk around and serve slices of the cake while Mrs. Kelly did the cutting and dishing out, exchanged a guilty look.

"Smashing is the word," Mary Ellen muttered out of the side of her mouth.

"Quiet, and be thankful she started cutting on the east wing of the cake," Justine replied under her breath.

"I'm so glad, Laura," Mrs. Kelly was saying, smiling as she expertly dismantled the building and cut trim, even slices. "The turnout is even better than you'd anticipated, isn't it? I hope it gives you a good start with the fundraising."

"It's given us more than a good start," Dr. Bobowick said. "See that man over there?"

Mary Ellen followed the direction of her mother's gaze, as did Justine and Mrs. Kelly, to a shortish, balding man wearing a three-piece gray pinstripe suit, and talking to a woman who looked like a model about half his age.

"Robert Grumman, of Grumman Publishing, and his wife. He's a Dickerson alumnus. And he told me his firm is going to seed the building fund with half-a-million dollars." Dr. Bobowick beamed. As if he sensed he was being discussed, Mr. Grumman turned to the group near the model and the cake, and strolled over, with a jovial expression on his face.

"I really have to congratulate you on this spread, Dr. Bobowick," he said in a strong Southern accent. "Is the caterer responsible for this gastronomic creation as well? Where did you find 'em? My wife wants to hire 'em for our daughter's debutante party."

"Yes, one caterer did the whole show, from soup to nuts as it were. And I found her next door," Mary Ellen's mother said, turning toward Mrs. Kelly. "Corrine Kelly, Robert Grumman."

"An astonishing piece of culinary creativity," Mr. Grumman said, holding out his hand, which Mrs. Kelly shook, blushing slightly. "Architecture you can eat. Now THAT would make a good book. Is it really all suitable for consumption? Even the flowers and the shrubs? "

"Oh, yes." Mrs. Kelly assured him. "From the roof to the landscaping. Even the columns are edible. They're meringue."

"Isn't that a coincidence. Meringues are one of my favorite things. Haven't had a decent one since my last trip to Paris. May I?"

"Please." Mrs. Kelly smiled again. "By all means. That's what it's here for."

As Mr. Grumman reached toward the west-wing entrance columns, Mary Ellen and Justine stiffened, and shot each other a frantic look, but it was too late. He'd grasped one of the columns between his thumb and index finger and pulled it out. A frown creased his forehead, as he took in the fact that it wasn't dry, light, and powdery, but gooey

with a solid core. Hesitantly he moved it toward his mouth, stopping halfway to stare some more, then continuing, while a puzzled look crossed Mrs. Kelly's face, and a suspicious one came over Dr. Bobowick's face.

"Don't," Mary Ellen blurted out.

"Wait," Justine said at the same time.

All three of the adults turned to stare at them.

"All I can say to you two is that it's a good thing Mr. Grumman has three daughters of his own and a well-developed sense of humor," Dr. Bobowick said. They were all sitting around the Kellys' kitchen, after having unloaded Mrs. Kelly's equipment and tons of leftovers from the station wagon. "Why didn't you girls *tell* poor Corrine? Give her a chance to participate in the great cream-cheese coverup?"

Mrs. Kelly, over at the computer on the kitchen desk, burst out laughing. "At least they had the sense to stop Mr. Grumman before he put it in his mouth. I can't imagine what conniptions you would have put his taste buds through, expecting meringue, and getting horseradish spread. But actually, I have to say it was a very resourceful method of damage control."

Mr. Bobowick chuckled, too. "And when you think about it, it was technically edible."

"And it was still carrot cake, too," Olivia put in. "And you see, Mom? Aren't you glad you had your business card ready?"

Mrs. Kelly laughed again. "Yes, I am, although I can see I need to educate myself about the business aspect of catering." She did some calculations in the financial program, then laughed again. "Well, after adding up the expenses, my profit came to about twenty-seven cents an hour."

"Oh, Corrine," Dr. Bobowick exclaimed, concerned. "I'll put in to the department for more money."

"Absolutely not," Mrs. Kelly said. "It was a learning experience for one thing, and I plan to be a person of my word as a business person. I'm chalking it up to a crash course in 'Real World 101.' "

Olivia patted her mother on the shoulder. "I bet you'll ace it, too."

Chapter 17

"I know, I know," Justine said anxiously, bursting into the Bobowicks' kitchen, where Mary Ellen was waiting impatiently. "I'm late—"

"Twenty minutes," Mary Ellen put in. "Jason's party started ten minutes ago."

"I'm sorry. Really. You can put it on my tombstone— 'The Late Justine Kelly.' But we didn't want to be the first ones there, anyway."

"I don't want to be the last ones, either." But Mary Ellen toned down her annoyance. She didn't want to get in a fight before the party.

"Look." Justine pulled off the scarf she'd worn on her head. "I decided at the last minute to have Livie cut my hair. I was getting so tired of trying to figure out what do with that bottom half." It was shorter than Mary Ellen's now, in fluffy blonde waves, parted just off center with a silver barrette holding part of it back. "What do you think?"

"I think it looks fantastic," Mary Ellen had said truthfully. The frizzy ends were gone, and it didn't look like a schizophrenic wig that couldn't decide if it wanted to be short or long, anymore.

"Ready?" Mr. Bobowick came in from the living room. "Bobowick's Taxi, at your service, ladies."

"We're ready," Mary Ellen confirmed, sticking her arms into her coat sleeves and making a beeline for the back door.

"I'll pick you up at 10:30 sharp," Mary Ellen's father said, as he pulled up in front of the Hodges' split-level ranch. "If you don't want to be embarrassed by the appearance of a flabby old party-pooping geezer coming in to cut the rug in the midst of the festivities, be out on the porch on time."

"You're not flabby and you're not old," Mary Ellen said, leaning over to give him a kiss on the cheek. "But we'll be out on time." She held up her arm to show her wristwatch. Justine opened the door and got out first, and Mary Ellen slid out after her.

Mrs. Hodges greeted them at the door, looking flustered. Jason's little brother Andy was peeking out from behind her legs. He was rubbing his finger on a balloon, making squeaky noises that made Mrs. Hodges wince every time she heard them, though she didn't seem to register where the noise was coming from. Well, living with Jason and his little brother, if he was anything like him, would be enough to make a pretty frazzled mother, Mary Ellen imagined.

"Come right in, girls, " she said, smiling a distracted smile as the phone started ringing somewhere in the house. "Everything's set up in the family room, down the hall," she pointed with a hand that had smears of dried chocolate cake batter on it. The Hodges' golden retriever nosed up to the two girls, enthusiastically sniffing their knees and drooling on their shoes. Mrs. Hodges grabbed him by the collar and pulled him back, smiling. "Don't worry, he's friendly. He might slobber you to death, but he'd never hurt you. Just follow the music and the yelling." Then she turned and ran to answer the phone, almost tripping over Andy, who stuck his tongue out at the two girls.

"I got him the new Rancid Rockers CD," Justine said as they went down the hallway. "What did you get him?"

"I got him a pair of those imitation Vuarnet glacier glasses at Eyewear Outlet," Mary Ellen said. "You know, the dark sunglasses with the leather flaps on the side? It reminded me of the jacket he bought when we saw him at the mall that day."

"Oh, that's such a good idea," Justine said. "I wish I thought of it. What if he hates Rancid Rockers? Or what if he already has the CD?" She stopped in the hall, and looked like she was thinking of turning around and leaving before she even went in. Mary Ellen had a sudden flash of how awful it must feel to be Justine right now. She worried about *everything*. It had to be exhausting. On impulse, she held out the small wrapped package and pulled off the card.

"Here. Switch. I don't care that much one way or the other. If he already has the CD or doesn't like it, he can exchange it."

"Really?" Justine asked. "You wouldn't mind?"

"No. Yes. I mean, yes, really, and no I wouldn't mind." She hurriedly took the wrapped CD, took Justine's gift card off it, and stuck her card to Jason on it, and Justine's card on on the other package. "Now come on."

Mary Ellen went first down the half-flight of stairs to the family room. It was packed with kids, and the stereo was blaring, but no one was dancing. A fluorescent light over the pool table was on, and most of the guys were gathered around that. The girls were huddled around a three-sided couch arrangement that wound around the other side of the room, dipping into salsa and tortilla chips, bowls of popcorn, and potato chips. On a paper-tablecloth-covered table, a buffet was set out. The girls saw two six-foot-long deli sandwiches sliced and set on foil-covered boards, with a colorfully fringed toothpick stuck into the top of each sandwich section, an immense bowl of pasta salad, stacks of paper cups and plates and plastic silverware, and a huge chocolate sheet cake.

"Hi, Mary Ellen, hi, Justine," Jason greeted them as he opened a cooler filled with ice and soda, and took out a root beer. "Hey, your hair looks good that way." He stuck out his hand and gave a lock a tug.

"Thanks," Justine said, blushing.

As Jason headed back toward the pool table, Mary Ellen noticed Amy shooting a dirty look at Justine.

"Hey guys!" a familiar voice squeaked out from across the room.

"Oh, no," Justine groaned. "I bet Amy got Jason to invite Kevin just to torture me."

Mary Ellen ignored the comment and went over to put the Rancid Rockers on the table with the other presents. Kevin came up beside her.

"Ready for the speeches on Monday?" he asked, then said in a lower, conspiratorial tone, "I've been taking an informal poll with the kids that are here from our homeroom. It's a close race so far, half, half, and half."

"That's three halves, Kevin," Mary Ellen pointed out.

"Oh. True. Well, what I mean is, it's split pretty evenly between kids who want you, kids who want Amy, and kids who don't know who or what they want. Undecided. Hey Justine, I like your hair," he said as Justine came up and added the switched gift to the pile.

"I'm thrilled, Kevin," Justine said dryly. "I'm going to go grab some food," she said to Mary Ellen, and headed toward the buffet.

Mary Ellen saw Kevin's face fall as he watched Justine

walk away, and she felt a stab of major irritation with Justine. It was one thing not to want to give someone who had a crush on you the wrong idea that there might be hope. It was another thing to treat them like cow manure.

"Mary Ellen!"

She spun around. Could it be—sandy hair, great tan, and the smile that every once in a while, like now, caught Mary Ellen by surprise and made her heart do an actual thump?

Without even thinking, she took two steps, and they met in the middle of the room in a big bear hug!

"Ben! I didn't know you were coming!! When did you get here? How did you know about the party?"

"It was a last-minute thing," he said. "My grandfather went in for cataract surgery yesterday, and we came down for the weekend to see him and help my grandmother out. I called Jason to see what was going on, and he invited me."

They smiled at each other for a moment. Mary Ellen only realized they were still hugging when the whole room went silent. She and Ben both looked around.

"You get the feeling like we're in a fishbowl?" Ben asked.

Mary Ellen grinned and nodded. They let go of each other, and Mary Ellen waved her arm around the room. " 'Chat amongst yourselves,' " she quoted Mr. Gumble. "Need a topic? Consider this: Hamburger. Why isn't it made out of ham?" Jason started a round of whistles and applause, and Mary Ellen and Ben both joined in laughing.

"I'm sorry about your grandfather—but I'm so glad you're here. I've really missed you."

"Me, too," Ben said.

"Why didn't you write? I was waiting for you to write first."

"Have you checked your e-mail recently?" he asked.

Mary Ellen shook her head. "No," she admitted. "I've

been real busy, with school and all, and with Justine back, I didn't even think to."

"Check it when you get home," he said. "How's Bozo, by the way?"

"Bozo's great. The King of the Tank," Mary Ellen said with a smile.

"Okay everybody, it's Choice time," Amy said loudly. She'd commandeered Jason by the arm, and was dragging him toward the couch. "Everybody sit in a circle."

"Who died and left her social director?" Ben leaned close to Mary Ellen, whispering in her ear.

Mary Ellen grinned. "Some things never change. I have a feeling Amy's going to be like this when she's ninety, bossing all the other old people in the nursing home around." She looked around the circle of kids now. Justine was sitting cross-legged on the floor opposite her, with a plate of food balanced on her knee. Mary Ellen smiled and wiggled her fingers, suddenly feeling a little guilty, as if with Ben showing up, and kind of being with her, she was kind of deserting Justine. After all, they'd come together. Pointing to the couch next to her, she raised her eyebrows, signalling that they could squeeze over and make more room. Justine smiled and gave her head a little shake, then looked away, as if she'd suddenly noticed something interesting on the far side of the room.

"Jason, it's your birthday, so you get to start," Amy was saying.

"Okaaaaayyyy," Jason said, looking around the circle, his eyes lighting up at a likely victim. "Marcia, would you rather get a shampoo with Elmer's glue, or wear a live octopus on your head for three weeks?"

Marcia's face immediately scrunched up into an anxious frown. "Oh, no. Why did you start with such a hard one? Okay, okay, I'm thinking. Um—do I get to wash the glue out of my hair before it dries? And is the octopus de-inked?"

Everyone cracked up.

"No washing your hair before it dries, and the octopus has tons of ink," Jason told her.

"Ohh," she groaned. "I just don't know. I mean, if I waited till the glue dried, it might not come out at all and then I'd have to wait till it grew out, but I couldn't stand having all those octopus suction thingys on my face. Eeewww! Um—all right. I'd take the glue. But I'd wear a hat for six months. Okay. My turn. Um, Amy, would you rather . . . um . . . walk barefoot around a whole city block on a sidewalk made of . . . um . . . dead fish eyeballs, or . . . wait a sec, I'm thinking . . . or . . . or . . . have to go to school every single day, even weekends and summers, for the rest of junior high?"

"That's a dumb one, Marcia," Amy said.

"You have to answer anyway, Amy, that's the rule. You made it up," Jason said.

"Oh, okay. I'll do the sidewalk. But on stilts."

"No fair, Colter, you can't use stilts," Robbie said.

"Yes, I can," Amy retorted. "I'll still have bare feet. If Marcia can wear a hat over her gluehead, I can use stilts. So there."

"It'd still be gross," Kevin piped up. "Even on stilts. The eyes would be squashing and popping all over the—"

"EEEEEWWWWWW!!!!! KEVIN!!!!!!" A chorus of groans filled the room. Kevin grinned from ear to ear.

"Okay, I ask now," Amy said loudly. "Justine. Would you rather eat ten pounds of tunafish-flavored jelly beans, or drink a quart of dead squashed fly-flavored iced tea?" Amy said sweetly.

"I wouldn't rather do either," Justine said, wrinkling her nose in disgust.

"You *have* to choose," Amy said. "That's the game."

"Could she put sugar in the fly iced tea?" Mary Ellen sensed Amy going into hyper-mean mode, and wanted to deflect the tension if she could. "Hey, that would make it Fl-Iced Tea," she joked.

"No sugar," Amy said. "But that should be an easy choice for you, Justine. You'll eat anything, anyway." She looked pointedly at the heaped plate on Justine's knee, then said to Debra, but in a voice they were all meant to hear, "I mean, oink oink, or what."

Debra and Robbie snickered with Amy, as Justine reddened and slumped down, with a pasted-on smile on her face. But most of the other kids didn't laugh. And Mary Ellen saw Jason give Amy a kind of disgusted look.

"Hey, I've got a choice," Kevin spoke up loudly. "Would everyone rather play a game of Choice with Amy or get rolled in honey and stuck in a cave with ten hungry grizzly bears? Me—I'd take my chances with the bears any day."

"Okay, last choice," Jason shouted. "You guys wanna play Twister or Twister?"

"Yeah, Twister, and I get to do the spinner, right Jason? Right? You said I could do the—"

Jason picked up his little brother. "Yep, Andy, buddy, you get to be the spinner."

"Aren't there too many of us to play?" Debra asked. She did a quick head count. "There's sixteen, not including your little brother."

"S'okay," Jason said. "We've got three boards."

Mrs. Hodges got the Twister boxes from a utility closet, and set them on the pool table. Jason and Robbie pounced on them, opened them, and spread the plastic mats with the rows of red, blue, green and yellow circles on them out on the carpeting between the pool table and the couches.

"Okay, everybody ready? Go ahead, Andy, spin," Mrs. Hodges said. She watched while he spun the plastic arrow. "Right foot red, everyone!" she said.

Immediately the scramble for territory began. Mary Ellen and Ben went for the same circle, and she wound up stepping on his foot.

"Oh, sorry!"

"You're not supposed to say you're sorry. This is supposed to be war. Every man for himself." But he grinned and slid his foot out from under hers and onto the next circle.

"Yellow, left hand!" Mrs. Hodges called out.

Mary Ellen slid under Ben's stomach and planted her hand on the circle next to Shane Daly's.

"Ooops!" She grinned as she heard Kevin's trademark "I goofed" exclamation.

"Kevin, you just headbutted me. Watch out!" Marcia complained. "Boy, how can somebody so skinny have such a heavy head?"

"Because he's got twenty pounds of brains in there," Mary Ellen called over to the neighboring mat.

"Right hand, red!"

Everyone scrambled to squeeze a hand on the same circle as a foot.

"Now's when the fun starts," Ben said, leaning over Mary Ellen's back while she curled up in a semi-cannonball position to try and keep her balance.

"I feel like a human pretzel," Jason said.

Mary Ellen heard Amy giggling, and under her arm, could see the two of them pretty well wound up together.

"This is like—ooof!—organized Pig Pile," Kevin said breathlessly. "Hey, easy with the elbows there, Debra."

By the tenth round, everyone was so breathless from laughing that they all collapsed in a tangle of limbs on the floor.

"Okay, everyone, I think you've exhausted the possibilities of this game," Mrs. Hodges said. "Ready for cake?"

"Yeah!" Jason shouted. "And open the loot time!"

Mrs. Hodges went over to the table and started lighting the candles on the cake. Mary Ellen and Ben settled on one corner of the couch, as all the kids made their way over to the couch area. Mary Ellen looked around the room for Justine. She hadn't been on the same mat for Twister. In fact—Mary Ellen thought hard—had she been on any of the mats? Had she played at all?

Mrs. Hodges carried the cake over to the coffee table, and everyone joined in on different pitches to sing a sloppy version of "Happy Birthday," Jason singing the loudest of all, "Happy Birthday to Me!"

As he blew out the candles, with Amy bugging him to tell what his wish was, Mary Ellen felt a tap on her shoulder from behind the couch. She craned her neck around. Kevin was standing behind her, with an oddly worried frown on his face. He jerked his head toward the stairs. Mary Ellen raised her eyebrows questioningly.

"Justine," he mouthed back, without saying it out loud, then jerked his head again.

"I'll be right back," Mary Ellen said into Ben's ear, then stood and carefully picked her way over legs and around bodies, while Jason opened his first present.

She went up the stairs, and followed Kevin to the kitchen.

"What's the matter?" she asked.

Kevin looked down at his shoes for a minute, fidgeting with his hands stuck in his pockets, then back up at Mary Ellen.

"Look, maybe I shouldn't open my big mouth, but I've been noticing some things," he began, his words coming out in a rush. "Things that remind me of my sister, and I thought, you know, maybe I should say something, just in case, so they could tell someone, if they hadn't noticed, check it out—"

"Kevin, what are you trying to say?" Mary Ellen interrupted, mystified.

He looked toward the doorway, as if to make sure no

one was within eavesdropping range, then said in a voice so low Mary Ellen could hardly hear him.

"I came up to use the bathroom right after we played Twister, when everyone else was still downstairs. And I heard water running in the bathroom, so I waited, you know, so whoever it was could finish washing their hands. Then the toilet flushed, with the water still running. And then again, two more times. And it sounded like someone, you know, getting sick."

"I don't get it, Kevin," Mary Ellen said. "Are you saying Justine is sick?" She looked toward the bathroom door. It was open and the light was off. "Why didn't she tell me if she didn't feel well? I would have called my father to come pick us up early."

Kevin was shaking his head. "Listen. The water was running. The toilet flushed three times, not in a row, with time in between when it sounded like someone was puking."

"What the heck were you doing listening outside the bathroom door, anyway, Kevin?" Mary Ellen was beginning to get angry. "That's pretty creepy if you—"

"Mary Ellen, please listen to me." Kevin took a deep breath. "My sister Kathy is bulimic. That's what she used to do to try and hide it—run the water."

Mary Ellen stared at him. Justine? Making herself throw up on purpose? Mary Ellen couldn't think of anything she'd rather do less than throw up. How could anyone even *think* of doing it deliberately?

She stared at Kevin angrily. "I'm really surprised at you, Kevin. I mean, I know Justine's been mean to you, but to say something like that, to start a rumor, that's . . . that's . . ."

She started to march out of the room, but he grabbed her arm with surprising firmness.

"Mary Ellen, I hope I'm wrong, and I could be." His face was red, and he looked angry himself. "And I'm not starting any rumor—that's why I only told you. It's just I've noticed some other things that my sister used to do, like always talking about being on a diet, but never losing weight—not that I think Justine needs to," he inserted hastily. "But that, and doubling up on desserts and sweet stuff at lunch in school. And one other thing—look at the knuckle of her index finger on her right hand."

"What does that have to do with anything?" Mary Ellen stared at him.

Kevin looked down at his shoes. "It does. I'm not just making this up. You can talk to my sister if you want, she's in therapy now." He looked at Mary Ellen earnestly now. "Look, I know Justine hates my guts, but if she does have bulimia, it can be really serious, and she needs help. That's all." He let go of her arm and walked out of the room. Mary Ellen stared after him, then jumped a little as the kitchen door opened, and Justine came in from the deck.

"Hi. I just went out for some fresh air. What'd I miss?"

Mary Ellen tried to avoid staring at her. "Not much. Just the worst rendition of 'Happy Birthday' ever sung. And the cake."

"I don't really feel like having any cake right now," Justine said. As she went to walk past Mary Ellen, Mary Ellen couldn't keep from looking at her right hand. There was a sore-looking reddish mark, like she'd scraped her knuckle. Mary Ellen averted her eyes quickly, and took a deep breath, feeling slightly sick to her stomach herself. It couldn't be. She'd know for sure if her best friend was doing something like that. She walked slowly back to the family room.

"What's up?" Ben asked as she sat back down. She looked over at Kevin, but he avoided her glance.

"Nothing," Mary Ellen said slowly. Ben looked at her, like he knew that wasn't true. He snuck his hand over and held hers, while Jason opened the present Mary Ellen had picked out.

"Hey, Kelly! These are really cool! Thanks a lot." He put

the glacier glasses on and bobbed his head a few times. "Now I'm really baaaaad to the bone!" Everyone laughed, except Amy. Justine smiled brightly at Mary Ellen, but it seemed to Mary Ellen that there was something forced and false about it. She forced herself to smile back normally. If Kevin *was* right, what should she do? Who should she tell?

Chapter 18

Mary Ellen braced herself. *Don't duck this time!* a little voice in her head said. She and Ben were standing *very* close to each other, on the side of his grandparents' deck, behind the picnic table.

"My parents and I are taking my grandmother out to brunch," Ben had said when he called that morning, right after Mary Ellen and her family got home from church. "At the Bistro on the Beach. Can you come with us? We have a reservation for 12:30. I know it's kinda last minute but . . ." Mary Ellen had covered the phone with her hand and breathlessly asked her parents, who said yes without even a raised eyebrow.

Now Mr. and Mrs. Aldrich were having a last cup of coffee with his grandparents before getting back on the road for the return trip to Boston. And she and Ben were outside, where they'd been chatting on the deck. And Ben's face was getting closer and closer to hers! Mary Ellen held her breath. *What were you supposed to do with your arms?* Hers dangled uncertainly by her side, her fingers twitching. Then his right hand bumped her left, and after a little bit of finger groping, they were holding hands. Or hand, anyway. And he was looking at Mary Ellen kind of seriously, and as if he wanted to ask a question, but didn't know quite how to get it out.

Suddenly he closed his eyes. Quickly, Mary Ellen did the same. And in the next second she felt his lips just barely touching hers!

Now what? What was supposed to happen? Mary Ellen's brain scrambled for love scenes she'd seen in movies, but then it got distracted by Ben's lips moving a little, lightly, as if he were talking in slow motion, but with no words coming out. Mary Ellen made hers do the same thing. Then he moved his head a little bit sideways. She followed suit again, thinking maybe it was like Simon Says. If she just did what Ben did, she wouldn't make a complete idiot of herself. *Yeah—a lip version of Simon Says.* Without thinking, Mary Ellen giggled, in mid-kiss. She opened her eyes when Ben drew back a little. His brown eyes were open now, and nervousness showed in them.

"What?" he said. "What were you thinking?"

"Huh?" Mary Ellen stalled, trying to think of an answer that wouldn't sound insulting.

"What made you laugh?" he asked.

"Oh, not you," Mary Ellen said. "Really." *What an idiot you are,* the head voice said. *You probably hurt his feelings! Damage control, quick!* If she messed up this second kiss, there probably would never *be* a third. "I mean," she stammered. "It's just I was thinking—well—"

"Well, what?" He tilted his head curiously.

"About Simon Says," Mary Ellen told him, then smiled

sheepishly. "I mean, not that I wasn't—you know—enjoying—I mean—but I was trying to figure out how to do this right, and trying to do what you did, and that made me think of Simon Says and . . ."

Now Ben smiled back. "I'm not sure this is the kind of thing you're supposed to think about too much. Or analyze scientifically to see if you're doing it right. But if you want to stop that's ok—"

"No," Mary Ellen said quickly. "I don't want to. Stop, I mean. I mean . . ."

Ben let go of her hand. Then he took a step closer, and this time, put both his arms around her waist. Mary Ellen bit her lip, then put her hands on his arms, right near his shoulders.

"Okay?" he whispered.

Mary Ellen nodded. And closed her eyes. And tilted her chin up a little, to get in the right position. And waited. And waited. After about ten seconds, she opened one eye to peek. Now Ben was grinning.

"What?" she asked. "What are *you* thinking?"

He gave his head a little shake, and tried to stop grinning, but couldn't quite manage it.

"Tell me," Mary Ellen said. *Had she ruined the whole thing?*

"Nah," he said. "It was just something really stupid that came into my head."

"Come on, you have to tell," Mary Ellen said. "I did. It can't be stupider than what I was thinking."

"Well, I was looking at your mouth, to aim right, you know? So I wouldn't miss like that first time. And it just flashed through my head that up close, lips kind of look like worms, and—-"

"You think my lips look like *worms*?" Mary Ellen took an indignant step back.

"No, no, not yours—everybody's—you know, the little ridges and the smooth skin . . ." He was talking fast and

now *he* looked worried. "Not yours at all—not unless there were pink worms—really *really* pretty pink worms—"

They stared at each other, then both burst out laughing. After a second, Mary Ellen moved close to him again, and they put their arms around each other. And this time, it fit as comfortably as her favorite pair of old worn-out blue jeans.

"I think maybe we were both thinking about it too much," Ben said in a low voice. "What do you think?"

"I think so, too," Mary Ellen whispered.

"Ben!" Mrs. Aldrich's voice called over from the driveway. "Time to get moving. We can drop Mary Ellen off at her house."

"Be right there," Ben called back. Then he tightened his arms around Mary Ellen and looked right into her eyes.

All of a sudden the strings in Mary Ellen's knees got a little wobbly.

"I don't want to say good-bye in front of my parents," he said.

"I don't want to say good-bye at all," Mary Ellen said.

"Me neither."

This time Ben didn't hesitate at all. When Mary Ellen felt his mouth on hers, her lips weren't sending "what should we do?" signals back to her brain. In fact . . . her brain . . . kind of . . . stopped!

"Hmmmm," Ben said after a moment that seemed so long to Mary Ellen while they were in it, but much too short once it was over. "I guess it gets better with a little practice." He grinned.

"Ben, we don't want to hit weekend back-to-the-city traffic," his dad called.

"Coming," he called over his shoulder, then turned back to Mary Ellen and squeezed her in a tight hug. "I'll write. Check your e-mail," he whispered. Then he kissed her hair, right next to her ear, let go, put one hand in his pocket, and held tight to one of Mary Ellen's with the other, as they walked slowly toward the car.

"That's a *date*, Mary Ellen," Justine said. "I can't believe it. You've gone out on your first date."

Mary Ellen had cut through the hedge to go tell Justine, after the Aldriches dropped her off.

"I don't think it counts," she said. "I mean, it was with his parents and his grandmother."

"But he asked you, right?" Justine put her pencil down on her math homework notebook. "He called you on the phone and invited you."

"Yeah, he did," Mary Ellen admitted. She grinned.

"Then it definitely counts," Justine declared.

Olivia came into the kitchen and opened the refrigerator, leaned in to pull out a bottle of soda, then stood up and stared accusingly at Justine.

"There were two-dozen Chocolate Decadence Brownies on a tray in here this morning. I know there were two dozen because I arranged them myself. And then I wrapped up the platter in colored cellophane and put a ribbon around it, to bring to the juniors' bake sale at school tomorrow," she said.

Justine shrugged. "So?" She suddenly sounded very tense.

"So the arrangement is different, and the bow is tied differently, and it looks like there are half-a-dozen missing. Do you have any idea what happened to them?" Olivia demanded.

"No, I have no idea," Justine said.

From her tone of voice, as defensive as it was snotty, Mary Ellen suspected that Justine might be lying. And *that* was totally unlike the old Justine, who might do something dumb, or something she wasn't supposed to, but wouldn't ever have lied about it.

Olivia put her hands on her hips and let the refrigerator

door close. "There are only three people living in this house. Me, and I know I didn't touch them, Mother, and she made them specifically for the bake sale, so I assume she didn't touch them. That leaves you!"

Justine stood abruptly and slammed her math book shut. "You know, Olivia, I am getting *sick* and *tired* of you picking on me all the time! You ride in here on your high horse, and tell everyone how they should do things, and nothing I ever do is ever good enough, or done the right way, or is politically correct enough for you. Why don't you go take a *long* walk off a *short* pier?"

She stomped out of the room. Mary Ellen and Olivia both winced a little as she stomped up each step, down the hall, then slammed her bedroom door shut so hard the light fixture hanging over the breakfast nook table trembled.

"Shwew," Olivia said, sounding astonished at the intensity of Justine's reaction. "Was it something I said, or what?"

Mary Ellen shrugged slowly, and stood up. "I don't know. She's been kind of moody lately. At school and stuff. I'll see you later, Olivia. Tell Justine to call me when you guys are speaking again, okay?"

Olivia nodded soberly, and Mary Ellen could tell she was really upset. Justine and her sister bickered a lot over unimportant things, but they rarely had big fights.

Dr. Bobowick was sitting at her desk grading quizzes when Mary Ellen walked in. "Wrong, wrong." Her red pen flicked and she sighed, and looked up at Mary Ellen. "I have a feeling this is going to be a looooo-ooong semester. How was brunch?"

"Brunch was good. *Very* good," Mary Ellen said, smiling at the memory that had been pushed aside by Justine's outburst. And besides being able to count her first official date, she could now count her first official kiss—not a near miss. "Mind if I use the computer for a little while?" she asked. "I want to do some research on Parlinet."

"That's fine. As long as you're not over your budget for the month," her mother replied.

Mary Ellen pulled the chair over in front of the computer desk, sat down, booted up, and logged on.

"You have mail!" the cyber-receptionist said.

She clicked her mailbox open, and grinned. A letter, dated a few days ago, from another Parlinet user who went by the screen name of BozoB. Grinning at the name, she opened the letter and read it quickly.

Dear Mary Ellen,

Sorry it took me so long to write, but I didn't get online till yesterday. Wish I was going to Dexter with all you guys. But my new school up here's not bad, and it's pretty cool living right in the middle of the city. We have an apartment in a brownstone in Back Bay, which is near the river. What's great is being able to get around to so many places on the subway. I went to the Museum of Science last Saturday. Ever been there? You'd love it. Maybe if you happen to ever get up this way, we could go together. Hey, that's an idea. Maybe you could come up to visit. Take the train or something. We've got a spare room in the apartment.

Anyway, how's Bozo doing? I haven't had a chance to set my tank up yet. Write back when you get this letter, okay? I miss you.

*:o) ← BozoB (Ben)

Mary Ellen smiled back at the little sideways smiley face. Ben missed her! She copied his e-mail address into her online address book, then clicked on the return mail icon, opened a blank letter field, and started to write back.

Dear Ben,

It was so great to see you last night and today was even

better. I went to the Museum of Science when I was little, but the only two things I remember are the vacuum tube where the feather drops like a lead balloon, and the population counter, and thinking about every one of those rising numbers meaning a real baby was being born somewhere in the world. I would LOVE to go again. I'm so glad you signed up for Parlinet—living in the same cyberhood is almost as good as living in the same neighborhood. I'll write longer soon, I have to do some research. And even though I just saw you, I miss you, too.

: D ← Mary Ellen with a BIG smile because she got e-mail.

After sending the letter on its way, she went to Parlinet's research area. Her search with the word bulimia turned up a *lot* of information. The first source to pop up was a general definition of eating disorders, both bulimia and anorexia, with a Frequently Asked Questions section. Mary Ellen hit *print* and the printer whirred into action. Eight articles and ten minutes later, she thought she had enough to give her at least an idea of whether or not Kevin might be right.

"You going to use the computer tonight, Mom, or do you want me to put it to bed?" Mary Ellen asked, standing and removing the papers from the printer tray.

"I have to use it to record these grades when I'm finished correcting, so you can leave it on. What's all that about?" She pointed to the stack of documents Mary Ellen was holding. "Research? For homework?"

"Mmmm," Mary Ellen murmured noncommittally, not wanting to tell an outright lie, but not wanting to open up the topic. She left her mother's study and went up to her room.

It took her over half an hour to read what she'd had printed out. Bulimia wasn't just forcing yourself to get sick once in a while if you ate way too much. From what Mary Ellen read, it seemed like it could take over a person's whole life, in a vicious cycle, bingeing on food, then getting rid of the calories any way you could.

One of the articles said it had more to do with how a person looked at herself, her own self-image (because most sufferers were female), than with an actual appetite for food, for nutritional requirements. Several of the articles dicussed anorexia nervosa—people literally starving themselves, sometimes to death. Mary Ellen knew all the basics about the four food groups, and that people needed to fuel their bodies with the right food. But she had had no idea how badly it could mess up someone's body if she developed an eating disorder. A few of the articles talked about people with both anorexia *and* bulimia. But one thing almost all the articles made reference to—eating disorders often developed as a way for a person to try and control her own life, if for some reason they felt it was out of control. And the worst thing was that the disorder itself often turned into the most out-of-control part of her life.

When Mary Ellen finished combing through all the material, she set the papers down on her quilt, plumped her pillow, and leaned back again, staring out her open window at Justine's bedroom window, right across the driveways from hers. Nothing in any of the articles contradicted Kevin's suspicions. In fact, a number of things suggested he might be right. The constant dieting, or trying to diet, and obsessing about her weight, even though she looked to Mary Ellen pretty much the same, weight-wise, as she always had. One of the most surprising facts she'd read was that although people with anorexia got really, really thin, people with bulimia didn't necessarily lose weight. Sometimes they even gained weight, because of the way too much dieting messed up their metabolisms.

And there were more symptoms. The way Justine was always so dissatisfied with the way she looked. The way she didn't want to be seen in any clothes that weren't baggy enough to hide her figure, and her getting more and more private about getting dressed or undressed in front of anyone.

Mary Ellen thought back to the night Justine had slept over, and the really long shower she'd taken after they both pigged out on pizza. There was no way she could have made the connection with bulimic behavior then, but it fit the pattern the articles described. Most of all, though, it was the low self-esteem—the way Justine was always putting herself down—that fit. Mary Ellen looked out her window at Justine's house.

The light went on in her best friend's room, and Mary Ellen saw her come in, and stand in front of her mirror, not moving for what seemed like forever. She wondered what Justine was thinking. And she couldn't imagine. And she still couldn't figure out what she should do. Stuffing the papers under her bed so her mother wouldn't find them and ask questions, Mary Ellen opened her English book. But she just sat staring at the page for a long time.

Chapter 19

Right after morning announcements and attendance, Mr. Gumble beat out a long, loud rhythm to bring the class to order.

"All right, everybody, let's settle down. We have about fourteen minutes left to listen to our candidates outline their platforms. We'll flip to see who goes first." He pulled a quarter out of his pocket. "Heads, Mary Ellen goes first, tails, Amy. Ready?" He flipped the coin from his right into the palm of his left then turned it over onto his right arm, and looked. "Okay, tails wins. Amy, the floor's yours."

"That fits," Robbie said in a loud stage whisper. "Bobowick gets heads, and Colter gets tails." Amy got up from her desk, and walked with a practiced model runway sashay up the aisle, bopping Robbie on the shoulder on her way up front. She was wearing a short skirt, and a loose matching top that Mary Ellen had seen put together with exactly the same accessories, down to the same green sandals, in a spread in one of Justine's magazines. Holding her index cards in front of her, Amy first looked around the whole room and smiled, then started reading her speech.

"The primary purpose of school is, of course, education."

"Of course," Justine mimicked under her breath. "Right. From the queen of airheads."

"But school is also a place where we students build all our social foundations. The academic side of Dexter is already very good. We have one of the best reputations of all the junior highs in the county." She paused as some of the kids erupted into mini-cheers of school spirit.

Mary Ellen looked at Justine, who rolled her eyes as Amy went on.

"But what I would like to see are more opportunities for social interaction, for a larger part of the student body—"

"Hey, student bodies interacting," Jason said in a stage whisper. "I like the sound of that!" Mr. Gumble gave him a dry look, and shook his head.

"Namely, the SEVENTH GRADERS!" Amy sang it out like a cheerleader, and most of the kids responded with shouts of approval. Kevin kept glancing at Mary Ellen, and she could tell he was thinking the same thing she was: this isn't a totally horrible, stupid speech, and she might win.

"At this time, the seventh grade is allowed only one dance at the end of the school year, while the eighth grade has three, the Harvest Dance, the Valentine's Dance, and the Graduation Dance, to which seventh graders are only allowed to go if they get invited by an eighth grader. This is actual discrimination against the socially disadvantaged students of the seventh grade—"

"What's socially disadvantaged?" Justine whispered.

"Is that supposed to be some politically correct phrase for *clod*?"

"And if I am elected, I promise to try and get at least one more, if not two more dances for the seventh grade!" Amy beamed a bright smile as most of the kids in the class clapped.

"Another area," she went on after the clapping died down, "in which I would like to try and improve Dexter is in the area of health."

Health? Amy going for the healthy vote? Mary Ellen looked at Kevin, who now gave her a worried shrug.

"It's the rule here that students are not allowed to go outside during study hall modules. It's a well-known fact that fresh air is a healthy thing for human beings, especially kids. So if I'm elected, I promise I'll try and get that rule changed so we can all go outside during study hall."

There was another burst of clapping, but Mary Ellen could see that a few of the kids still thought Amy's promises might be as full of hot air as her ego.

"The other healthy thing I would try and do is get a frozen-yogurt machine in the cafeteria. Glenville Junior High has one, and they get two different flavors every week. This would provide a healthier diet with extra calcium for Dexter students."

Actually, that wasn't a bad idea at all, Mary Ellen had to admit. She wasn't against frozen yogurt. She liked it, in fact, although she had no idea how much a homeroom representative could influence the school caterer.

"And last, but not least," Amy said, then paused dramatically. "The uniform of the Dexter cheerleading squad is the *tackiest* in the whole league. It represents our school in a negative way and reflects poorly on our student body."

"I never heard of anybody winning an election based on an anti-tacky-uniform platform," Kevin said to Mary Ellen. She knew he was trying to give her a boost of confidence to follow Amy's act.

"And just so nobody thinks I'm prejudiced against boys . . ." here she stopped and—Mary Ellen couldn't believe it—actually batted her eyelashes, flirting at all the boys in the class! "I think the football and basketball teams deserve new uniforms too. And if I'm elected, I promise I'll try to convince the student council and the administration to hold a schoolwide vote so everyone can have a say in what our new school colors will be. I mean—maroon and orange? Puh-leeeze! Thank you."

Most of the class laughed, and Amy got a good round of applause when she sat down.

"Thank you very much, Amy," Mr. Gumble gave her a nod and a big smile.

Great, Mary Ellen thought. Amy'd won the teacher's vote, it looked like, for whatever that was worth. "Now let's hear from our other candidate. Mary Ellen, come on up."

Mary Ellen took a deep breath, stood, and started resolutely up the aisle. With no warning, her heart did a few thuds, and she felt herself blushing. At the same time, her knees felt like the hamstrings had just come loose. Stage fright? What lousy timing for her first attack ever. When she was almost to the front of the room, she realized she'd left her index cards on her desk. She'd look like a completely incompetent idiot if she went back! Who'd vote for someone as class rep to give reports of the student council meetings if that someone couldn't remember to bring the notes for her speech? And got stage fright besides?

She turned around and took a deep breath, scanning the classroom, which was going a little blurry around the edges of her vision. Standing up there, she suddenly felt gawky and awkward, especially compared to Amy. The kids were getting a little restless, as if they were getting uncomfortable with her hesitation as she rummaged desperately through her brain trying to connect with the first line of what she'd wanted to say. Kevin was looking positively panicked for her, Justine was looking embarrassed and sympathetic. Then her eyes met Jason's. He winked at her and gave her a thumbs-up and a little nod. Spontaneously, she grinned. And the frozen moment thawed out. She knew basically what she wanted to say. She knew most of the kids in here. She was who she was, and there was no use going through a huge dog-and-pony show to pretend she was someone else.

"Okay." Taking another deep breath, Mary Ellen just started talking. "Over the past couple of weeks of this campaign, I've tried to pay attention to some things at Dexter that I think could be improved. And I guess the main specific thing I noticed was that we could do a lot better job of recycling. Especially in the cafeteria, where we're supposed to separate the trash, and we have the containers to do it, but most of us are too busy trying to get to our next class before the module starts. But if everyone took about ten extra seconds to do it, the system would work. I mean, what good's having an environmental policy if we don't use it?"

She looked around the class. While no one was clapping or cheering, all the kids seemed to be listening to what she was saying.

"It's one of the rules we don't get in trouble for not following—at least not here in school. But if you think about it, not following it on a small scale, as individuals, is one of the reasons the whole world is in trouble today. So I think maybe reminding kids about the rule might be something the student council could sponsor. If we made it work in one area, and the administration saw we were serious, maybe they'd listen to us about bigger things, like getting the catering company to use less packaging, or even putting in a frozen-yogurt machine."

Mary Ellen saw Amy frown in puzzlement at her opponent's saying something good about her speech. She paused a moment, trying to figure out exactly where she was going with this point. Everyone else seemed to be wondering, too, because they were paying attention.

"There's a lot of specific things to deal with, I'm sure, but I don't think I've been here at Dexter long enough to really know what they are. I guess I think being a home-room representative should be more about representing what you guys think, than just what me, myself, and I think. So if I'm elected, I'd like to put a suggestion box in here, and that's what I'll do—represent you, all of you, not just the cheerleaders and the jocks, and I'll try to do a good job of it. That's all, I guess. Thanks." She shrugged, and smiled, then headed back for her desk, startled by the strength of the applause from the class. Kevin had his hand up to give her a high five as she went by.

"Sincerity!" he said. "What a great campaign strategy."

As soon as Mary Ellen sat down and saw the cards, all the other things she'd meant to say came flooding back into her brain. But they didn't really matter that much—she'd gotten her main point across. The bell signaling the end of homeroom sounded, and Mr. Gumble called out over the noise, "Be thinking about what your candidates had to say. Next Monday we vote."

Mary Ellen had pushed what Kevin said about Justine at the party to the back of her mind because she didn't know what to do with it. But it came forcefully to the forefront at lunchtime, when Justine came and sat down with her and Kevin. That, at least, seemed to have become a usual thing, and Justine seemed to be tolerating his presence a little better. She sat next to Mary Ellen with four brownies and two cartons of milk on her tray.

"Ugh," she said. "Did you see what today's choices were for lunch? Fried clams or Eggplant Parmesan that looks like a meltdown at a tomato cannery."

Mary Ellen nodded. "Disgusting and disgustinger. It's a good thing they always have peanut butter and jelly." She unwrapped her sandwich.

"I haven't been able to eat peanut butter since the first

time I saw Kevin eat one of those." She pointed to his usual lunch.

He grinned, and took a bite of his sandwich. "Don't knock it till you've tried it. It definitely beats fried clams that bounce a foot and a half off the floor when they fall off your plate. Wouldn't surprise me if they were deep fried rubber bands."

Justine rolled her eyes, but Mary Ellen saw she couldn't help smiling.

"It's true!" Kevin said, catching her smile. "I swear. It happened to the kid in front of me in line."

As Justine looked down to unwrap her first brownie, Kevin gave Mary Ellen a quick and pointed frown. She frowned back, and gave a slight shake of her head. She didn't want to think about that. Especially not at lunch.

"So," Kevin said casually. "You g—" he stopped and corrected himself before Justine could do it. "You two thought about what you're going to do for Hat Day? It's the same day as the homeroom elections, Mary Ellen. You might be able to use it as a last promotion."

"I haven't thought about it yet," she said. "What are you going to do?"

"Mine's already done. I took my old Mickey Mouse hat and glued two CD-ROMS to the ears, and a SIMM from my old computer on the top."

"What's a simm?" Justine asked.

"Extra RAM—Random Access Memory. SIMM stands for Standard Integrated Memory Module. I feel like I'm wired wearing it, like my brain can run extra applications. Wouldn't that be cool, if we could attach computers to our brains?"

"Sounds like a modern version of Frankenstein to me," Justine said with a laugh.

"I don't know, Kevin," Mary Ellen said, grinning at him. "I think your brain is scary enough as it is!"

"How 'bout you, Justine?" Kevin asked. "You have your Hat idea yet?"

Justine started on her second brownie. "Yeah. I'm going to poke two holes in a paper bag and put it over my head," she said sarcastically, her brighter mood of the previous moment gone.

Kevin caught Mary Ellen's eye, and raised an eyebrow. She deliberately looked away from him, feeling a sudden rush of anger. Even if there was something in what he'd said, what did he expect her to be able to do about it?

Chapter 20

"Ugh," Justine grunted. She slowed her already sluggish jogging pace even more.

"Come on," Mary Ellen urged. "We're only halfway around the first lap. Those guys are gonna pass us, and we'll end up being stuck running the last one all by ourselves."

"I can't." Now Justine stopped behind the end zone of the hockey field. "This ... is ... student abuse ..." she panted.

Mary Ellen looked at her closely. Usually Justine's face got reddish and blotchy during the Phys. Ed. warm-up laps. Today she just looked pale.

"You know, even if you just wore the T-shirt, instead of

the whole sweat suit—" she started to say but Justine cut her off.

"I'm not going to run around bouncing all over the place, for everyone to see."

"At least you have something to bounce," Mary Ellen joked. "Only kidding," she said when Justine didn't even crack a smile. "You could get one of the sports bras—"

A long shrill blast from Ms. Musanti's whistle caught their attention.

"Anyone who dogs it will be running two extra laps," she called sternly to the two girls.

Mary Ellen looked up the field and saw the frontrunners of the pack almost ready to cross the line, completing their first lap.

"Come on," she urged. "I don't want to run two extra laps."

She started jogging again, relieved when Justine took a few halfhearted steps to catch up with her. As she got to the corner of the field, she slowed to a trot, and looked back over her shoulder. Justine had stopped running again, and Mary Ellen saw her wavering where she stood, as if she were about to topple over. Immediately she ran back, reaching Justine at the same time as Ms. Dart, who'd apparently seen it from the middle of the field, where she'd been standing.

Justine looked at both of them. Her eyes looked bleary, as if she was having trouble focusing, and her face looked even paler.

"I don't feel well," she whispered in a weak voice.

"Here, head down," Ms. Dart ordered. She supported Justine around the waist with one arm, and helped her bend over so her head was upside down. Ms. Musanti jogged over as Mary Ellen stood by helplessly.

After a long moment, Ms. Dart helped Justine straighten up. "Any better?" she asked.

Justine nodded, still pale, but not quite as shaky looking.

"Have them finish their laps, then get started with a scrimmage," Ms. Dart said to her assistant.

Ms. Musanti nodded, and stepped aside and started steering the herd of jogging girls around Mary Ellen, Ms. Dart, and Justine.

"Let's go, women, keep it moving, we don't need any rubberneckers, move it along," Ms. Musanti shouted, giving her whistle a few blasts.

Mary Ellen watched as Ms. Dart pushed Justine's sleeves up past her elbows, and took her pulse. "Okay, I'll take care of things here; you go back with the group now," she said to Mary Ellen. Mary Ellen nodded.

"I'll see you later, okay?" she said to Justine, who nodded weakly. Then she slowly walked toward the end of the field where Ms. Musanti was organizing the squads into teams, while Ms. Dart, holding Justine by the arm, started back toward the school building.

With three minutes left in the last module of class, Ms. Dart appeared at the end of Mary Ellen's locker row just as she was stuffing her gym clothes and shower things into her locker.

"I'd like to see you in my office. Bring your books. I'll give you a late pass for your next class," she said in an oddly neutral tone of voice.

Nervously, Mary Ellen obeyed, walking across the locker room, while other kids stared curiously at her. "Maybe Justine was doing drugs or something," she heard Debra whisper to Amy as she walked by them. Mary Ellen was too concerned to stop and address the comment, but she gave both of them a withering look as she passed. She went through the door into the gym office, and Ms. Dart, who was sitting behind her gray steel desk, motioned for her to close the door between the office and the locker room, and take one of the two steel-framed, vinyl-seated chairs.

She sat down, hugging her backpack in front of her as a shield.

"Is Justine okay?" she asked. "Did she go home?"

"Her mother came to pick her up," Ms. Dart said. She folded her hands on her desk and fixed a serious gaze on her. "Mary Ellen, I've suspected Justine of having an eating disorder since the second day of gym class. I've taught young women Phys. Ed. for ten years. I've seen the problem before. I've also seen the problem increasing, especially in your age group. So you tell me . . . *is* Justine okay?"

Mary Ellen stared at her shoes, not even registering for a few seconds that Ms. Dart had actually called both her and Justine by their first names. Justine had never said a word about it to Mary Ellen. So if there was a problem, obviously she didn't want to talk about it. The opposite in fact—if it was true, she was trying really hard to keep it a secret. And Mary Ellen couldn't blame her. It was pretty horrible.

Ms. Dart was waiting patiently for her answer.

"Anything you tell me will be held in the strictest of confidence, Mary Ellen. And I want you to know that given my suspicion, I'll be contacting Justine's guidance counselor and the school psychologist, anyway. That decision's already made, and I won't mention our conversation to them," Ms. Dart said in a gentle tone of voice Mary Ellen had *never* heard her speak in before. "But I thought you might be able to enlarge my understanding of the situation."

"I don't know," Mary Ellen finally said. "I mean, she hasn't said anything to me."

"I want you to listen carefully to me, Mary Ellen," Ms. Dart said. "If you think you're showing loyalty to Justine by keeping her secret, you need to know that she's engaging in a behavior that is not just mildly unhealthy, it can be very dangerous, with serious side effects and lasting damage. You saw one of the results today outside. I suspect she almost passed out from an electrolyte imbalance and dehydration. Those would be two symptoms that went along with bulimia."

Mary Ellen winced at hearing the word out loud. She let out a slow sigh. "I know," she said, her voice almost a whisper. "I looked it up."

"So it has occurred to you, then," Ms. Dart said.

Reluctantly, Mary Ellen nodded. "One of our friends said something at a party. His sister is bulimic, and he said he noticed some of the same things with Justine as with his sister—her hand." She looked up at Ms. Dart again. "But I still can't believe that Justine—" she started to blurt out, when Ms. Dart held up her hand and gently stopped her.

"Yes, you can believe it. That's why you looked it up, and that shows what a very good friend you are to her. All right, Mary Ellen, thank you for being honest with me." As Ms. Dart started writing out a late pass, she kept speaking, but back in her more businesslike manner. "The psychologist will be calling Justine's parents—"

"Justine's father isn't living with them anymore," Mary Ellen said.

Ms. Dart looked surprised. "Is that a recent development?"

Mary Ellen nodded.

Ms. Dart nodded back, as if it made some sense to her in some way. "So it's Justine, her mother, and Olivia?

Mary Ellen nodded.

Ms. Dart chuckled, as if remembering something that amused her, then a surprisingly sympathetic expression came over her face. "I wouldn't imagine Olivia's act would be easy for a younger sister to follow." Then it was back to her brisk business tone. "Here's your late pass for your next class."

Mary Ellen stood up slowly, put the paper in the pocket of her jeans, and turned to leave. When she had her hand on the doorknob that led straight out into the corridor, Ms. Dart called one last thing after her.

"Mary Ellen . . ."

Mary Ellen looked over her shoulder questioningly.

"I know this was a difficult thing for you to do. As I said, I won't mention this conversation when I talk to the guidance counselor. But if you want to tell Justine yourself, that's up to you. I wouldn't want it to turn into something that interfered with your friendship. So you may want to tell her."

Mary Ellen bit her lip. If the situation were reversed, would she want Justine to talk to her about it? What if Justine considered it a huge betrayal?

"I'll think about it," she said after a minute. "I'm not sure."

Mary Ellen looked at the basket of garlic bread she was holding as if it had materialized out of thin air. "Huh?" she said to her mother.

"I said, could you please pass the garlic bread to Nicky?" Now Dr. Bobowick looked at her closely. "Ground control to Mary Ellen. Are you with us?"

Mary Ellen gave her head a little shake, as if to shake loose the thoughts that were clamoring. Should she tell Justine her secret was about to be out? Had Ms. Dart talked to the people and had they already called Mrs. Kelly? She pushed her plate of lasagna back from the edge of the table. "Not really. Sorry, I have things on my mind."

"Is there anything you want to run by us, honey?" her father asked.

She thought for a second, then shook her head. "Can I be excused?"

Dr. Bobowick took in her half-eaten dinner, but nodded. Her parents exchanged concerned glances as she stood up, but they didn't say anything else. She picked up her plate, scraped it into the compost bin in the sink, stuck her plate in the dishwasher, then went out the back door, and sat on the back steps.

The sun had set already, but the sky was still lightish behind the Kellys' house. The light was on in Justine's bedroom but the window shades were down. She felt like the shades were down inside Justine's mind, these days, too. For as long back as she could remember, up until Justine had gone away to Paris for the year, the two of them had always shared a wavelength. Sometimes they could guess almost exactly what the other one was thinking without it being said out loud, like Mary Ellen and her mother could. Whatever was going on with Justine, it felt like they were almost farther apart than they had been over the past year when they were e-penpals, an ocean apart.

The Kellys' back door opened as Mary Ellen sat there, and Olivia came out, and headed for their garage, carrying a bag of trash. She watched for a moment, then jumped up before she could change her mind, and cut through the gap in the hedge between the two driveways.

"Hi, Mary Ellen, what's up?" Olivia said cheerfully. "Did Justine tell you the great news? About Mr. Grumman calling my mother with the idea to do this big coffee table book on stylishly elegant yet homey entertaining? She has to go into New York to meet with him next week!!"

Mary Ellen's spirits sagged. The last thing she wanted to do was throw something unpleasant into the picture for Mrs. Kelly's sake. She bit her lip and tried to figure out how to bring up the subject.

"That's great, Olivia. No, she didn't tell me," she said. "Maybe because she came home sick from school and all. Did she tell you what happened?"

"She said she got overheated in gym class, and the Poison Dart made a huge big deal out of nothing," Olivia said. "Well, gotta get back to—"

"Olivia," Mary Ellen said abruptly, grabbing her arm. "I have to talk to you. It's really important."

Olivia looked puzzled. "Okay. Well, come on in—"

"No, I don't want Justine to know. Or my parents either. Or your mom—yet. But I have to—now—in private. How about—" She looked around, trying to figure out a place where they could talk without being overheard, and saw the top of Nicky's swing fort over the hedge. "Nicky's fort."

Olivia was giving her an extremely hairy eyeball now. "Mary Ellen, you are going very weird on me here . . ."

"Remember the other day when you got mad at Justine when your bake sale brownies were missing?" she asked urgently. "It's related to that."

The beginnings of a look of comprehension started creeping into Olivia's expression. She nodded. "Okay." She cut through the hedge, and Mary Ellen went right behind her.

Up in the fort, sitting cross-legged across from Olivia, Mary Ellen took a deep breath, and began sketching the details. Justine's eating habits at lunch in school. Jason's party. What Kevin had said. The not wanting to change in front of anyone in gym, and always wearing clothes that hid her figure. And finally, what Ms. Dart had said today.

"You know, I didn't put it all together, but it fits," Olivia said slowly. "At the end of the school year in Paris, Justine started hanging around with this girl named Theresa—older than her, younger than me. One of my friends was friends with her older brother, and I heard she had some kind of eating disorder. But I didn't think—that's right around the time Justine started trying all these crazy diets. And things between my parents started falling apart."

Olivia sat silently for a minute, then laughed softly.

"I don't think it's anything to laugh about, Livie," Mary Ellen said soberly.

"No, no. I was just remembering something. You know, when I was at Dexter, Francine Rinaldi and I snuck into the gym office one day, and dipped Ms. Dart's whistle into clear dishwashing liquid. You should have seen the face she made when she went to do roll call."

"Did you get caught?" Mary Ellen asked curiously.

Olivia shook her head. "Uh uh. But this is the first time I've ever felt bad about it. Shwew. . . ." She let out a long slow sigh. "This is very heavy-duty stuff."

"Livie, phone," Justine called from the Kellys' back steps.

"Coming," Olivia said loudly. She scrambled out the fort's entrance, and slid down the slide. Mary Ellen followed her.

"What the heck were you two doing in there?" Justine asked, walking up the Kellys' driveway and spotting the two of them together through the hedge. She frowned a puzzled frown, looking back and forth from Mary Ellen's face to her sister's. Neither of them spoke. "What, were you having some kind of secret powwow? How come you didn't invite me?" She laughed a little, but Mary Ellen knew it was forced, and could see a panicky look coming into Justine's eyes.

"Justine," Olivia said quietly, putting a hand on Justine's arm. "I think we should talk about some stuff, okay?"

"Justine," Mary Ellen put in hastily. "Ms. Dart called me in to talk today, and somebody's going to be calling your mother, because she's worried—"

"I don't need any drill-sergeant gym teacher worrying about me!" Justine shook Olivia's hand off angrily. "And as for talking, it looks like you two have already been talking about *stuff!*" She glared at Mary Ellen. "*Some* best friend. Thanks a *lot*." Furious, she turned and stalked toward the house.

"I'll talk to you later, Mary Ellen." Olivia took off after Justine.

Mary Ellen nodded, very upset, but at the same time, very relieved. Maybe the whole thing was too complicated for a best friend to figure out.

Chapter 21

"Mary Ellen, what is wrong?" Dr. Bobowick stood in the doorway to Mary Ellen's bedroom Friday night. "Did you and Justine have a fight? She hasn't come over to meet you for the bus in two days, you two haven't spoken on the phone, and you've been broodier than a hen."

"We didn't have a fight, exactly," Mary Ellen said slowly.

Justine hadn't been in school for the whole rest of the week. Mary Ellen had no idea what had happened when Olivia went back into the Kellys' house after the swing fort talk. She assumed Ms. Dart had followed through telling the guidance counselor, and that someone from Dexter had called Mrs. Kelly. But she still didn't know if Justine had admitted it—or even if it were actually true, for that matter. And she was afraid to call the Kellys' house, not sure if Justine was ever going to speak to her again.

"Do you want to talk about it?" Mary Ellen's mother said now.

Mary Ellen let out a long, slow sigh. Part of her wanted to unload the burden. Maybe that would keep it from weighing so heavily on her mind. But the best friend part of her thought she didn't have the right to talk about Justine's personal business.

"I can't talk about it, really, Mom," she said. "It's—kind of confidential."

Dr. Bobowick frowned slightly with concern, but she nodded. "Okay, sweetie. But you know I'm here to listen, if you change your mind. I'm off to the University—department meeting. Would you help Daddy get Nicky squared away for bedtime? The last place I saw *Go Dog Go* was sticking out of the couch cushions in the living room."

Mary Ellen nodded. After one more worried glance, her mother left.

Go Dog Go. That poor poodle, with all the attempts to come up with a hat that her dog friend would like, and all his negative responses. A low-self-esteem cartoon dog-woman. Mary Ellen shook her head, and for the first time, felt a flash of annoyance at the guy dog, who kept insulting her, then ditching her. What business of his was it what kind of hat she wore? And why did she care? Hats. She sighed. Ms. Coville's Hat Day project was due next class, and she still had no idea what she was going to put together for it.

The phone rang twice, then stopped.

"Mary Ellen, phone," her father called up from downstairs.

"I'll take it up here," she hollered back, jumping off her bed, and running down the hall to her parents' bedroom.

Maybe it was Justine. Maybe it was even Ben! She picked up the phone.

"You can hang up now, Dad." The extension clicked. "Hello?" she said breathlessly.

"Mary Ellen? It's me." Kevin's unmistakable squeaky voice came back.

Suppressing a surge of disappointment, she tried to make her voice sound cheerful. "What's up, Kevin?"

He hesitated for a minute, then plunged ahead. "I was wondering if, you know, Justine was okay. Have you found out yet if—"

"No." She cut him off. "I haven't found out anything."

"Oh."

Mary Ellen wasn't sure what else to say, so she waited.

"Okay, here's the thing," he blurted out after an uncomfortable pause. "I have the name of the person my sister goes to—her therapist."

"Did you *tell* your sister?" Mary Ellen asked anxiously.

"Uh uh. I wouldn't tell anyone, Mary Ellen. Geez, did you think I would?" He sounded almost disappointed in her.

"No, I guess not. I'm sorry, Kevin. I know you wouldn't." All of a sudden something burst in Mary Ellen. She had to talk to someone. The words came pouring out, telling Kevin about Ms. Dart calling her in, and her talk with Olivia, and Justine's reaction, and now the silence, the no contact at all from Justine. "I'm wondering if I've lost my best friend again—for good this time," she finished up.

Kevin's voice came back surprisingly firm. "Mary Ellen, if you *didn't* get involved, you might lose your best friend forever—the worst way. People *die* from eating disorders. So maybe Justine is mad at you—but would you rather have her mad or dead?"

And for the first time since that gym class, Mary Ellen felt a little better.

"Listen, my sister was furious at all of us when we found out. I mean, she exploded like a volcano. But she's getting better now. You definitely did the right thing," Kevin said. "Don't feel guilty. Besides, Dart said she was going to tell the guidance counselor no matter what you said, right?"

"Right," Mary Ellen said quietly.

"I gotta go—if you find out that Justine needs the name of someone to see, you can tell her about my sister, and call me and I'll give you the name and number."

"Thanks, Kevin," Mary Ellen said. "You know something?"

"What?"

"You're a really good person."

There was a short pause this time, and then Mary Ellen could almost hear the grin in his voice.

"Yeah, for someone with peanut butter pickle breath. I'll seeya on the bus. Bye."

After he hung up, Mary Ellen took a deep breath. She wasn't going to stew in this wondering what was what with Justine anymore. She dialed the Kellys' phone number.

"I'm not mad, Mary Ellen, honest," Justine said. "I mean I was. But not at you, really." The two girls sat side by side on Justine's bed. Right after the confrontation in the driveway, Justine had locked herself in her room, refusing to talk to either Olivia or her mother. But then the school guidance counselor had called Mrs. Kelly, and the whole thing was out in the open.

"She gave my mother the name of three eating disorder specialists. I didn't like the first one at all, so we went to see the second one. She was pretty cool."

"I wonder if one of them is the one Kevin's sister goes to," Mary Ellen wondered out loud, then bit her lip when she saw Justine's suspicious, ready-to-get-mad again reaction.

"You told Kevin Middendorf???"

"No, no—it wasn't like that at all—I swear," Mary Ellen

said hastily. "Just listen for a minute without getting mad, okay?"

Justine frowned, but nodded.

Mary Ellen filled her in on all the conversations, the ones with Kevin, at the party and on the phone, the one with Ms. Dart, and finally the one with Olivia.

"Do you think Kevin will tell?" Justine said soberly. "At school, I mean? I've been pretty rotten to him . . ." Her voice trailed off uncertainly.

Mary Ellen shook her head. "I'm positive he won't. He's been really, really worried about you—I guess he knew how serious it could be because of his sister and all. But would you mind if I just call him back and tell him you're okay? That way he won't be giving you worried hairy eyeball looks in school."

"You can call him." Justine said. "It's weird. I don't mind him knowing as much as I'd mind a lot of other people knowing. He may be the geekiest kid at Dexter, but there's something about him that's kind of growing on me."

Mary Ellen raised both eyebrows.

"Don't even think it!" Justine laughed. "Growing on me like a friendly fungus. That's all."

"What's your therapist like?" Mary Ellen changed the subject.

"She's really nice," Justine said. "I mean, she didn't come on all stern and say 'You must stop this at once!' or anything like that. She wants to know how I feel about a lot of different stuff."

"Did she say when you can come back to school?" Mary Ellen asked. "It was horrible last week without you—like a repeat of sixth grade when you left for Paris."

"Monday. I'm kind of nervous about it." She rubbed the bandaid that was on her hand now. "I mean, do you think people suspect? What if Amy guesses and—"

"Don't worry about Amy," Mary Ellen said. "I've still got something on her. I'll blackmail her if I have to."

"Huh?" Justine said.

"The ShapeShifter, remember?" Mary Ellen grinned. "I didn't want to just throw it away. I mean, it's worth sixty dollars!"

Justine laughed. "That makes me feel a little better," she said. "I forgot about it."

Mary Ellen smiled back, then turned serious again. "I was worried you were going to have to go away, like to a hospital or something," she said.

"No. I guess some kids do, but Mrs. Lennon said I don't have to. I haven't been doing it for all that long, so the real bad physical things hadn't started to happen to me yet. But I have to see her twice a week for a while."

"Ms. Dart said to tell you she's looking forward to having you back in class."

Justine laughed out loud at that. "Well, I can't say the same, that I'm looking forward to being back in her class," she said, and shook her head. "Old Poison Dart." She bit her lip. "You know, I'm kind of glad she figured it out. It was starting to get kind of scary. I mean, I wanted to stop, a bunch of times, but I couldn't. It felt out of my control after a while, like my body was going ahead and doing it, even though my head didn't want to. You know what I mean?"

Mary Ellen thought for a minute, then shook her head. "No," she said. "I don't know. But I can imagine it would feel awful. So what kind of stuff do you talk about with Mrs. Lennon?" she asked curiously.

"All kinds of stuff," Justine said. "I didn't think I'd be able to talk about it at all. But somehow she works the conversation around and I wind up saying things I didn't even know were in my head." She stared at the poster of Sabrina Kelsey, the British supermodel, that hung on the wall above her desk for a moment. It was slightly crooked, the way Mary Ellen had hung it for her that first Saturday morning after she'd gotten home from Paris. Mary Ellen watched as she went over, carefully unstuck it from the wall, realigned it and stuck it back on.

"I can't believe you left it like that for almost a month," Mary Ellen said with a grin. "That should have clued me in that something wasn't right."

Justine stepped back, looked at it critically, then went back over and took it off the wall, rolled it up and slipped an elastic from her desk over it, then stashed it in the closet.

"Much better," Mary Ellen said.

"I'm hungry—let's go downstairs and grab a snack."

Mary Ellen shot her a nervous look.

"It's okay, Mary Ellen. Really. Fat free double carob frozen yogurt! Olivia stocked up on it for me."

Mary Ellen smiled.

Down in the kitchen, Mrs. Kelly was sitting at the breakfast nook table, with a very strange look on her face, like she'd either just won the lottery, or been stunned by a phaser.

"What's the matter, Mom?" Justine asked

"Your father . . ." She stopped speaking, and tilted her head a little, as if puzzled.

"Daddy what? Mom, what is it?" Now Justine sounded alarmed. "Did something happen? Is he okay?"

"Do you want me to leave so you can talk to Justine alone, Mrs. Kelly?" Mary Ellen asked.

"No, no, Mary Ellen. You count as family." She looked up at Justine. "Your father's all right. I mean, he's not sick. Well, at least not physically sick . . . His mind? I'm not so sure about that, but—"

"Mom, this suspense is killing me. Spit it out! Please!" Justine said in exasperation.

"He wants to come home."

Justine did a double take. "When did you find that out?"

"Just now. He called. I called him on Friday to tell him about, you know—the problem. Mrs. Lennon thought he should know," Mrs. Kelly said, in an almost wondering voice. "He just called back. It's the middle of the night in Paris. He said he made a terrible mistake, and wants to know if he can move back. He's already told the company he plans to relocate back to the U.S."

"It's a good thing Olivia didn't answer the phone," Justine said. "She would have told him to relocate to the moon."

Mrs. Kelly shook her head, still seeming dazed.

"So, what did you tell him?" Justine asked. Mary Ellen could see she was holding her breath as she waited for the answer.

"I told him," Mrs. Kelly said, "that I'd be open to the possibility of considering it, but that I didn't want to make a hasty decision." She sounded like she was almost amazed at her own response. "I told him he'd have to take an apartment or a condo or something and go into marriage counseling, and we'd see how things worked out."

Just in time to hear the last part of Mrs. Kelly's sentence, Olivia came bouncing through the kitchen door. She dropped her backpack on the floor, and stared at her mother.

"You told Daddy that?" she asked, incredulous.

Mrs. Kelly nodded. "Yes. I did. Can you believe it?"

Mary Ellen couldn't imagine Mr. Kelly's reaction.

"And what did he say?" Olivia asked.

Mrs. Kelly gave a tiny shrug. "He said, 'Okay.' "

"Go, Mom, Go!" Olivia said, laughing out loud.

Chapter 22

"I wonder if anybody will say anything," Justine said worriedly as she and Mary Ellen stood at the bus stop Monday morning.

"Why should they?" Mary Ellen said, trying to reassure her. "Anybody that asked, I told them you had a wicked case of the flu."

The bus screeched around the corner, the doors opened, and as they climbed up the steps, they heard the familiar, squeaky greeting. "Hey—" Mary Ellen saw Kevin's mind clamp his mouth shut till his brain could come up with a collective noun that wouldn't make Justine mad. "Kids!" he said, scoping out Justine, to check her reaction. "Seats right here."

"We're not baby goats, Kevin," she said, but to Mary Ellen's relief, she smiled at him.

Mary Ellen headed down the aisle first, and slid in next to Kevin, just to be a buffer zone in case Justine needed it. But Kevin acted completely normal. *Well, normal for Kevin.* Mary Ellen had to laugh as he blew the hugest green bubble she'd ever seen him do yet, and almost caught it, but not quite, before it popped on his nose, getting on his glasses.

"Ooops!" she said, as he wrinkled his nose and, taking them off, started scraping away the gum.

"If she had such a bad case of flu, I'm glad she's not sitting near me," Amy said from a few seats back.

"Yeah, who wants to breathe her germs?" Mary Ellen heard Debra chime in.

She looked nervously across the aisle at Justine, who was still sitting by herself. Justine gave her a little "It's okay" smile, as the bus pulled up in front of Robbie and Jason's stop, and opened the doors.

"Are you sure you've got the right bus here?" Tina the Bus Driver said loudly as a very strange passenger got on board. It had the body of a boy wearing blue jeans and a T-shirt; but the head was concealed inside a basketball, cut out to fit like a space helmet. As he turned to come down the aisle, his face became visible, though his eyes were concealed behind imitation Vuarnet glacier glasses.

"Hey Jason, did you block a shot someone was trying to stuff in the net?" Mary Ellen asked. "With your head?"

The mouth under the disguise grinned, and Jason walked down the aisle, stopping between Mary Ellen's and Justine's seats.

"There's seats back here, if you don't want to catch germs, Jason," Amy called to him.

He turned the dark glasses in her direction for a second, then patted his homemade helmet. "I got protection," he said. "So Kelly, move in and make room, wouldya?"

Justine blushed, and moved in against the window as Jason sat down next to her.

"So, Mary Ellen, Justine, you have your Hat Day projects all set?" Kevin asked. He'd scraped enough of the gum off that he could partially see through his glasses again. Reaching down inside a paper bag on the floor at his feet, he pulled out his Hat Day project, and put it on his head.

"What do you think?" he asked.

"I think they should quarantine you, Kevin, before whatever bug you've got in your brain spreads," Justine called across the aisle.

Kevin grinned. "Does that mean you like it?"

Justine smiled. "Welllll . . . it suits you, Kevin."

"Let's see yours," he said.

Mary Ellen and Justine both shook their heads. "Not until class this afternoon."

"Aw, come on," he wheedled.

"Yeah, put 'em on," Jason said.

"Nope," Mary Ellen told him. "But I have Kevin to thank for the idea."

"What'd I say? Huh?"

"Not what you said. From one of my campaign posters." That's all she'd tell him.

Mr. Gumble stood in front of the class holding out a shoebox as the kids filed past him and dropped in their votes. Mary Ellen looked over at the group gathered around Amy, who was acting like she'd already won the election, talking about the colors *she'd* recommend for the new uniforms. Kevin was pacing up and down the aisle, looking worried, and apologizing, in case he hadn't done a good enough job as campaign co-manager.

"If I had a scanner, I could have put your picture on the flyers," he said glumly.

"Don't worry about it, Kevin," Mary Ellen said. "I'm not going to be crushed if I don't win. I'm not really expecting to."

"All right everybody, you can chat while I tally up the votes," Mr. Gumble said. He walked around behind his desk with the shoebox, and sat down. "Consider this: Infinity— if you had it, where would you put it all?"

"I bet Mr. Gumble was a lot like you when he was growing up, Kevin," Justine said.

"You think?" His face lit up with a huge smile.

"I'm not sure that's a compliment, Kevin," Mary Ellen joked.

"Hey, I'll take what I can get," he said, grinning at them both.

"Listen up everybody, we have a new homeroom representative." Mr. Gumble stood up.

Mary Ellen inhaled sharply and held her breath. Everyone quieted down immediately.

"Before I announce the winning candidate, I want to say how well I think you both ran your campaigns, and to congratulate you both. It was a very, very close race. Either one of you would make a terrific class rep, and I hope the person who came in second today will consider running for class officer next semester, or for student council again next year. Okay everybody, salute your new homeroom representative, Mary Ellen Bobowick!"

"Yay!!!!!!"

As Kevin yelled a victory yell, and came over to shake her hand, pumping it up and down vigorously, Mary Ellen exhaled.

"So Bobowick, I'll give you your first suggestion to represent for us," Jason shouted from his corner of the room. "MTV in every classroom, and two Kentucky Fried chickens in every desk."

Mary Ellen laughed, and pretended to write it down in one of her notebooks. Across the room, with all the bustle, she caught Amy's eye. Her face looked kind of stiff, and she was clearly trying not to show her disappointment.

"Excuse me, " Mary Ellen said, working her way

through the crowd, and walking over to the other side of the room. Debra gave her a snotty look as she approached.

"What do *you* want?" she said huffily.

"I just want to say you were a really good opponent, Amy. I was pretty sure I'd be congratulating you this morning."

Amy nodded a little stiffly. "Well, maybe next year. Anyhow, you'll have a lot of work to do with all the suggestions I'm going to stuff in the suggestion box." Then she smiled. Not a huge smile, but not a fake one, either.

"HAT DAY, PEOPLE!! Is everyone ready?" Ms. Coville sang out after their affirmations. "Don your millinery creations then."

As Mary Ellen pulled the paper bag with her Hat Day hat in it out from under her chair, she got a little worried, for the first time, that the idea she'd come up with late yesterday afternoon was stupid. It started when she checked her e-mail. There was a letter from Ben, not saying much, but just enough to make her cheeks feel warm, and signed with his screen name, BozoB. She'd looked at hers, plain old MaryE582, and decided to change it to something at least a little less . . . generic, to use Justine's word. And then she'd remembered one of Kevin's campaign flyers. And that had given her the idea for the hats. She called Justine to ask her what she thought, and then a new idea blossomed. The results of which were hidden inside identical brown paper bags.

Now, with her bag in her hand, Mary Ellen looked at Justine. She was holding hers, the other half of the idea, on her lap.

"Ready?" she mouthed.

Justine smiled, and nodded. They both reached into their paper bags at the same time, and pulled out matching yellow baseball caps, each with bright-colored letters cut out of poster board glued over the brims. They held them

behind their backs, while Ms. Coville went around and exclaimed over each person's hat.

"Ours kind of go together, Ms. Coville," Mary Ellen told the teacher when she reached them.

"Is that okay?" Justine asked.

"That is perfectly okay," Ms. Coville said with a smile. "Wear them with pride."

Justine swept her left hand out from behind her back at the same time as Mary Ellen swept her right, and they put the hats on at the same time. Above Justine's face, in bright red, upper-case letters, her cap said "JUST" and above Mary Ellen's, in bright green, "M.E." They put their arms around each other's shoulders, and shouted together: "JUST . . . ME!"

From out of the Shadows…
Stories Filled with Mystery
and Suspense by

MARY DOWNING HAHN

TIME FOR ANDREW
72469-3/$4.50 US/$5.99 Can

DAPHNE'S BOOK
72355-7/$4.50 US/$5.99 Can

THE TIME OF THE WITCH
71116-8/ $4.50 US/ $5.99 Can

STEPPING ON THE CRACKS
71900-2/ $4.50 US/ $5.99 Can

THE DEAD MAN IN INDIAN CREEK
71362-4/ $4.50 US/ $5.99 Can

THE DOLL IN THE GARDEN
70865-5/ $4.50 US/ $5.99 Can

FOLLOWING THE MYSTERY MAN
70677-6/ $4.50 US/ $5.99 Can

TALLAHASSEE HIGGINS
70500-1/ $4.50 US/ $5.99 Can

WAIT TILL HELEN COMES
70442-0/ $4.50 US/ $5.99 Can

THE SPANISH KIDNAPPING DISASTER
71712-3/ $4.50 US/ $5.99 Can

THE JELLYFISH SEASON
71635-6/ $3.99 US/ $5.50 Can

THE SARA SUMMER
72354-9/ $4.50 US/ $5.99 Can

Buy these books at your local bookstore or use this coupon for ordering:

Mail to: Avon Books, Dept BP, Box 767, Rte 2, Dresden, TN 38225   G
Please send me the book(s) I have checked above.
❑ My check or money order—no cash or CODs please—for $_____is enclosed (please
add $1.50 per order to cover postage and handling—Canadian residents add 7% GST). U.S.
residents make checks payable to Avon Books; Canada residents make checks payable to
Hearst Book Group of Canada.
❑ Charge my VISA/MC Acct#_____Exp Date_____
Minimum credit card order is two books or $7.50 (please add postage and handling
charge of $1.50 per order—Canadian residents add 7% GST). For faster service, call
1-800-762-0779. Prices and numbers are subject to change without notice. Please allow six to
eight weeks for delivery.
Name_____
Address_____
City_____State/Zip_____
Telephone No._____   MDH 1097

THE MAGIC CONTINUES...
WITH
LYNNE REID BANKS

THE INDIAN IN THE CUPBOARD

60012-9/$4.50 US/$5.99 Can

THE RETURN OF THE INDIAN   70284-3/$3.99 US

THE SECRET OF THE INDIAN   71040-4/$4.50 US

THE MYSTERY OF THE CUPBOARD

72013-2/$4.50 US/$5.99 Can

I, HOUDINI   70649-0/$4.50 US

THE FAIRY REBEL   70650-4/$4.50 US

THE FARTHEST-AWAY MOUNTAIN   71303-9/$4.50 US

ONE MORE RIVER   71563-5/$3.99 US

THE ADVENTURES OF KING MIDAS

71564-3/$4.50 US

THE MAGIC HARE   71562-7/$5.99 US

ANGELA AND DIABOLA   79409-8/$4.50 US/$5.99 Can

Buy these books at your local bookstore or use this coupon for ordering:

Mail to: Avon Books, Dept BP, Box 767, Rte 2, Dresden, TN 38225   G
Please send me the book(s) I have checked above.
❑ My check or money order—no cash or CODs please—for $_____is enclosed (please add $1.50 per order to cover postage and handling—Canadian residents add 7% GST). U.S. residents make checks payable to Avon Books; Canada residents make checks payable to Hearst Book Group of Canada.
❑ Charge my VISA/MC Acct#_____Exp Date_____
Minimum credit card order is two books or $7.50 (please add postage and handling charge of $1.50 per order—Canadian residents add 7% GST). For faster service, call 1-800-762-0779. Prices and numbers are subject to change without notice. Please allow six to eight weeks for delivery.
Name_____
Address_____
City_____State/Zip_____
Telephone No._____   LRB 0198

They're super-smart, they're super-cool, and they're *aliens*!
Their job on our planet? To try and resuce the...

RU1:2
79729-1/$3.99 US/$4.99 Can

One day, Xela, Arms Akimbo, Rubidoux, and Gogol discover a
wormhole leading to Planet RU1:2 (better known to its inhab-
itants as "Earth") where long ago, all 175 members of a secret
diplomatic mission disappeared. The mission specialists scattered through time all over the planet. They're Goners—and
it's up to four galactic travelers to find them.

THE HUNT IS ON
79730-5/$3.99 US/$4.99 Can

The space travelers have located a Goner. He lives in Virginia
in 1775 and goes by the name "Thomas Jefferson." Can they
convince the revolutionary Goner to return to their home
planet with them?

ALL HANDS ON DECK
79732-1/$3.99 US/$4.99 Can

In a port of the Canary Islands in 1492, the space travelers
find themselves aboard something called the *Santa Maria*, with
Arms pressed into service as a cabin boy.

Buy these books at your local bookstore or use this coupon for ordering:

Mail to: Avon Books, Dept BP, Box 767, Rte 2, Dresden, TN 38225   G
Please send me the book(s) I have checked above.
❑ My check or money order—no cash or CODs please—for $_____is enclosed (please
add $1.50 per order to cover postage and handling—Canadian residents add 7% GST). U.S.
residents make checks payable to Avon Books; Canada residents make checks payable to
Hearst Book Group of Canada.
❑ Charge my VISA/MC Acct#_____Exp Date_____
Minimum credit card order is two books or $7.50 (please add postage and handling
charge of $1.50 per order—Canadian residents add 7% GST). For faster service, call
1-800-762-0779. Prices and numbers are subject to change without notice. Please allow six to
eight weeks for delivery.
Name_____
Address_____
City_____State/Zip_____ ___
Telephone No._____   GON 0498

Read All the Stories by
Beverly Cleary

☐ **HENRY HUGGINS**
70912-0 ($4.50 US/ $5.99 Can)

☐ **HENRY AND BEEZUS**
70914-7 ($4.50 US/ $5.99 Can)

☐ **HENRY AND THE CLUBHOUSE**
70915-5 ($4.50 US/ $6.50 Can)

☐ **ELLEN TEBBITS**
70913-9 ($4.50 US/ $5.99 Can)

☐ **HENRY AND RIBSY**
70917-1 ($4.50 US/ $5.99 Can)

☐ **BEEZUS AND RAMONA**
70918-X ($4.50 US/ $5.99 Can)

☐ **RAMONA AND HER FATHER**
70916-3 ($4.50 US/ $6.50 Can)

☐ **MITCH AND AMY**
70925-2 ($4.50 US/ $5.99 Can)

☐ **RUNAWAY RALPH**
70953-8 ($4.50 US/ $5.99 Can)

☐ **RAMONA QUIMBY, AGE 8**
70956-2 ($4.50 US/ $5.99 Can)

☐ **RIBSY**
70955-4 ($4.50 US/ $5.99 Can)

☐ **STRIDER**
71236-9 ($4.50 US/ $5.99 Can)

☐ **HENRY AND THE PAPER ROUTE**
70921-X ($4.50 US/ $5.99 Can)

☐ **RAMONA AND HER MOTHER**
70952-X ($4.50 US/ $5.99 Can)

☐ **OTIS SPOFFORD**
70919-8 ($4.50 US/ $5.99 Can)

☐ **THE MOUSE AND THE MOTORCYCLE**
70924-4 ($4.50 US/ $5.99 Can)

☐ **SOCKS**
70926-0 ($4.50 US/ $5.99 Can)

☐ **EMILY'S RUNAWAY IMAGINATION**
70923-6 ($4.50 US/ $5.99 Can)

☐ **MUGGIE MAGGIE**
71087-0 ($4.50 US/ $5.99 Can)

☐ **RAMONA THE PEST**
70954-6 ($4.50 US/ $5.99 Can)

☐ **RALPH S. MOUSE**
70957-0 ($4.50 US/ $5.99 Can)

☐ **DEAR MR. HENSHAW**
70958-9 ($4.50 US/ $5.99 Can)

☐ **RAMONA THE BRAVE**
70959-7 ($4.50 US/ $5.99 Can)

☐ **RAMONA FOREVER**
70960-6 ($4.50 US/ $5.99 Can)

Buy these books at your local bookstore or use this coupon for ordering:

Mail to: Avon Books, Dept BP, Box 767, Rte 2, Dresden, TN 38225   G
Please send me the book(s) I have checked above.
☐ My check or money order—no cash or CODs please—for $_____is enclosed (please add $1.50 per order to cover postage and handling—Canadian residents add 7% GST). U.S. residents make checks payable to Avon Books; Canada residents make checks payable to Hearst Book Group of Canada.
☐ Charge my VISA/MC Acct#_____Exp Date_____
Minimum credit card order is two books or $7.50 (please add postage and handling charge of $1.50 per order—Canadian residents add 7% GST). For faster service, call 1-800-762-0779. Prices and numbers are subject to change without notice. Please allow six to eight weeks for delivery.
Name_____
Address_____
City_____State/Zip_____
Telephone No._____   BEV 0597